2-

THE LAST AMEN

A DETECTIVE KATE MURPHY MYSTERY

C.C. JAMESON

The Last Amen

By C.C. Jameson

WARNING: This book is intended for mature audiences and contains disturbing and potentially offensive material.

Thank you for taking the time to read this book. Please leave a review wherever you bought it or help spread the word by telling your friends about it. Thank you for your support.

Published by Creative Communication Solutions Ltd.

eBook Edition last updated October 6th, 2019

Editing by Claire Taylor

e-book ISBN: 978-1-988639-40-6

Print Book ISBN: 978-1-988639-41-3

CHAPTER ONE

Boston, Massachusetts
Sunday, June 3rd, 2018

THE POP of the cork echoed in the dining room as he opened the 2011 bottle of *Terre Rouge Tête-à-Tête*. If one type of alcohol made his life easier, it was red wine. It pleased his taste buds and suited his profession. The blood of Christ.

Whether early priests had begun drinking it due to alcoholism, epicurism, or simple lack of clean drinking water was debatable, but one thing was certain: blends were better for his budget than expensive dry wines. And they offered the perfect cover for the first step of his cleansing process.

She sat cross-legged at a proper distance from him, with her Sunday best on. Her manicured hands rested together on one of her knees, but he knew she hadn't kept her distance from other men before… At least she had the decency to keep her filthy digits away from him.

For a second, he reconsidered whether he should proceed with his plan.

"Your parents have been out of town, you said. Are they back?" he asked, his eyes scanning the rest of the dining room decor, which was adorned with family photos. In the neatly tiled frames, she and her parents beamed in various settings: by the harbor, at graduation, at the beach. Her blonde hair ran in the family.

When she started speaking, he returned his eyes to her. A hint of pink had reached her cheeks.

"They're away on a cruise. They've been gone for a week already, but they should be back in two weeks."

Her reply returned him to his senses. If he let her be, she'd only worsen her situation. She'd have too much time to continue sinning. If he waited any longer, she'd forever be damned and stuck in Hell, rotting with…

He couldn't even bring himself to think about her name anymore.

A soul could only stand so much staining before the gates of paradise would forever seal shut, preventing trespassing by those who didn't deserve entry.

He moved the empty wine glasses closer, away from the pen and pad of paper she'd placed on the table minutes earlier.

As he poured an inch of red liquid into the first glass, he spoke. "You said your parents had a special Bible they liked to read from, as a family. Could you please get it? I'd love to see it."

"Of course." She grinned, got up from her chair, and headed into the adjacent living room, her footsteps fading away as she walked out of sight.

He knew she could be back any second. A practicing family like hers had to have Bibles nearby at all times. After retrieving the tiny vial he'd hidden, his fingers swiftly dumped its contents into the empty glass. By the time the creaks of her footsteps got closer, he'd already poured wine over it, hiding his special ingredient.

"Here it is," she said, handing the worn-out, leather-bound book to him and beaming as though it was an Olympic medal she'd just earned.

"Ah, the Revised Standard Version, Catholic Edition. Is this one of the original printings?"

She nodded. "Daddy says so. He's had it since he was a child."

"Very nice. Please join me." He indicated to the chair she'd previously occupied next to him.

"You are so… fun." She sat and grabbed her pen and paper. "You're right. It will be much easier to work on the social calendar here, away from the screaming children waiting for their parents to be done socializing. And while drinking wine? You're the coolest!"

Such a lovely young woman, but so easily tempted.

Her soul deserved to rest in peace. Unlike the one whose name he dared not think about anymore, he had time to save this young woman's soul, if he acted now.

"Shall I bless this wine before we get started?"

CHAPTER TWO

Friday, June 15th, 2018

DETECTIVE KATE MURPHY stepped out of Detective Lieutenant Mark Fuller's office, her heart pounding in her chest, her fists still clenched. She stood still in the middle of the vacant hallway for a second before finally stretching out her fingers. Her nails—while kept short compared to most women's—had left deep, white grooves in her palms. But she hadn't drawn blood, and—most importantly—she hadn't lost her temper in front of both her partner and Fuller.

At least no one was sitting right here in the hall to overhear all of that screaming, she thought, a detail that brightened her mood, however slightly.

Concentrating on her breathing, she inhaled, counted to four, then exhaled slowly.

Snap out of it, Kate!

Then the muffled voices behind the door turned into deep, guttural laughter, and Detective Malvin Rosebud joined her in the hall a few minutes later. It seemed that, without Kate around, their conversation had lightened.

"Walk with me, Murphy," he said, tapping her on the shoulder.

Kate shook her head but nonetheless caught up to her partner as he headed toward the lunchroom.

"How did you get him out of his pissy mood?"

"Trade secret."

"Come on! You know I work my ass off. I don't deserve to be treated that way."

"Fuller's old school. He likes his detectives burly and stubborn—"

"Come on—"

"Wait, before you call him a misogynist prick—which I could agree with—you qualify as both those things in his head."

"What?" Kate looked down at her body, suddenly worried that her fairly recent lack of running had morphed her athletic body into a blob.

"If tiny burly existed, that is. You and I both know you'd kick my ass."

"Then why is he so fucking upset at me?"

"The part that he didn't say while you were in there—something I discovered a few hours ago myself—is the reason why he was away two days ago. Remember?"

"Yeah, but what could that possibly have to do with my performance at work?"

He headed toward the vending machine, shaking his head, his wallet in hand. "You missed the entire point of the conversation."

Kate avoided the sugar-laden treats and went directly for the coffee dispenser. She pressed the button and waited for her large serving of Colombian blend as Rosebud droned on.

"He wasn't giving you hell for *not* doing your job; he was upset at you for putting in *too many* hours."

"What does he care if I choose to spend my personal time on open cases? I'm helping make Boston safer." She grabbed her drink out of the machine and dared to dip her lips into the boiling hot liquid. There was nothing like the lunchroom's tar-like substance to jolt her out of her crappy mood. No other coffee she'd ever tasted had been quite as potent (and foul-tasting), and she went back to it once or twice daily, like a true addict.

"The job will kill you if you don't balance it out with happy things."

"Oh, please…" Kate stirred her coffee in an effort to cool it off a tad.

"Murphy, I'm not joking. Fuller attended a funeral a few days ago. His old partner from back in the day. The man ate his gun."

"Oh…" Kate walked over to the garbage to toss her stick.

"I reassured him. Told him I'd convince you to have a kid so you can have something to occupy your free time. That's when he started laughing. He told me he'd be willing to bet on you never having a baby." Rosebud tossed two snacks on one of the tables: a blueberry muffin and a packet of Skittles. "His comment was weird, but then I remembered your uncle's murder case. He'd adopted you, right? Did you lose more than your parents back then?"

Rosebud sat and stayed quiet, as though expecting Kate to answer. "Come on, Murphy! If we're going to keep working together, you gotta tell me what could make your head spin. I can't protect your back if I don't know your weakness."

Kate leaned against the counter and looked at her partner, trying to gauge if she should or not. The last thing she wanted was for her own partner to think of her as the weakest link in their team. "What's *your* Achilles' heel?"

"Look at me!" He leaned back on his chair, making his rounded gut stick out more than it normally did. "Sugar. Fat. Bad eating habits. But I know you've got my back. You can fucking outrun anyone I know. Not that I've had to run after many suspects since becoming a homicide detective, but that's my number one weakness. Speaking of which, I should really make use of that stupid gym." He ripped the top off his muffin and broke it in half before stuffing it in his mouth. His closed eyes and growing smile made it obvious he was enjoying his calorie-dense treat. But he reopened his eyes and his expression turned stern.

"So, are you ever going to invite me to your house for drinks? Maybe I can talk your lab guy into picking you up early every evening from now on."

Kate rolled her eyes at him. "Please don't."

"So, what's your story?"

"Like I told Fuller before. I promise it won't affect my work. I'll focus. I'll set aside my emotions."

"Stop feeding me bullshit. I'm not Fuller. What is it?"

"Okay," she said before taking a seat in front of him.

"I'll give you the CliffsNotes, but I don't want everyone in the department to know about it. It's gotta stay between us. The last thing I need is some stupid prank played on me again."

"Deal."

Kate sat at the table and inhaled deeply, preparing herself to discuss a part of her past she preferred to keep hidden.

~

WHEN KATE UNLOCKED the door and walked into Luke's house, a delightful aroma of garlic and tomato reached her nostrils.

"Luke? Mrs. O'Brien? I'm home."

"I'm in the kitchen, Kate," Mrs. O'Brien yelled. "Luke's not home yet."

Kate locked the door behind her, hung her jacket on the coatrack, and unlocked the safe in the back of the closet before securing her firearm for the night. Every time she pressed the buttons on it—their high-pitch beeps echoing through the entire house—her heart filled with gratitude for having Luke in her life. He was the one who'd insisted on having the safe installed right in his vestibule since his mother had wanted nothing to do with guns in their house.

Mrs. O'Brien had already pushed aside her Irish Catholic values and reluctantly agreed to let Kate move in and share Luke's bedroom (it was *his* house after all). Sure, the installation of a safe wasn't a particularly romantic gesture, but that was Luke's perfect solution to keep everyone happy and enjoy a secure home where they wouldn't have to worry about intruders coming in to rob them… Or worse.

She shook her head as though the movement could prevent her recent conversation with Rosebud from returning to the forefront of her mind, where it threatened to fill her eyes with tears. She was definitely going to have nightmares again tonight.

And as she pressed one more button to lock the safe, the clink of a key through the lock made her turn her head just in time to see Luke come in.

"Hey, baby!" She bridged the gap between them to wrap

her arms around his tall frame. Their lips met for a brief kiss, interrupted by Mrs. O'Brien yelling from the kitchen.

"Luke? Is that you?"

He pulled away from Kate, rolled his eyes, then yelled back toward the kitchen. "Yes, Mom. Who else are you expecting?" He turned to Kate again and smiled. "I had a great idea at work today. After dinner, remind me to tell you about it, okay?"

"Why don't you tell me now?"

He took off his jacket and added it to the other side of the coatrack. "Because I know you, Katie. And I know my mom. It will lead to a topic that isn't suitable for dinner conversation."

"Ah!" Kate said, stealing another kiss from Luke. "Now I'll just keep imagining all sorts of stuff." She stood on her tippy-toes to whisper in his ears, "Or is it something you want to do to me? Or me to do to you?"

She bit his earlobe before returning her heels to the floor, realizing she'd forgotten to take off her shoes, again.

"Shoot! It's like my mind doesn't want to get with the program." Kate took off her shoes and replaced them with a pair of Mrs. O'Brien's hand-knitted slippers.

"My mom is just trying her best to domesticate you. Careful, she may try to teach you how to knit them next."

"Argh! Don't you dare suggest that to her. It's bad enough I have to behave myself all the time because she lives with you, I don't want to turn into a housewife!"

"Are you complaining about my mom?" he asked, a twisted smile on his lips.

Kate knew it was slippery territory, but she also understood the value of family. Especially since the only relatives she had left were distant cousins who lived in Ireland. "You know I love your mom. She's fantastic. You're lucky to still have her."

"Well, remember that thought for when we talk later," he said, kissing her and heading toward the kitchen.

Kate followed, grinning.

What had she done to deserve him? Luke reappearing in her life a few years prior had been nothing short of miraculous. Well, save for the fact that she didn't believe in miracles.

"Mom, how was your day?" Luke asked before walking over to the chubby woman in the apron who was retrieving a dish from the oven.

"Wonderful, as usual. But careful, this is really hot." She turned around and walked over to the kitchen table to rest the steamy lasagna on top of the pot holder in the middle of the table. "Now, dear. I'll take my hug."

Luke smiled and wrapped his arms around his mother before kissing her forehead.

Every time Kate saw him do it, it pinched a little part of her heart. It wasn't jealousy. More like her own faint memories of simpler times pinging in her chest, trying to resurface. The pleasures and comforts of having a mother had long ago disappeared from Kate's life, so joining Luke and his mom in their home made her nothing but joyful and grateful.

"Come on, Kate. You know the rules. I make you guys dinner, but you pay me back in hugs. Pay up, Kate!"

The daily charade was cheesy, but it was what they did. She hugged the woman who'd raised the man she loved.

"And you have to stop calling me Mrs. O'Brien!" After the hug ended, she turned to her son. "Luke, please make her call me Marjorie. She won't listen to me."

Luke raised his palms in the air before taking a seat at the table. "That's between the two of you, I'm afraid."

"I promise I'll work on it! It's just that I've known you as Mrs. O'Brien since I was a kid! It's a little weird," Kate said as she opened the cupboard where they stored the alcohol. "Who wants red wine?"

Her dinner cohorts replied in the affirmative, so she grabbed the bottle, along with three glasses, and brought it all to the table.

"Do you mind grabbing the salad from the fridge, Katie?" Mrs. O'Brien asked.

"Not at all."

A minute later, with a decadent dinner spread in front of them, Mrs. O'Brien reached to grab Luke's and Kate's hands, then lowered her head.

"Dear Lord, thank you for bringing my Luke and his Katie home safely. I know they both work hard to make this world a better place. Thank you for providing us with the means to feed ourselves and live in such a wonderful, safe home. Thank you to the farmers who grew this food and to the merchants who brought it to us. Bless us, Lord, and bless the food we are about to receive. Through Christ, our Lord. Amen."

"Amen," Luke said while Kate stared at her food, her mind wandering.

He kicked her under the table.

"Ouch!" Kate said, her eyes sending daggers toward her boyfriend. But she'd understood the message. "Amen!" she said before smiling at Mrs. O'Brien. "Let's dig in! I'm starving."

CHAPTER THREE

LUKE O'BRIEN WAS SITTING in bed with his computer on his lap when the en-suite bathroom door opened. Surrounded by a mist of steam, the woman he loved walked out wearing nothing but a towel wrapped around her petite frame and another tied around her head.

"All yours," she said as she undid her turban and let her wet blonde hair dangle down to her shoulders.

While the bigger part of him wanted nothing more than to make love to her, he talked himself out of it. At least for a few minutes until he could discuss his idea with her.

He closed his laptop and set it aside while she traded her wet towel for one of his large T-shirts. Seconds later, she'd hopped onto the bed.

"Do you think you can be really quiet? I think your mom's still awake."

"Kate…" He bit his lip, then exhaled loudly, closing his eyes to muster some courage.

"What's up? You're acting all weird."

He reopened his eyes and moved to sit in front of her. He rubbed his hands against her shoulders, as though trying to protect her from what he was about to say. Or possibly to protect himself from her reaction. He didn't know which of the two he feared the most.

"Luko, you're starting to freak me out."

She'd used his childhood nickname, which eased him into finally talking.

"Okay. Please promise you won't get upset at me for what I'm about to suggest."

"Why would I get upset? Is this about me tuning out while your mom was saying grace? I'm sorry about that. I was just thinking about something else. I respect her. I promise I'll pay attention next time." She extended her leg. "I think I'll get a bruise out of your kick, though. Not cool, mister!"

"Come on, Kate. I didn't kick you that hard. You know it."

"Just kidding." She brushed his lips with a kiss. "What do you want to tell me?"

He exhaled loudly. "Well, two things, actually."

"Okay. Bad news, good news? Start with the bad."

"No, no." He shook his head, even though the movement didn't ease what he was about to do. Good thing he spent most of his time in a lab, avoiding the social interactions some people enjoyed so much, for whatever reason. "Here goes. You know the nightmares you keep having?"

As though his words had deflated her body, she shriveled away from him and leaned back against the headboard. "Yeah. Hard to forget about them." She scrunched up her nose. "Do you have problems sleeping because of me having nightmares next to you? 'Cause if it's bothering you, I can go back to living in my own place."

"No, Katie. That's not where I'm going with this. I love you sleeping next to me. I love waking up next to you. I don't want to change that."

She lifted her shoulders and frowned. "Then what's your point?"

"Well, first, a colleague of mine recommended a hypnotherapist—"

"What? You talked about my nightmares to your colleagues at work?" Kate's volume had raised a notch, and Luke moved closer to her.

"No, don't worry. I know how you feel about it. Totally random how it came up. This guy, Frank, he's been trying to quit smoking for years. Decades, even. I can't remember him without a cigarette in his mouth. Anyways, he mentioned how he's been smoke-free for nearly a month now. And without cravings."

"So? It's not like I can will myself to stop dreaming, no matter how good this therapist is."

Luke nodded. "I know, I know. But turns out a big part of this lady's process involves taking her patients back through their past and identifying the trigger that started their smoking in the first place."

"Okay. Still not following."

"She's really good at helping people work through the past."

"And..." Kate squinted as though she knew where Luke was headed.

"While it would not be pleasant—far from it—I just thought that, with proper guidance from this hypnotherapist, you might be able to remember details that you may have pushed away in the dark corners of your mind."

She brought her hands up to her face, hiding her eyes while she shook her head. When she finally peeled them off, her eyes were red. "Why do that? Do you know how hard I worked at forgetting that day?"

"I know, baby." He repositioned himself so he could hug and rock her in his arms.

"Fifteen years of therapy it took, and the memories still haunt me."

He pressed her body closer to his. "But—bear with me for just a few more minutes—if you could identify one little clue—one tiny detail—you could potentially find the person who killed your parents and your baby brother. Wouldn't putting that man in prison end your nightmares for good?"

He continued rocking her, as though the motion could remove the pain he knew he'd inflicted just by talking about it.

She inhaled deeply, then asked, "What's the second thing you wanted to tell me?"

"Oh, I probably should have started with it... But every summer, the staff at our DNA lab have a big party. It's not something we invite people to. We just celebrate the advances that have been made in our field with free food and drinks. I mean, DNA profiling began in 1984. Your parents died in 1995. That's more than two decades of improvements in technology. If we were to reanalyze the evidence, perhaps there's something new we could discover."

"Luke… I appreciate what you're trying to do for me. But whatever DNA existed is probably deteriorated beyond use. They've already tested what they had."

"But—and that's a big but—if you were to see that hypnotherapist, perhaps we could uncover new leads, new evidence, or run new tests on the old evidence based on new memories that you'd bring back to the surface. You're the one who discovered them, first at the scene. You were just thirteen then, but now you're a detective. And a smart one. If you could relive that day with your current expertise, don't you think you could uncover new clues or new leads?"

CHAPTER FOUR

KATE TRIED TO SLEEP, but images of her dead baby brother haunted her every time she closed her eyes. Her chat with Rosebud combined with Luke's far-fetched idea, and a glance at the bright digits of her alarm clock—2:32 a.m.—made it clear she wasn't going to sleep tonight.

Rolling quietly out of bed, she donned a pair of jeans and a sweater, left a note on the kitchen counter for Luke, then drove away to her uncle's old place.

Might as well put her insomnia to good use.

After Kenny's death, she'd waded through all the red tape associated with his will, but finally his house had become hers. While there was sentimental value to it, it was a crumbling mess. She'd talked it over with Luke. Turning it into a rental property would require so much work. She didn't have the skills or time to do it herself, and Luke wasn't the type of guy to make good use of power tools. He was a nerd through and through, and she loved him for that. She dealt with enough machismo from some of her colleagues at work.

As she unlocked the door to the house where so many happy and sad memories had been shared, she realized she had to deal with it as quickly as possible. Rip off the Band-Aid, strip away the memories worth saving, and then put it up for sale.

Whatever cash would come out of it would be a bonus.

So she picked up a garbage bag and one of the boxes Luke

and she had brought over during a previous visit. She unfolded the box, taped the bottom shut, and carried it with her to the living room to see what was worth salvaging and what needed tossing.

She could get a lot of things sorted while the rest of the neighborhood still rested in darkness and silence.

CHAPTER FIVE

Saturday, June 16th, 2018

AFTER OPENING the panels of the antique toaster on the kitchen counter, Luke put a slice of sprouted-grain bread into each then closed them up.

How he loved that old toaster!

It was a serious fire hazard, but every time he used it, he thought of his dad, hoping the man was resting in peace. And he got to enjoy perfectly toasted bread. Every time.

"Mom, can I ask you something?"

She sat at the kitchen table, sipping on her orange juice, her hair still in rollers from the previous night. As she put her drink down, she nodded. "Sure, dear."

Luke checked if his toast was ready then returned his attention to his mom. "Kate and I have been seeing each other for a while now. We're coming up on an anniversary of sorts. I was thinking of doing something special for her. What do you think about me getting her a dog?"

"A dog?" Her fork cut into the soft yolk that rested on top of her bread, making the yellow liquid ooze out into the toast.

Luke peered into the antique appliance again. *Not ready yet.*

"Well, she's already living here. I know she doesn't want children. At least not until she gets over those nightmares. Wouldn't a dog be a great stepping stone?"

"You realize I'd be the one taking care of it. Walking it. Training it. Cleaning up after it…"

Luke opened the panels and flipped his bread to expose the soft sides to the central element.

"Yeah… You're probably right." His mom was getting up there in years, and that was something that had begun to worry him a little. He definitely didn't want to burden her with anything. "I don't know what to get her."

His mom's fingers fidgeted with the silver cross that hung around her neck. "You know what would make me the happiest person on earth?"

"What?"

"Make an honest woman out of her!"

Luke moved toward the table. "Come on, Mom! Kate's not religious. And I can't blame her for losing whatever faith she may have had after her family got killed." He reached for the cup of coffee he'd left on the table minutes earlier. "No, I can't do that." He poured in some sugar then stirred.

Mrs. O'Brien shook her head, looked up to the sky, then back down to Luke as she exhaled. "Well, if you don't want to make it official under the eyes of God, then at least make it official at City Hall."

"But don't you think it's a little too fast—"

"Luke Stewart O'Brien, you've known and loved this woman for over twenty-five years! Sure, she wasn't in your life for a solid twenty of those years, but I know you never stopped loving her. She's special. She gets you, and you get her. Don't you dare—"

The smoke detector shrilled over the rest of her words as smoke escaped the toaster behind Luke.

"Shit!" he muttered, rushing to unplug the machine and flip the panels open.

Two blackened squares stared back at him. *Well… Perfect toast 99.9% of the time.*

Following the annoying sound, he stepped into the living room and waved a newspaper under the detector, hoping to make the damn thing shut up.

A long minute later, he was finally rewarded by silence. He walked back into the kitchen just as his mother was closing the window, the smoke now cleared.

Luke tossed his failed toast into the garbage, reloaded the toaster and plugged it back in.

"You know my birthday's coming up," she said to Luke as she returned to her seat to finish her breakfast.

"Yes, of course. But same as last year, I don't know what to get you."

"I half-expected as much, so I thought of something I'd like you to do for me. For my birthday."

"What?" he said, heading toward the table.

"Better stay back there, son. That alarm was bad enough the first time."

Luke shrugged but nonetheless obeyed. "What do you want?"

"The church is arranging a fundraiser to support the community. I'd like you to accompany me."

"What?" Luke asked as he flipped his toast. When he returned his glance her way, she was finishing the last bite on her plate. "What kind of fundraiser? When?"

"Tomorrow evening. It'll be from six to nine."

"Why?"

"Luke, be a good Christian and accompany your mom. It's for the good of the community. I'll be selling my baked goods."

"It will be packed with people," Luke said, his face shriveling.

"We certainly hope so!"

After checking that the bread was toasted enough—although not perfectly—he unplugged the device, loaded his slices onto a plate, then joined his mom at the table.

Her wide eyes were hopeful, her smile genuine. "You could ask Kate to join us, if you want."

Luke's eyes inadvertently widened. "I'm pretty sure she's not going to be interested in that."

His mom's brows descended as she frowned. She got up from her chair and carried her dirty dishes to the sink.

Luke began spreading peanut butter on his toast while considering her request. His extreme introverted nature wouldn't enjoy it at all, but he couldn't disappoint his mom. That would just be selfish of him. "Okay, Mom. I'll go with you."

She walked back to the table to squeeze his hand, a large smile on her increasingly wrinkled face as he himself forced a grin to last long enough to please her.

Suck it up, Luke. She's the only mother you have. If spending a ridiculous number of hours surrounded by way too many people is going to make her happy, then so be it.

CHAPTER SIX

Sunday, June 17th, 2018

IN FRONT OF HIM, the congregation stood, dressed to the nines, their booming voices joining the choir to chant:

> *"Lord, my savior,*
> *Lord, my liberator,*
> *Guide me toward your light,*
> *Together our souls will unite.*
> *Your spirit calls, through the dark times it beckons,*
> *With open arms, you'll greet me in the heavens.*
> *Glorious is your name,*
> *Glorious is your flame.*
> *Lord, while I walk with shame,*
> *My sins you forgive the same,*
> *I look up to you and your name I'll forever proclaim."*

As he and the crowd repeated the last five lines of his favorite hymn—words he'd memorized decades ago—he relished his most recent success, rubbing the beads of his wooden rosary between his right thumb and forefinger.

It had been two weeks already and nobody had come and spoken to him. He hadn't heard anything on the news either, but he knew that it'd be just a matter of time.

The cleansing ceremony had gone off without a hitch.

He'd had time to clean up everything. He'd been cautious not to leave fingerprints on anything he'd touched. Not the Bible, not the kitchen table, not the door handle on his way out. Not a thing.

The minute after she'd passed out, he'd donned his gloves and covered his head with a surgeon's cap to avoid leaving any hair behind. He'd cleaned everything, including the wine glasses from which they'd drank. He'd thought about placing them in the dishwasher and letting the hot steam remove both his prints and the chemicals from his homemade brew, but the appliance had been empty. He'd hand washed them instead and stored them away.

Everything had been left as it was before he'd arrived. Nobody had heard a thing, and nobody had seen him leave the house in broad daylight with the rest of his wine bottle in hand.

Well, almost everything had been left as it had been. The family's precious Bible now rested on Mary Magdalene's breathless chest in her bedroom.

The hymn ended, and creaking noises echoed in the nave of the church as everyone took a seat in front of him.

He inhaled deeply, soaking in his pride. Her soul now rested in Heaven. No more would she sin. No more would she bring shame upon herself, her family, and her community.

While everyone else turned their attention to the visiting bishop, he scanned the crowd for his next sinner.

Who else deserves a seat at God's side?

CHAPTER SEVEN

KATE SWORE under her breath as she kicked off her shoes while holding a large brown box. “Stupid no-shoe rule.”

Seconds later, she walked into the living room in her socks. “Hey, babe,” she said to Luke.

“What’s that?” he asked as she dropped the heavy box near the TV he was watching. The news was on, by the sounds of it.

She walked over to the couch. “Well, I made a lot of progress at Kenny’s house yesterday and today. I dumped a bunch of old, worthless stuff and I packed a few boxes’ worth of items I want to go through. Photo albums, tax papers, letters, trinkets…”

“You have more?”

Kate nodded. “Lots more.” She left the room and put on her shoes again.

“I’ll help you,” he said as he joined her in the entrance.

Ten minutes later, the two of them stared at the mini wall they’d built between the TV and the couch.

“Can’t believe you managed to cram all of these in your Subaru. Good packing! But you should have called me. I’d have helped you load your car.”

“Nah. I needed some alone time. It was good.” Kate looked around, surprised that Mrs. O’Brien hadn’t once appeared to check that Kate was adhering to her no-shoe rule. “Where’s your mom?”

“She’s still at church.”

"Ah! I've been getting up so early I didn't realize what time it was." She eyed the room, then Luke. "She's not going to like seeing these boxes here, right? Where can I put them?"

Luke's lips twisted as he brought a finger to scratch the growing stubble on his chin. "My office?"

"You won't mind the clutter?"

He shrugged. "I don't spend that much time in there."

"I promise I'll go through them as fast as I can. I won't keep all of it. I just wanted to clear Kenny's house so I can list it and start showing it."

He wrapped his arms around Kate and rested his chin on top of her head. "I know." He inhaled deeply as he squeezed her closer to his chest. "Since Mom isn't around, what do you say we move those boxes fast, then make the most of our alone time? We have…" Luke checked his watch. "Thirty minutes?"

Kate moved out of his embrace to look him in the eyes. "And we wouldn't have to worry about being quiet?"

"We can be as loud as we want," Luke said, his eyebrows bouncing up and down as he grinned.

Kate got on her toes to kiss him but her phone brought a swift end to their embrace. It was the ringtone she'd assigned to Detective Lieutenant Fuller. She could not ignore it.

"Sorry, babe. We're understaffed right now." She rushed to the entryway and brought the device to her ear. "Detective Murphy."

"We've got a body. Young woman, no obvious signs of struggle at the scene, but the death is very suspicious. Most likely a homicide."

"I'm on my way. What's the address?"

CHAPTER EIGHT

DETECTIVE MALVIN ROSEBUD took in the renovated house's decor and furnishing: earth tones, leather and solid wood furniture, plush carpeting, hardwood floors, expensive television and stereo system. To date, other than the police tape surrounding the property, one broken glass panel on the front door, and the BPD, medical examiner, and crime lab technicians on scene, nothing seemed wrong in the middle-class family home.

Well, save for the stench. *That* was horribly wrong.

Decomposition had a certain pungency that couldn't be ignored, even by those fighting the nastiest of head colds. But, chewing on three sticks of mint gum with his mouth open behind his face mask, he did his best to ignore it.

After asking a crime scene tech to document the broken glass in the entrance and getting another to dust the front door for prints, Rosebud inspected the main floor instead of joining the rest of the crew upstairs. He liked to soak in as wide an area around the crime scene as possible. As he pondered on the family's CD and DVD collection, he remembered a handful of instances where little details like those, just outside the area where the victim had been left, had lost their meaning once he'd stared at the dead body.

But, most importantly today, he wasn't quite sure his burrito was going to stay put once he approached the origin of the stench. Testing that new food truck no longer seemed like the smartest idea.

"Hey, Rosebud. What do we have?" Murphy asked a few feet away from where he stood in the living room.

He turned to face her. "The vic's upstairs. I haven't seen her yet. I just got here myself."

She adjusted her right glove then looked back at him. "Fuller?"

"Upstairs, with the medical examiner."

"Wang? Chainey?"

"Don't know."

"I'm heading up."

He continued looking at the walls: picture after picture of a family of three blonds, and a large crucifix right above the fireplace.

Rosebud continued his inspection of the ground floor, moving into the dining room, paying attention to where his bootie-covered feet stepped, carefully avoiding touching any potential evidence. The department's photographer had already placed numbers around various footprints that had been left on the carpet, some bigger and some smaller than his. He suddenly realized that he wasn't sweating as much as he normally did under the one-use coveralls he'd donned minutes earlier. A glance at the thermometer on the wall explained why: the air conditioning was on, and the temperature had been set to 65 degrees.

He thanked his lucky stars. The stench could have been much, much worse. The family's electric bill would probably be huge, though. Then he realized the killer may have played with the thermostat to mess with their estimated time of death.

After getting a tech to pull fingerprints from it, Rosebud moved along to the next room.

Just like the living room, the dining room was clean and orderly. Absolutely no signs of struggle anywhere on this floor. Or at least not anywhere he'd seen. He bent sideways to inspect the table's glass surface and noticed how immaculate the top was. A light dusting of particles had landed on the surface, but not one smear was in sight.

"Hmm," he said to himself before heading into the kitchen.

The stainless steel fridge grabbed his attention next. Not a single fingerprint there either.

"Really? How?" With his gloved hand, he opened the cupboard under the sink, curious as to what brand of cleaners the family used. A pair of yellow rubber gloves, a sponge, a dish rack and tray, a spray can of oven cleaner, and a bottle of dishwashing liquid occupied the space. The family's miracle product couldn't be any of those, so he closed the cupboard, disappointed that he hadn't magically stumbled upon the solution for the unsightly smears on his own stainless steel appliances.

Do they use a maid service that carries their own products?

"Rosebud, get up here!" Fuller yelled from upstairs.

"I'm coming!" he answered before returning to the entrance and heading up the stairs, the potency of the stench increasing with every step.

Knowing fair well how Fuller would react if he saw him with his oversized piece of gum, Rosebud swallowed his now flavorless chunk then inhaled deeply before finally stepping into the pink room where the body was. There were already half a dozen people in there.

"What took you so long?" Fuller asked, a deep line between his bushy brows.

Rosebud ignored him for now, his eyes unable to look away from the vic's body. Several things looked wrong here. She was lying on top of her bright magenta comforter, wearing a faded orange nightgown with yellow flowers. The long fabric was spread out symmetrically around her swollen ankles. With her elbows bent at ninety-degrees, her hands were joined in a prayer position, a bright blue rosary wrapped around them. Her fingers were bloated with a tinge of green. Just above her hands rested an open Bible, pages facing down and upright, as though she'd been reading it.

Rosebud closed his eyes for a second and concentrated on breathing through his mouth. But it didn't help. Behind his mask, he inhaled his own bean and spicy garlic breath.

He knew from her stench and the bloat of the extremities that she'd been dead for at least a week, so bugs had most likely begun feasting and reproducing in her mouth, nose, and eyes. Looking up past her hands wasn't going to be pretty.

Mustering his mental strength—and pushing down his burrito—he finally glanced at her face.

But it wasn't as bad as he'd expected. It seemed very flew flies had managed to get to her in the closed home. He turned to her bedroom window and noticed the typical gathering of bugs on the other side of it. Those insects sure had a strong sense of smell.

Very few of them had sneaked their ways into the house, or the air conditioning had slowed her decomposition rate quite a bit. But her skin was discolored and bloated, well past rigor mortis. Her blonde hair was tied and orderly. No visible signs of struggle there. However, her glazed over eyeballs, sunken sockets, and open mouth did not offer a pretty sight, nor did they suggest a peaceful passing. When he spotted a few squirming larvae in the corner of her mouth, he turned away, swallowing the recycled sample of food that had darted up his throat.

His eyes met Murphy's. She seemed to handle the stench much better than him.

"Her name's Lori Davis. Twenty-two years old," she recited, looking at her pad. "Her driver's license confirms she lives here. I found it in her wallet, in her purse, over there on the desk." She pointed to a piece of vintage, solid-wood furniture.

Rosebud headed over to the desk, eager to distance himself from the vic's body and its new occupants.

Under the purse and neatly arranged books and pencils, the desk looked like something his own parents could have used when they'd gone to school. The light wood—birch or maple—surface was scarred from decades of overuse. An uncomfortable-looking wooden chair with a straight back completed the set. His gloved fingers perused through the contents of her purse. He retrieved a cellphone, its battery dead.

Once he ensured his stomach was okay, he spoke up, his eyes still aimed at the desk. "She must be the daughter of Doug and Francine Davis," he said. "Lots of photos with her between two older adults downstairs and lots of mail addressed to them as well. It seems the last batch brought into the home was dated Friday, June 1st. The mail overflowing out of the box on the porch is dated Wednesday, June 6th. That's probably a good start on the time of death."

Fuller walked over to him. "Rosebud, since the Sarge is on holiday, I want you to take the lead on this—"

"With all due respect, sir," Rosebud started, then paused once again, swallowing more acid reflux.

"What? Quick. I wanna get out of here."

"You and I both. I'd like Murphy to lead this one."

"Why? Not up for it?" Fuller asked, his fist bumping against Rosebud's shoulder. "About to toss your cookies again?"

Rosebud shook his head, sick and tired of his sensitive stomach being made fun of. "No. I just think Murphy's ready. I've been working alongside her for nearly a year now. She knows what she's doing. Just give her a chance to prove it to you."

Fuller looked to Murphy, who stood right next to the vic. She was speaking to the medical examiner and taking notes.

He turned back to Rosebud. "At least her gut's stronger than yours. You're as pale as a ghost. Get out and breathe some fresh air. I'll give her the lead, but you stay right on her ass. I want this case solved ASAP. This looks like a young woman from a good family. We're not talking about a drug deal or a B&E gone bad. We'll need to find out if this was random or not. The district commander's gonna ride my ass."

"Got it," Rosebud said, nodding vehemently as he dashed out of the room, down the stairs, and out the front door just in time to empty his gut behind a thorny green bush.

Shit, he thought after wiping his mouth, his eyes meeting those of Detective Gabriel Chainey who'd just ducked under the police tape, laughing.

Even though Rosebud had almost reached a two-year, vomit-free streak, Chainey wasn't going to let him live this down.

CHAPTER NINE

THE VICTIM'S neck was bruised with a pattern that led Kate to believe the rosary wrapped around the hands could have been the strangulation weapon. The vic's blonde braid was tied with a blue elastic band, the kind you'd find on broccoli. Faded and oversized, the nightgown looked out of place on the vic's petite body, as if she'd borrowed it from her grandmother.

There was no blood at the scene.

No sign of struggle.

Her nightstand was orderly, holding a reading light and a photo of the vic and a handsome young brown-haired man who appeared to be in his early twenties. Kate knew that man. She'd just seen him outside the house, secured in a squad car. He was the boyfriend, the one who'd broken into the house and discovered the body. The first one to see her dead.

But was he also the one who'd killed her?

Only the evidence would say once they'd analyzed it all.

"Scorfosi, did you take a photo of her hands?" Kate asked the photographer.

"Yep. Got all of it. I'm done with the body."

Turning to the medical examiner, she asked, "Is it okay if I just lift the end here?"

Dr. George Cooper shrugged, a paper bag in hand. "Go ahead. I was just about to seal her extremities."

Kate used a pen to lift the cross at the end of the rosary off the vic's hands. Her brightly colored manicured nails didn't seem damaged at all. "You'll retrieve whatever DNA you can from under her nails?" she asked, even though her hopes weren't high based on their immaculate state.

Kate turned to Detective Rosebud when he re-entered the room.

"Where did you go?" she asked him.

"Out. You're the lead. Do you need me here? I'd rather be downstairs."

"Tell me what you think. Doesn't look like there's been any struggle in here."

"Or anywhere in the house, really," Rosebud added.

"So what do you think about the religious theme?"

"Which part? The golden crucifix above the bed looks like it belongs here. Lots more religious items downstairs. The small cross around her neck looks like it could be something she'd wear. We'll check with the parents. As for the rosary wrapped around her hands? It could be hers."

"I don't think so. It's blue."

"Hate to break it to you, Murphy, but girls normally go past the monochrome tones you seem to limit yourself to. They can have blue things. Times have changed."

"I'm not being sexist here. Just look around the room. Everything here is peach, salmon, magenta, or some other shade of pink. If you look in her closet, she doesn't own anything blue, except for jeans. Why would she have a blue rosary?"

"Maybe you have a point. We'll just ask the parents," he said heading to the closet to open it. "Did you notice that?" he asked Kate.

"What?" she asked, heading toward him, her feet sinking into the plush carpeting.

"I'd say this girl has some sort of OCD or very strict parents."

"The evenly spaced hangers?"

"Yeah. And everything is hanging the same way, from longest to shortest outfits."

"And look at her desk," Kate said without bothering to finish her thought. Rosebud had undoubtedly noticed how the chair had been put in its rightful place, resting flush against the edge of the desk. The books' spines perfectly aligned, their backs flushed with each other. Three pencils, all of which were freshly sharpened and spaced evenly, perfectly parallel to each other. The purse had been aligned perfectly, too, but it no longer was after she'd gone through it.

"But there's one thing that's not perfect," Kate said after the medical examiner and his team had finally bagged and taken the body out of the bedroom.

"Other than the stench and the dead woman?"

"Look by the bed. The marks on the carpet. The murderer, he must have sat next to her."

Kate looked at the desk again, then the marks by the bed. Since both the photographer and medical examiner had cleared the area, she considered moving the chair to prove her point, but decided to shine her Alternate Light Source LED on it. With her gloved hand, she touched as little as she could to drag the chair back away from the desk so she could have a better look.

Sure enough, the back, the sides, and the underside of the chair were littered with visible prints. Many smudged but some as clear as day.

"Scorfosi! Get back in here, please!" she yelled out.

The photographer came back into the room. "What's up, Murphy?"

"Did you take photos of all those prints?" she asked, her blue light with the orange filter now illuminating the back of the chair.

He shook his head. "Fuller had me take photos of the nightstand and the Bible that rested on the vic, but not the chair. We already dusted for prints on the nightstand and took photos of those."

"I think we may have hit the jackpot. Loads will be the vic's, but if my guess is right, that chair was where the killer sat next to the victim when she died."

By now Rosebud had relocated to the side of the bed, a tape measure in hand, comparing the distance between the sections of flattened fibers and the legs of the chair. Kate was still illuminating the chair while the photographer recorded the evidence.

"Looks right to me," Rosebud said. "But who's to say these marks weren't from before?"

"I don't think so," Murphy said. "Look at the rest of the carpet. The lines. Other than our own footsteps, it looks freshly vacuumed. I doubt she would've left her chair there. It probably would have bothered her to see it out of place.

"So the killer sat next to her?"

"And for quite a while," Kate added, noting how flattened the carpet fibers were. Turning to the photographer, she asked. "Did you get a few good shots of the carpet before we stepped all over the crime scene?"

"A few. I'll share them with you when we get back, but I wouldn't get your hopes up."

CHAPTER TEN

"HOW MANY DOZENS did you bake, Mom?" Luke asked as he loaded yet another Rubbermaid container into his car.

"Don't you worry about it and just load it all up. Oh shoot!" she said, looking around. "I almost forgot my purse. I'll be right back!"

Five minutes later, Luke opened the driver's door, muttering to himself as his mother commented on his choice of clothing.

"I don't care what your fellow parishioners think of the way I dress," he said after she closed the passenger door. "Aren't they supposed to be all loving and accepting? Isn't that what religion is supposed to be about?"

"Watch your mouth."

"I'm not changing, Mom. These jeans are clean, and so is my T-shirt. If I'm going to be socially uncomfortable, at least let me do it in comfortable clothes."

~

AFTER DROPPING off his mother at the front entrance of the school where the fundraiser was being held, Luke drove to park his vehicle.

A few minutes later, one large container in hand, he found his mother chatting with a young, brown-haired man at a registration table. He, too, had dressed as fancy as his mother had, wearing a buttoned-down shirt even though his right arm was in a cast and pinned against his chest in a sling.

"Mrs. O'Brien, you're at table twenty. Go ahead and get yourself set up. Harold will come by later to collect more information and discuss an upcoming project we're excited about. I see you've brought someone to help." He looked at Luke.

"I'm her son. Table twenty, you said?" Luke turned his attention to his mother. "I'll go put this first box at your table, Mom."

As he walked away, he could hear his mom beginning the embarrassing speech that always came next. Sure, there were much worse things than having a mother who constantly bragged about how smart her son was. But decades of hearing the spiel hadn't made it less embarrassing. And his mother never listened to his numerous requests to end that behavior.

Best get this evening over with as fast as possible.

After several trips to the car, Luke had carried all of his mom's precious muffins, pies, and cupcakes to her table. Thankfully, she had already displayed a fair amount of her selection of goods and then organized the other Rubbermaid containers behind her table so she could presumably replenish her items as needed.

Either that or he'd have to carry all of those containers back home and he, Kate, and his mom would be stuffing their faces with baked goods for weeks to come. That wouldn't really be a problem, though. His mom's baked goods were delicious. He still had lots of spare notches in his belt, but Luke didn't want to put on weight. *Worst comes to worst, I'll talk her into offering free samples.*

Already, even though the doors had yet to open, his head was buzzing. The incessant jabber of mingled small talk, especially from the loud lady one table over, made him regret his decision to help his mother.

"Hey, Mrs. O'Brien!" she practically yelled. "Looks like we'll be neighbors again!" Her chirpy voice was as loud as her bright red dress. "And who's that nice man you brought with you today?"

Although the woman had technically addressed his mom,

her deep brown eyes were dead locked onto Luke. Her lips arched upward after she gave him the once over.

"I'm her son, Luke," he said, extending his hand toward her even though starting a conversation with the bubbly woman was the last thing he wanted to do.

"Adrianna Johnston. Nice to meet you. And you're not married?" she said as they shook, her eyes glued to his left hand.

Best to end this right here.

"Nope. But not single either," Luke said in a tone as flat as his interest toward the woman.

"Luke Stewart O'Brien, I didn't raise you to be impolite." His mom turned her attention to the woman.

"Adrianna, please don't mind him. My son's not much for social gatherings, but he's helping me tonight. It's his birthday present to me."

"Oh! Just like my son! I know how that goes. When did young people stop liking other people? Happy birthday, Mrs. O'Brien."

"Thank you. It's not today, per se, but I couldn't think of a better birthday present than getting my Luke to spend quality time with me."

"And helping the community," Adrianna added.

"Sure," Luke said, doing his best to not roll his eyes at the woman who was still looking at him strangely.

"Too bad you're not single. If things don't work out, please ask your mom to let me know." She winked at Luke then was about to walk back toward her table when Luke's mom spoke.

"Oh, Adrianna. I wouldn't get your hopes up. My Luke is dating a detective, you know? She's quite the catch—"

"Mom!" Luke said, doing his best to keep his voice low. "Enough about sharing my private life with strangers!"

"She's not a stranger! She's a friend from church."

"My offer remains in case things don't work out with your smart detective friend."

After giving one last wink, she returned to her table—the very next one over—where a young man sat quietly, his arms crossed on his chest. In front of him rested a colorful selection of rosaries made out of knotted strings.

He appeared as uncomfortable as Luke, but at least he'd

found himself a chair. Scanning the room, Luke spotted two stacks of chairs against the far wall.

"I'm gonna get us some chairs, Mom. I'll be right back."

He grabbed two, noticing several large plastic bins nearby. A sign read "Clothing donations" and he made a mental note to tell Kate she could donate her uncle's clothing to the church. He remembered her mentioning how much she'd found. Sure, Kenny hadn't been the most fashionable man he'd met, but he understood lack of income had contributed to him never updating his wardrobe.

Beggars can't be choosers, he thought. Kate had enough to sort through already—an entire houseful—the church volunteers could go through and decide if Kenny's old clothes were worth anything to them.

When he returned with the chairs, a broad-shouldered man with a clipboard was chatting up his mother.

"So, if you'd like to support our cause, then please write your name, address, and phone number. We're hoping to get two hundred signatures tonight."

Hoping to avoid an awkward conversation in front of his mother—and definitely not willing to listen to whatever pitch the man had been tasked with—Luke retrieved his phone and brought it to his ear, feigning to be on a call as he, one by one, moved the chairs over to the table. A polite nod later, he stepped away from his mom's table, then decided he might as well check on Kate.

She'd been called to work hours ago. Perhaps she was nearly done? Having her by his side would most definitely make the whole fundraiser much easier to stand. Spending time in social settings was at the bottom of his list of enjoyable activities. He already saw plenty of people at work.

But with Kate around, the world always seemed to fade away. How she achieved that, he had no idea, but he wished she were with him now.

His stomach twisted at the thought of how uncomfortable he'd soon be, once the doors officially opened to the public.

After dialing her number, it went straight to voicemail. "Hey, Katie, I was just thinking of you. You're probably still working, or maybe you're driving back home. Anyways, Mom and I are in a school basement for the next five hours. Selling baked goods to raise funds for something or other. You know how much fun I'll be having. So, it'd be nice to see you, if you can make it. But you might still be at work. Either way. It's cool. Love you."

He returned the phone to his pocket, saw that the man had moved on to table eighteen, so Luke deemed it safe to return to his mom.

"Luke, you should talk to Harold and sign his petition."

"Maybe later. I'm sure he'll find plenty of willing parishioners tonight. How many people did you say are expected?"

"About three hundred."

He took a seat and looked at Adrianna's son behind the next table. The young man hadn't moved a hair, it seemed. He hadn't even looked his way. Crossing his arms on his chest, Luke decided he'd follow the kid's lead. But he added a fake smile. Psychological disguise or not, he'd read that smiling increased one's happiness.

And he was going to need all the help he could get for the long social evening that was about to start.

CHAPTER ELEVEN

"MURPHY, YOU'RE IT. SUMMARY. NOW!" Detective Lieutenant Fuller barked as he walked into conference room two, ending the chatter among the four detectives in attendance.

Kate cleared her throat as she walked toward the board where she'd pinned several pictures.

"Lori Davis, age twenty-two, only child of Doug and Francine Davis, was found dead in her bedroom earlier today at her family home by her boyfriend of two years, David Dempsey. She still resided with her parents—"

"Parents," Fuller repeated. "Have you notified them?"

"No, sir." Kate looked at her watch. "They're still traveling as we speak, coming back from a Caribbean cruise. Their flight is expected to land in two hours. I'll be at the airport when they arrive"—Kate swallowed hard—"to tell them their only daughter is dead."

"Fun times ahead," Detective Jenny Wang said, tucking a long strand of black hair behind her ear. Her face was as solemn as a monk's.

"Yep. Moving on." Kate tapped her finger on the zoomed-in version of the map and the photo of the vic's body lying in bed.

"This is the cleanest photo of footprints left on the carpet. We don't know for sure, but this here"—she circled an area with the tip of her pen—"could be a sign that the victim was dragged into the room or it could be someone trying to wipe the footprints from the carpet. We've got at least two shoe sizes. Could be the victim's, the killer's, and/or the boyfriend's."

"The latter two could be one and the same," Chainey chimed in.

"Too early to say." Kate stepped back to point to a large photo of a brown-haired man with bright blue eyes. "Meet David Dempsey. He's the one who broke into the home." Kate referred to her notepad for a second. "I quote, 'I hadn't heard from her in over two weeks and I knew she had to pick up her parents at the airport tonight.' End quote." Kate closed her pad. "Scene markers like the overflowing mailbox confirm this as a plausible timeline. Boyfriend didn't have a key to her house. Broken glass on the floor says forced entry from the outside. The fingerprints lifted on both the outside and inside latch will likely confirm that story. We'll know soon enough."

"A suspect?" Fuller asked.

"For now, but we didn't arrest him. No way we could collect sufficient evidence to prove *probable cause*, let alone *without a doubt*, within twenty-four hours. We'll keep an eye on him then try to build a case once we get a time of death."

"Isn't it weird that he hadn't spoken to his girlfriend for two weeks?" Wang asked.

"Tough to tell. Items found in the vic's house all point to religion being important. Perhaps it was typical for them to only see each other once or twice a month. I'll interview David Dempsey again tomorrow. Give him a chance to digest the news and possibly contradict himself on record based on what we got from the squad car camera today. He seemed genuinely affected by his discovery."

"What else?" Fuller prompted.

Kate pointed to a map of the area. "The residential neighborhood is mostly multi-dwelling buildings. The vic's home appears to be an exception. One of the rare homes that hasn't been converted into multi-family housing, and based on renovations, the family probably has money. Wang will comb through the parents' financial situation and insurance policies for potential motives. Possibly a large life insurance payout. She'll check to see if there are more relatives who could have stood to gain from her death."

"Security footage?" Fuller asked, a line between his brows.

Kate shook her head. "The house isn't equipped with anything. No alarm, no cameras. I checked the streets in the neighborhood. No luck. I'll canvas the neighborhood over the coming days, but with so many tenants, many of whom could work various day and night shifts, it will take a while."

"I'll approve a few extra officers to help," Fuller said. "Businesses nearby?"

"Nothing for a few blocks."

"What are your priorities?" Fuller prompted.

"I'll attend the autopsy first thing tomorrow morning. There was no sign of struggle, but perhaps the medical examiner will find something underneath the nails—a lose hair, or some other fiber. Rosebud will look into the boyfriend—his whereabouts for the past two weeks, their history, any potential motives. In addition to the recorded interview we did earlier today, we'll get him to commit to a timeline on record again, to see if he contradicts himself. Tough to confirm an alibi until we get an estimated time of death."

"Go with your scene markers for now. You said Wang's on the parents. What about Chainey? What's he looking into?"

"The vic. Her story, phone calls, credit card and bank statements. Tracking down her whereabouts for the past three weeks. Talking to friends—work and church—to see if we can narrow down the time of death."

"Warrants?" Fuller asked.

"Filled out and submitted already so we can look into the vic's past. I don't expect any issues. I doubt I'll get any information from the parents tonight. I'm hoping I can talk to them again after the autopsy and show them photos to ask about anything missing or out of place in their home, or potential enemies."

"You're going to break the news at the airport?" Fuller asked, his brows raised.

"I can't think of any other option. I checked with border control. Scene markers and witnesses say she was alive when they left. The death occurred while they were out of the country. Unless they hired someone to kill their daughter, they're not suspects. I don't want to bring them all the way here to tell them. They deserve to know before they learn about it on the news."

"Take Rosebud and do your best to avoid a public scene."

CHAPTER TWELVE

Bath, Maine
Friday, June 23rd, 1995

STANDING in the doorway of her brother's bedroom in jeans that she'd already outgrown—exposing a few too many inches of her crimson socks—Kate watched her mother hum a lullaby while cradling Bobby, rocking him to sleep in the chair that made the old floor creak.

"Mom?"

She looked up and smiled, her green eyes kind and loving. "Yes, dear?"

"Can I head out to play with my friend Luko?"

"Where are you planning to go?"

"To the park, maybe go all the way to the cave today."

"Promise that you'll be careful?"

"Of course, Mom! Luko and I always check both ways before crossing roads. We never talk to strangers. We just go and play explorers."

"You sure are a little tomboy, Katie. I certainly preferred to play with my dolls when I was your age."

"Dolls are boring."

"You know what you like. But come back on time today. I'm cooking a small turkey, so I don't want it to dry out while waiting for you."

"Yes, Mom. Can I hold Bobby for a few minutes before I go?"

"Sure, sweetie. But he's sleeping already, so be careful not to wake him up." She extended her arms so Kate could take him. "Put him down in his crib gently when you're done. I need to get started on my potatoes."

Kate beamed as she grabbed her baby brother. He was so little and light. His tiny nose barely flared as he breathed in and out.

Her hands now free, her mom got up from the rocking chair and started the mobile that hung over the crib. A tranquil melody soon filled the blue bedroom with its bells and soft notes.

Kate sat where her mom had seconds earlier, sensing the warmth of her mother's body still in the chair. Humming the tune of the mobile, Kate rocked her baby brother, letting him hold onto the tip of her index finger. His tiny fingers loved to grab ahold of everything. Even while he slept.

She leaned in and inhaled her brother's scent before brushing a kiss on his tiny forehead. His lack of hair—a thin layer of fuzz was all he had—had first worried Kate, but her mom had explained that she needn't worry about it. His real hair would grow in due time. Unlike Kate and her mom, Baby Bobby had brown fuzz, like their dad. Well, their dad had real hair, not baby fuzz.

She rocked and rocked, the melody soon dissipating in the air as the winding reached the end of its cycle—

CHAPTER THIRTEEN

Boston, Massachusetts
Monday, June 18th, 2018

BUT HER PEACEFUL memory ended just as suddenly as it had begun.

A horrible vision flashed in Kate's mind, that of Bobby's cold and limp body in her arms, pressed against her teenage chest.

Kate woke up in sweats, her limbs almost slapped Luke as she bolted upright. Beating out of control, her heart syncopated to the soundtrack of her recent nightmare.

"Kate?" Luke said.

But all Kate could do was concentrate on slowing down her heart, on pushing aside the horrific memories that had overtaken her mind like a flash flood.

Luke fumbled, one hand out, until he found and pulled the string hanging from the lamp on his nightstand. A soft light filled the room, and he stared at Kate.

She could feel the heat in her face, the uncontrollable heaving of her chest.

He worked his way to a sitting position then wrapped his arms around her. "Katie, you're okay. I'm here."

With one of her hands, she reached out to pull his arm closer, to get more of his body pressed against hers. She needed to feel his warmth, to know that he was real and the horrible things she'd just seen were old memories, far from the present.

"I think you're right," Kate said once she got her breathing under control.

"About what?" Luke asked.

"My nightmares. Who am I kidding? They're never going to go away. Maybe I should talk to that hypnotherapist."

Luke inhaled deeply then exhaled slowly, as though processing her words.

"I'll get the number tomorrow."

Kate rubbed her hands against one of his arms. "Sorry for waking you up."

"Don't apologize. Just get back to sleep."

Kate shook her head, then turned to look at the alarm clock: 3:47 a.m.

"There's no point. I know I won't be able to. I'll hop in the shower and head to work. I've got lots to do. Go back to sleep, Luko. I love you."

He muttered something, then turned off the light as she headed into their en-suite.

While the warm droplets hammered her back—the massage feature on the shower head was magically powerful—she did her best at flushing away the memories.

Focus on something else. Anything else.

And just like that, Lori's face came back to replace Bobby's lifeless body.

She squirmed, annoyed at what her subconscious had provided in response to her demand.

I really need to start meditating. Or find a hobby that involves happy, positive things.

But no matter how hard she tried, the vic's glazed-over eyes came to mind. The tiny little white spots in her faded irises, her dilated pupils…

The lack of struggle in the house. Her immaculate fingernails and braid. And that blue rubber band. No self-respecting woman would ever use one of those. That was just begging for split ends and damaged hair.

Someone likely drugged her, then strangled her, then dressed her up, did her hair, and laid her on the bed…

Or perhaps the struggle had occurred elsewhere, and the

murderer had cleaned her up and brought her into the house… She thought of the house's lack of garage. Bringing a dead body into that home unnoticed was not really plausible.

She just had to be patient and wait for today's autopsy. Perhaps unexpected lividity or bruising patterns would reveal something different.

Kate, now wide awake, turned off the water.

She had to solve Lori's murder, not just to bring her justice, but to make the city safer. And Fuller was going to judge her for it. Her first time being the lead. She had to rally the team and solve the case fast or she'd never earn Fuller's respect.

CHAPTER FOURTEEN

AFTER DONNING scrubs and face masks, Detectives Murphy and Rosebud walked into the large examination room. Although sterile, the stench was the furthest thing from bleach. It stank like death in the outdated, floor-to-ceiling tiled space.

Kate turned to Rosebud, the part of his face visible around his mask had a greenish hue to it.

"I'll be over there," he said pointing to the stainless steel sink along one of the walls.

"Detectives. Right on time," Dr. Cooper said from behind the full-face plastic mask that hung from his forehead, over his black-framed glasses. On top of his blue scrubs, he wore a white apron. Kate knew from experience that it wouldn't stay that way very long. It had nothing to do with the examiner's potential clumsiness; death and slippery organs made for a messy work environment.

"I got ahold of Lori Davis's health records," he started, a file in hand. "No problems there. As healthy as they come, based on her medical history. Twenty-two-year-old female, blonde hair, blue eyes." Dr. Cooper put down the file and, with a pair of scissors, began cutting open the worn-out nightgown. As he reached the part where the victim's hands had been joined together, he put his scissors down and grabbed an evidence bag. With his gloved hands, he carefully removed the rosary and placed it into the bag, which he offered Kate.

"Thanks," she said, taking it. "I was wondering if we could

try to match the marks on her neck with the knotted beads on the rosary."

"Give me a chance to finish undressing and cleaning the body, then we'll do that if you'd like."

"Fine," Kate said, swallowing hard and doing her best to keep her stomach steady.

The doc carefully parted the vic's bloated fingers. Their decomposed state made the discolored skin stick where fingers normally didn't.

Kate turned away for a few seconds until she was certain her stomach was okay. When she looked at the victim again, the vic's arms hung loosely on each side of her body. The gown hung open, exposing her discolored, swollen corpse and legs. Her white bra and panties had taken on unrecognizable colors that matched the stench.

"Do you think she was raped?" Kate asked.

"No damage to her underwear," the doctor said before snapping the sides open with scissors.

"Do you mind helping me lift her up while I remove the clothing and bag it?" Dr. Cooper asked.

"No, thanks!" Rosebud said from a distance.

Kate nodded, well aware that if she helped, they could leave faster. "Just tell me what you need me to do."

"When I say, just lift her up right here, like so," he said, showing Kate where she could grab the vic's ankles. "Wait."

He cut away each sleeve, then gave Kate the signal. Kate lifted the cold ankles, trying her best to ignore how much the texture and firmness of her limbs reminded her of legs of ham. Rotten ham. Together, they lifted the body and the doctor pulled away the nightgown, underwear, and bra, which he then placed in a paper bag.

Seeing the woman's body on the stainless steel slab made Kate close her eyes. This wasn't her first autopsy, and she knew it would most probably not be her last, but the thought didn't make it any easier for her to watch. Lori Davis's life had ended so early. Too early.

Kate walked over to Rosebud, who was now rinsing his mouth directly from the tap.

"Gravol not helping today?" she asked.

"I don't know how you can stand so close to it. Your stomach must be a lot stronger than mine."

"I'm having a hard time today. This body really reeks." Kate knew Rosebud wasn't going to say anything about her not witnessing all of the autopsy. Chainey had the gut of steel amongst their group of detectives. He would have laughed at both Kate and Rosebud hanging out by the sink. Kate was grateful to have been partnered up with Rosebud.

"I don't see any obvious signs of rape," the doctor said from behind Kate.

"Is he inspecting her private bits?" Kate asked Rosebud, not daring to look at the corpse. Perhaps it was her upbringing, but she had never been able to witness that particular part of the autopsy. Perhaps she felt staring at a stranger's genitals, whether dead or alive, was wrong.

Rosebud glanced behind Kate for a second before snapping his neck back to face the sink. "Yeah."

"No obvious bruising, but it will be easier to see once I rinse her off."

"Can you take samples from her nails and orifices before you do?" Kate asked.

"Already on it," the doctor said. "I got a hair sample and nail clippings, and I'm doing swabs right now. I swiped the underside of her nails, but they're immaculate, as though she'd gotten a manicure an hour prior to her death."

"Maybe she did. I'll look into nearby salons to try to pinpoint her time of death," Kate said as she added more to her notepad.

"I think it was a homemade job," Rosebud chimed in.

Kate turned to look at him. He was still hunched over the stainless steel sink.

"I saw nail polish, remover, and those thingies that go between the toes in the downstairs bathroom. There were also some cotton pads with nail polish on it."

"There goes that idea," Kate said. "Was it red?"

"Bright red like what she's got on."

"Did you bag it?"

"The garbage, yes. I didn't bag the polish, though."

"I'll get Chainey on it. We'll process it for fingerprints."

The sound of water running was what made Kate return to the corpse.

"Lividity indicates she likely died in the same position she was found in. Now, let's have a look at that neck," Dr. Cooper said before leaning in. "Hmm."

"What's that 'hmm' for?" Kate asked.

He walked around the corpse to inspect the other side of her neck. "I don't think that rosary alone was the murder weapon."

"What do you mean?"

"Do you have it?" Dr. Cooper asked.

Kate lifted up the bag he'd given her minutes earlier. It hadn't been sealed yet. The medical examiner took out the rosary and positioned it against the swollen neck of the victim. "See, it's barely long enough to go around once. So, at most, you'd have two beads in one location because of its circular shape. Also, you'd have at most, what? Fifty or sixty bead imprints since that's how many this one has? But without doing a thorough count, which I'll do shortly, along with photographs, I'm guessing there's close to a hundred of these little bruises against her neck. See this part of the neck here shows at least four beads imprinted very close to each other. It's hard to tell for sure due to the decomposition, but I'd say the killer used more rosaries. It would have also made the strangulation weapon sturdier."

The doctor once again returned the rosary to Kate, who tested the strength of the string with her gloved hands. She didn't exert too much pressure as she did not want to damage the evidence, but she agreed that one rosary alone may not be able to support the tension required to strangle someone.

"But two or three of these would make sense, right? Especially if the victim's not fighting back."

"I'd agree with that. Victim weighs… one hundred and twenty-six pounds." He took out a measuring tape. "And measures five feet, six inches and a half. Now, I'm going to open her chest cavity. Are you guys gonna stick around?"

Kate nodded as she watched Dr. Cooper place a rubber body block underneath the victim's back, pushing her chest forward and out.

With his scalpel, the doctor proceeded to pierce the

discolored skin and make the Y-shaped incision she'd seen too many times already. She did her best to ignore the waft of putrefaction that emanated from the bloated corpse. She turned to look away.

The cracking of the rib cage made Kate call out to her partner, "Rosebud, join me in the hall?"

"I thought you'd never ask."

"We'll be back shortly, Doc."

"Take your time. I'm not going anywhere," he said.

Once out in the relatively unscented corridor, Rosebud removed his mask. "I hate that part of the job."

"So, this murder weapon. There are more of them out there. Maybe that's what we should focus on. See if David Dempsey has some at home. Maybe see if he has any prescription drugs that could have been used to make his girlfriend pass out."

"We're eliminating the idea that the victim was moved post-mortem?"

"There was no garage at the house, no easy way to unload a body from a car. One of the neighbors would have seen something if anyone had unloaded a large bag, rolled up carpet, or anything that could have hidden a body from sight. And the vic's lividity settles it. She had to have been killed in her own house."

"You're going to seal that bag?" Rosebud asked.

"That and the bag of clothes we'll take to the lab. And whatever else the doc has for us."

"Why don't I take care of those, and you stay here with the doc and fill me in later?"

"Sure, we can do that," Kate said as they re-entered the examination room.

The doctor was weighing various organs by the look of things. His apron had gained extra colors from various smudges and wiped handprints.

Kate and Rosebud remained silent as the doctor dictated the weight of every organ into his audio recorder. The evidence was sealed and transferred over to Rosebud, who promptly fled the examination room, leaving Kate alone with the medical examiner and the corpse.

"After you rinsed her off, still no sign of rape?" Kate asked, her eyes darting to the floor instead of the victim's open chest cavity.

"I'd say no to rape."

"Recent sexual intercourse prior to death?"

"Hard to say, but the swab will confirm or deny the presence of sperm."

"What else did the body tell you?" Kate asked.

"The white spots and red lines in her eyes indicate asphyxia from strangulation. The manner of death is neither an accident nor a suicide; it's a homicide for sure. The victim was otherwise healthy. All her organs were as you'd expect for a young, healthy twenty-two-year-old woman. The dilated pupils are not from asphyxia, though. Most probably drugged. I cut open the stomach and didn't find anything there."

"How was she drugged, then?"

"Could have been food but eaten more than two to three hours prior to death. Or it could have been a liquid, which would have gone through her system."

"So, she died more than three hours after eating?"

"Correct. We'll run a test on her blood, see if there's any alcohol in there."

"I'll add Valium, Ketamine, and Rohypnol to the toxicology testing, along with all of the prescription drugs we found in the vic's house. See if the killer could have spiked a drink with one of those," Kate added. "What about the time of death?"

"As much as I'd love to tell you that, I can't really narrow it down much. I'll send a sample of the blow flies I took earlier to a forensic entomologist to get a better idea, but ambient temperature could have really sped up or slowed down that timeline."

"Rough idea?"

He shook his head. "It was quite chilly in that house. With the current state of decomposition, I'd say ten to twenty days."

Kate exhaled loudly while making notes on her pad. Not only had attending the autopsy made her lose her appetite, she'd also lost hope of finding the killer fast.

CHAPTER FIFTEEN

"MR. AND MRS. DAVIS," Detective Rosebud said, "thank you for coming down here." He noticed Mrs. Davis's red and swollen eyes. The husband didn't look as bad as his wife, but there was a certain absence in his stare. "We'll continue our discussion about Lori—"

"Looooriii," the mom sobbed, covering her face with one hand while her husband wrapped his arm around her slumped shoulders.

Rosebud cleared his throat then Murphy spoke up. "Mrs. Davis, I'm sorry." Murphy extended her hand to clasp the woman's clenched fist. "Let me assure you that we're on your team here. As I said when I announced the awful, awful news to you last night, we take no pleasure in this. No parent ever wants to hear that news. I'm sorry it happened to you, and our entire department is working really hard to catch the person who did this to Lori."

Mrs. Davis nodded then inhaled deeply.

Rosebud cleared his throat. "Now, I know this is a difficult time, but I'd like your DNA and fingerprints so that we can eliminate yours when we analyze the evidence. Is that all right with you?"

Both parents nodded in silence.

"Thank you, we'll collect and process those shortly. Also, do you have access to your daughter's cellphone bill and your home's landline statement?"

"Of course," Mr. Davis said. "We have a family plan on our cellphones. I thought detectives had access to those."

"Eventually we will, with the warrants we've already gotten, but it takes a while for companies to provide the information we need. If you don't mind sharing your latest bills and call history, it would buy us some valuable time."

"No problem. Anything we can do to help, detectives."

"Thanks," Rosebud said before opening the manila folder in front of him. "I want to ask you a few more questions and then show you some photos. Whatever you say, whatever tiny detail you mention could make a big difference and help us catch the killer faster."

"Are we going to see photos of our baby girl?" Mrs. Davis asked, part dread and part something else shining through her eyes.

"Only if you feel up to it," Rosebud said. "But first, I want to repeat a question my partner asked last night. I know you were in shock at the time, so I want to make sure we have our facts straight. Yesterday, you stated that you and your daughter were the only people with a key to your house. Is this correct?"

"Yes," the father said.

"Any relatives in town or neighbors with a key? Or spare keys hidden somewhere near the house?"

"No," Mr. Davis said. "The neighbors are all renters. New people come in and out all the time. It wouldn't be safe."

Rosebud noticed a strange look on the mother's face.

"Mrs. Davis?"

"Well, it's not totally accurate," she said.

"What do you mean?" The father's tone was more surprised than angry.

"Remember a few years ago when I kept losing my keys?"

Mr. Davis frowned at his wife. "Mm-hmm."

"Well, I had a spare made."

"Where is that spare now?" Rosebud asked.

"It's hidden about an inch or two in the largest flower pot on the front porch."

"What?" The father's voice had gone up a notch.

Rosebud rifled through the pile of photos to find one of the front porch. "This one?" he asked, pointing to the largest pot.

"Yes, it's buried in there, along the part of the rim closest to the door."

"What?" the father repeated.

"Don't worry. Nobody ever saw that key! I put it there in the middle of the night, and I've never had to use it since. It's probably all rusty anyway."

"We'll look into it. Thank you, Mrs. Davis. But, just to clarify, you said you'd lost your keys before. How long ago was that and any possibility someone could have used one of those lost keys in the past?"

The Davises looked at each other, then Mrs. Davis spoke. "I… I don't think so. Wouldn't they have stolen something? And why now?"

"How long ago did you last lose your keys?" Murphy repeated.

Mrs. Davis shook her head while exhaling. "I don't know. Two years ago?"

"Was there any identifying tag on your keys? Something that could point to your home address?"

The woman shook her head.

Rosebud made note of her reply on his pad as Murphy got up. "I'll get someone on the spare key right away." She grabbed the photo and exited the interview room.

"Do you think my key could have been used by the killer?" Mrs. Davis asked Rosebud as horror morphed her tired face.

"That's not what we're saying, but we need to look at all possibilities. We'll see if that key is still there, if there are fingerprints on it, if it looks like it's been used at all in the past week."

"Oh my god! Did my silly habit of misplacing my keys kill my daughter?"

Mr. Davis wrapped his arm around his shaky, weeping wife. "Don't do that to yourself, Fran."

Rosebud once again cleared his throat, not enjoying how the interview was unfolding. "I agree with your husband. Don't blame yourself. We'll find whoever did this to your daughter, but we need your help. Would you like a cup of coffee or something?" he asked as he got up, manila folder in hand.

"No, thank you," the man said as his wife silently shook her head. Nothing except sobbing came out of her.

"I'll go and get myself a cup, give you both a few minutes to collect yourselves. I'll be back shortly, and we'll start looking at photos, all right?"

"Thank you," the man said. Rosebud exited the interview room to walk into the smaller room that oversaw it.

Wang sat there alone, a steamy cup of green tea in front of her. "Hard to get info from them, isn't it?" she told Rosebud after he closed the door.

"Can't blame them for being emotional. I just have to give them time or they'll be totally useless."

"Why don't you go and get yourself that cup of coffee you talked about?"

"Could you have Murphy head in whenever she gets back?" Rosebud asked.

"Will do. She said she was going to get Chainey to recover that spare key."

"Great. Thanks, Wang."

Fifteen minutes later, his manila folder and a large cappuccino from the deli across the street in hand, Rosebud reentered the room.

"How are we doing now?" he asked.

Although the Davises remained quiet, they looked a little less worse for wear.

Rosebud sat down in front of them and reopened his photo folder. "Ready to continue?"

"Yes," the couple said in unison.

"We'll start with the easiest things, like the rest of your home."

As he finished his sentence, the door opened, and Murphy joined them again. She, too, had grabbed a cup of coffee, but a crappy one from the lunchroom's machine, according to the cup's label.

"Okay," the mom said. She made a noticeable effort at swallowing while reaching for a tissue from the box on the table.

"Your house was extremely orderly when we arrived at the scene. We don't know if it's how you leave it, or if the killer could have cleaned up after him or herself."

"Herself? You think a woman could have killed my baby girl?"

"We really don't know anything at this point, so we don't want to eliminate half the suspect pool."

The dad spoke up next. "So, that means that… she wasn't…"

The mom's breathing became erratic.

Rosebud looked at Kate in silence, knowing the trap they faced. Kate broke eye contact and spoke to the mother. "We're still waiting for the full autopsy report…"

"But? Say it, please!" the father begged.

"Based on what she wore and the autopsy we just—"

"Murphy," Rosebud interjected, closing the folder in front of him.

She turned to him, "I know I'm not supposed to state anything since it's not confirmed yet but…" Kate reached out to grab the woman's hand. "The body had begun the decomposition process—"

"Decomposition?" Tears burst forth from the mother like a fountain.

Rosebud moved the box of tissues closer to her.

When the mother got herself under control, Murphy spoke again. "The medical examiner stated that, based on the lack of bruising in that area and the state of the clothes she had on, it didn't seem as though she had been raped, but more tests will be conducted."

The woman continued weeping.

"This isn't an official statement by me, anyone at the Boston PD, or the medical examiner. This is just from one woman to another, and I ask that you keep this detail within the confines of this room. If this belief changes based on the test results, we'll let you know."

"Thank you," the mother said before reaching for another tissue.

"So, can we begin looking at photos now?" Rosebud asked after re-opening the manila folder in front of him.

The couple nodded.

He spread out various shots taken in the living room.

"Do you notice anything different. Either out of place or perhaps missing?"

The dad glanced at them all, a slight line between his brows. "Looks normal to me."

"It's always this tidy and organized?" Rosebud prompted. "No books, magazines, or anything on the coffee table?"

"Yeah, that's how we keep it. Hold on!" the mother said before grabbing one of the photos to take a closer look.

"Anything on that one?"

"The bookcase. There's a gap…" She brought the photo closer to her face, most likely trying to read the spines, then she finally lowered the photo. "Our Bible is missing!" She handed the photo to her husband."

"Why would someone steal our Bible?" he asked, agreeing with his wife's findings.

Murphy ruffled through the photographs and pulled out the close up of the Bible that had been left on the vic's body.

"Is this your Bible?" Murphy asked.

"Yes!" they exclaimed, their eyes widening with relief. "But what horrendous fabric is that underneath it? We don't have anything orange with yellow flowers like that."

Rosebud was grateful that the close up didn't reveal enough of the fabric for them to realize it was the gown their daughter had on. He knew that they were entering slippery territory, one more fact could mean their minds would re-enter the shock zone where they would no longer be able to offer any valuable information. So Rosebud tried to squeeze out a few answers first by being vague. "It was on a piece of clothing we found. It's not something either of you, or your daughter would have in the house?"

"Most definitely not," the woman said.

"Let me show you other rooms," Rosebud said.

A few minutes later, after going through the rest of the living room, kitchen, two bathrooms, and their master bedroom, the parents hadn't spotted anything that would help the detectives.

"Now, the next photos will be more difficult. Tell me if you need more time or if you've seen too much and we'll stop. Obviously, the more you can help us, the better."

"Okay," the mother said.

"I understand," the father said.

"Is there anything out of place on her desk?" Rosebud asked as he slipped a picture in front of them.

Both parents raised their shoulders.

"Was your daughter always aligning things like this or could this have been done after her death? We saw a similar display in her closet, with hangers evenly spaced." Rosebud added a new picture next to the previous one.

"No, that's our little girl. She's always liked things tidy and organized."

"Very well, and the limited color selection in the closet?"

"Also her, she only wore shades of pink."

"When we found her, she wore a nightgown made with the orange and yellow fabric we showed you earlier."

"She doesn't own anything like that."

"How about a rosary?" Murphy asked.

"She has a gorgeous one, made out of pink pearls. It's something we brought back from a trip to China years ago."

"How about this one?" Rosebud slid a new picture and took away the previous ones. "Did it come from anywhere in your house?"

The photo the parents looked at was a close-up shot of the rosary in the evidence bag.

"This blue thing?" the mother asked.

Kate nodded.

"No way. We never bought one of those, and most definitely not in blue."

"So you've seen rosaries like this before?" Rosebud asked.

"Of course. Lots of them. Our church fundraises to help some of our poorer parishioners. That's one of the items they make and sell."

So much for the one thing that could have been a good lead.

CHAPTER SIXTEEN

"IN THE NAME of the Father, the Son, and the Holy Spirit. My last confession was a week ago," whispered a female voice.

"Talk to me, my child," the father said, his voice strong and reassuring, even though his tone was hushed within the confessional.

"Forgive me, Father, for I have sinned."

"You can clear your conscience today. Through me, the Lord will forgive you."

A deep and long, ragged exhalation later—as though the woman was fighting tears—she spoke again. "I feel responsible for my friend's death."

More ragged breathing could be heard before the father spoke, prompting the woman. "Go on."

"I couldn't keep my tongue tied. Maybe I was just proud to be better than her for once."

"I'm not sure I follow, my child."

"She wasn't the perfect little prodigal daughter anymore. For once, I was better than her. Purer. I hadn't committed her sin of the flesh."

"What sin are you talking about?"

"She had given herself up. To a boy. Before marriage."

Another pause. "And you, my child, what sin are *you* here to confess? What have *you* done?"

More ragged breathing followed, as though the woman struggled to get herself together.

The father spoke up again. "Take your time. Facing the truth can be hard sometimes."

"I've told on her. Last week, I spoke evil of her. Here, during my confession, and with a few close friends afterwards. I've… I've ruined her reputation. Then, after she…" This time, her sobbing could be heard very clearly.

"Go on."

"After she… died…" More sobs and ragged breathing. "… I flirted with her boyfriend. She was my best friend. How did I dare do that? She hasn't even… been… buried yet!"

"Breathe, my child. The Lord will forgive you. Is there something else you'd like to confess today?"

"No," she said before snorting back her tears.

In a more solemn tone, the priest continued. "God, the Father of mercies, through the death and resurrection of his Son has reconciled the world to himself and sent the Holy Spirit among us for the forgiveness of sins; through the ministry of the Church may God give you pardon and peace, and I absolve you from your sins in the name of the Father, and of the Son, and of the Holy Spirit."

"What is my penance, Father?"

"Say one *Our Father* and ten *Hail Mary*'s, then have a conversation with God in your prayers. Examine your life, my child, but do forgive yourself because the good Lord forgives you."

"Thank you, Father."

"Remember to give thanks to the Lord for He is good."

"For His mercy endures forever."

The door creaked as she exited the confessional.

CHAPTER SEVENTEEN

WITHOUT A DOUBT, David Dempsey could state that he'd just had the worst week of his life.

While the month had started on the biggest high he'd ever had—his first sexual encounter—the following days and weeks had been… much less stellar, to say the least.

The death of his girlfriend had just…

Well, it had destroyed him. It had torn out his soul, ripped it away from him. It had taken his heart and shredded it into a thousand pieces. Pieces that could no longer be reassembled into a cohesive organ.

It'd only been hours since he'd found her. Since his life changed forever.

Hours.

Not even a full day.

He did his best *not* to think about her. About her death. About what he'd discovered after breaking into her home. The sight of her decomposing body. The reeking stench. He hadn't managed to sleep one bit the previous night.

This morning, when the sun peered through his bedroom window, his eyes hurting from crying his heart out, he'd decided to stop the pain in whatever way he could. He'd rummaged through his parents' medicine cabinet and tried everything in there to numb himself. To numb the memories.

He'd ended up taking something that had been prescribed to his mom. Something ending in *zone*. Something that managed to shrink the size of the gash in his heart. He didn't feel much at all. But he couldn't say that his thoughts were the clearest they'd ever been.

The two detectives sitting in front of him—a chubby man and a blonde woman—now forced him to re-hash what he'd already explained the previous day.

"As stated earlier, I'm recording the audio, could you please state your name for the record?" the woman asked.

"David Dempsey."

"Please repeat exactly what happened the last time you saw Lori," the chubby, curly-haired cop asked. His dark-framed glasses and spare tire didn't make him a believable-looking cop—at least not compared to those cops with buff bodies he saw on TV. But a badge was a badge.

"Like I said yesterday, I last saw her on Friday night, June 1st."

"That was over two weeks ago. What did you do with Lori that day?"

"Evening," David corrected the man.

"What time did you meet and where?"

"Like I said before, I met her at her house."

"Do you have keys to her house?"

"No! Why do you think I broke in yesterday?"

"You tell me," the chubby cop prodded.

"I was worried sick! I knew she was supposed to go pick up her parents at the airport that night. And…"

"And?" the female cop repeated.

"And since I hadn't heard from her for two weeks, I was scared that something had happened to her."

"You've been dating for over two years," the woman said, after flipping through a small notepad she kept referring to, jotting notes as he spoke.

"So?"

"You've been together for a while. Yet you can let two weeks go by without contacting her once?"

"It's… complicated."

"Enlighten us," the woman said.

David concentrated, trying to come up with an explanation that would appease the detectives without revealing what had really happened. Nobody needed to know that. Especially now.

"David," the woman resumed. "You just lost your girlfriend. The two of you were exclusive, right?"

David nodded, unsure where she was going.

"I know it's tough, the libido of young men such as yourself can be quite… active." She looked down at her notes. "You're twenty-two years old, just like she was. You guys probably got busy, right? That's just nature, if you ask me."

"What?" David had feigned offense the best he could. "Lori and I were in a chastity club. We were saving ourselves for marriage."

"David… David…" The woman shook her head.

David felt sweat beginning to bead on his forehead. His heartbeat had increased. Maybe he shouldn't have taken his mom's medicine. "What?"

"I've been there. Rosebud has too." She turned to the chubby cop, who spoke next.

"Come on, man. Tell me. Lori was a very pretty girl. You've been dating for two years! Her parents were away…" The chubby cop shrugged. "I lost my virginity a bit late in the game, but it was still gone the first opportunity I got."

David couldn't believe what the detectives were saying. How could they tell? Was his sin printed on his forehead in big crimson letters?

"David, I'm going to offer you one chance to do the right thing, to not add perjury to your record," the woman said. "The medical examiner performed the autopsy this morning. He took a swab. I've already spoken to the parents. I've seen the strong religious theme going on in their household. I'm not going to go and rat you out to them. But I want to know the facts going in. We have your DNA and we have your fingerprints. If we find evidence of Lori having had a sexual encounter, and then have that swab we took analyzed for DNA, are we going to find yours?"

"You could find that? So many days after?" David asked.

"Are you telling us that you and Lori had sex?" Rosebud asked.

David cracked his neck once, twice, three times. He had no way out. His heart had never beat so fast. His mouth was dry.

He made fists with his hands. Perhaps the pills were making him weak-willed, but he was still clear-headed enough to know that he had to confess.

He stared down at the stainless steel table, not daring to look either of the detectives in the eyes. "Yes, I had sex with Lori. But you can't tell her parents."

"David, thank you for your honesty," she said. "Her parents don't need to know about it. But did you see her between the time you had sex with her and the day you discovered her body?"

His glance met the woman again and he shook his head.

"Please state your answer verbally for the record."

"No," he said.

"Did you call her?"

"I tried to. She never picked up."

"What about Facebook? Snapchat or whatever you kids use these days?"

"I tried to contact her every possible way I could. I even called her home phone. But she ignored me."

"Why do you think that was?" the woman asked, her voice soft, nothing like what his own mother would use after learning that he'd lost his virginity. And to a girl who was now dead.

David broke down crying, holding his hand over his face before lowering his head to the interrogation table.

"Rosebud, give us a minute, will you?" the woman said before joining David on his side of the table.

"I know… It's tough. I'm sorry," she said, rubbing his shoulder.

He tried to swallow a few times, his Adam's apple bobbing in his throat in between sobs.

"I just thought I'd hurt her. It was awkward. It was fast. I don't think she enjoyed it. She even cried."

The woman exhaled loudly before taking a seat in front of him again. "You know, a woman's first sexual experience can be… weird."

"Weird?" David repeated.

"Just between the two of us, I can't speak for every woman on earth, and I can't say that Lori felt that way, but for me, it was as though I'd let someone 'in' in all possible senses of the word: physically, emotionally, mentally. It was weird. Or at least very new."

"So you don't think I hurt her?"

"Well, I wasn't there. I don't know how things unfolded, but if you were a decent guy, went slowly, and were kind to her, then probably not."

"I was!"

"Then why do you think she would have ignored your calls for two weeks? Why didn't you show up at her door earlier?"

"Well… Lori… I loved her to bits, you know?"

The woman nodded but stayed silent.

"Lori had a fiery temperament at times."

"What do you mean, fiery?"

"Whenever we had a disagreement, I had to give her room to cool off."

"You've had disagreements before?"

"Sure. Every couple has a few of those, right?"

The detective returned her attention to her notepad, her pen at the ready. "Sure. Why don't you give me some examples?"

David racked his brain, trying to come up with something. Then prom came to mind.

"Once I went shopping with her. She was trying on a bunch of dresses for prom. I gave her my honest opinion on one of them. That proved to be a bad call."

"What did you say exactly?"

"Well. Not much, really. She asked if the dress made her ass look big."

"All I said was 'a little,' then I got the silent treatment for a whole week."

The woman shook her head at him. "David, you've got a few things to learn about women. You're still young. But here's a tip: Never answer that question. There's no right answer. Always change topics."

The detective got up and opened the door to let her partner back in.

The chubby man spoke up next after tossing a photo of a blue rosary onto the table.

"If we search your house and your car, would we find rosaries like this?"

David shrugged. "I don't own any of these. I've seen them at church, though. My parents may have bought some. I don't know."

"How about drugs? Any roofies or other fun pills like that?"

"No!" he said, wondering if his altered state was also written on his forehead.

"Well, then. We'll have to let the evidence point us toward the right person. But we found something else at the scene that leads us to believe that Lori was murdered because of her... looser morals, shall we say. Do you know if she would have told anyone about what had happened between the two of you?"

"You mean about losing her cherry?" David asked, his eyes once again on the table.

"If you want to call it that," the woman said.

David tilted his head. "Certainly not her parents, but maybe Amanda. They're best friends. I don't know how much they shared with each other, but if she told anyone, then I'd bet on Amanda."

"And what's Amanda's last name?" the woman asked, half-smiling.

CHAPTER EIGHTEEN

Tuesday, June 19th, 2018

ROSEBUD SAT ALONE in the interrogation room, sipping his coffee and nibbling on the rest of his chocolate chip muffin, when Murphy finally walked in with their latest lead in tow after getting fingerprints and a DNA swab.

The brunette wore a neon pink sundress with a neckline that dove deep enough to expose the lacy border of her bra, all the while highlighting the crucifix that hung low between her—more than likely—pushed-up breasts. All in all, she didn't look like a grieving best friend. More like a young adult in heat.

"Amanda, this is Detective Rosebud," Murphy said. "Please take a seat. We're recording this session. Please state your full name for the record."

"Amanda McCutcheon. Am I a suspect?"

"Right now, you're of interest to us," Rosebud said flatly. "We'd like you to answer a few questions."

Amanda sat, her expression as unreadable as that of a poker player.

Murphy took out her small notepad as she joined Rosebud on his side of the table. "Where were you between June 2nd and 6th?"

One of her eyebrows went up. "Uh… In Boston?"

"Can you be a bit more precise?" Rosebud asked.

"When was that? What days of the week?"

Rosebud took out his phone and turned on the calendar app. "Let's start with Sunday, June 3rd. What did you do that day?"

The young woman glanced off to the side and her right hand went up to fidget with the crucifix that hung around her neck.

A tell or just a nervous habit? Rosebud wondered.

"Hmm. I went to mass in the morning, then… Is it bad that I can't remember? Should I call a lawyer?"

"We're not accusing you of anything," Rosebud said. "You're free to call a lawyer if you wish. But those people cost money, and if you've got nothing to hide, then you shouldn't have to."

"I have nothing to hide."

"Then let's proceed. Did you see Lori Davis at mass that Sunday?"

"Yes," Amanda said.

"Was it the last time you saw her alive?"

Amanda bowed her head, looking at the table as she quietly voiced her affirmative reply.

"Did you talk to her?"

She looked sideways, swallowed hard, then shook her head. "No."

"Why didn't you talk to her?" Murphy asked. "I heard from other people we've interviewed that you were quite close."

"We had a disagreement the previous night."

"Disagreement?" Rosebud echoed, straightening his back.

"More like a small fight."

"About what?" Rosebud probed.

"I…" She shook her head. "I really can't recall."

"Come on, Amanda," Rosebud said. "Your best friend was found dead, and you don't recall your last conversation? If I were you, I'd be replaying that stupid fight over and over in my head—"

"Rosebud!" Murphy interjected, lifting her hand up and splitting the tension between him and Amanda. She turned to the girl. "I get that it's tough. Nobody wants to remember their last words with someone, especially when they were mean. But let's face it. We don't control when death hits. You can't change the past. But if you tell us what your fight was about, it may help us find the person who killed her. Okay?"

Amanda nodded.

"So where and when did you last talk with her?" Murphy asked.

"In her house on Saturday night, over two weeks ago. We hung out there sometimes. Her parents have a good bar selection, so we often played around and made cocktails of our own."

"Were her parents away?"

"Yeah. They were on a cruise."

"Good, so that's something. Do you recall what you talked about while making those cocktails?"

"Hmmm, I don't really want to say."

"Could you tell me if you talked about her boyfriend, David?"

She nodded. "We often talked about him."

"Did she share with you something specific that happened between David and her?" Rosebud asked.

Amanda's cheeks flushed as though someone had just turned on a bright light. Her fidgety fingers once again reached for her crucifix.

"Amanda," Murphy said with a softer voice. "Between us girls. Ignore Detective Rosebud."

"Want me to step out?" Rosebud asked, even though they'd made it plenty clear that the interview was being recorded.

"Would you mind?" Murphy asked with a smile.

Rosebud knew the false intimacy she could create if he stepped away. She'd done it before. "I'll get myself another cup of coffee. You've got five minutes."

"Great, thanks."

Rosebud walked out of the interrogation room and headed straight into the monitoring room that looked into it. Taking a seat, he watched Murphy work her woman-to-woman magic, getting Amanda to confirm what David Dempsey had already stated: Lori did talk about losing her virginity to Amanda the day after it had happened. Their fight was about Amanda disagreeing with her and calling her a slut.

Just what one would expect out of a chastity club member.

Flipping through his notes, Rosebud noticed that the special night in question had been Friday, June 1st. That meant she'd seen the victim on June 2nd, after David Dempsey. She and all of the parishioners who'd attended mass on that Sunday. Had David also done so and forgotten to mention it? Had something happened after mass? Would there be video footage near the church?

Looking at his watch, Rosebud left those questions unattended for now and returned to the interview room just as Amanda was finishing up a sentence that had Murphy making notes on her pad.

"So, Amanda, what did you do after mass that day?" Rosebud asked, hoping for some sort of lead to either pinpoint the time of death or point to the actual killer.

"I went back home."

"Alone?"

"Yes."

"And what did you do?"

Her eyes darted up and she frowned, then she finally replied. "I think I watched Netflix."

"All day?"

"Yeah."

"What was so interesting that you stayed glued to the TV?"

"I've been watching loads of *Jane the Virgin* lately."

"And what about Sunday evening?"

"I probably watched more of it."

"And Monday?"

"I don't think it was a holiday, so I went to work."

"And Monday evening?"

Her eyes grew round. "I don't know! Why does it matter?"

"Perhaps you were jealous of Lori and angry at her for not having stuck with the chastity oath. Could you have gone back to her house and killed her?"

"What? No!—How do you know?" Her high-pitched question was aimed at Rosebud.

"Remember that this is all being recorded," he said, pointing to the camera.

She exhaled loudly, her nostrils flaring. "Sure, I was upset at her—and I still maintain that what she did was wrong—but I would have never physically hurt her for it."

"Can anyone confirm your whereabouts for Sunday and Monday?"

"Like I said, I was home alone. Watching Netflix. Can you look up my IP? I'll give you the email associated with my account. Maybe Netflix can give you my viewing history or something."

"I'm afraid what you're suggesting wouldn't prove anything. Only that your device was playing one episode after another. Your presence in front of the screen can't be proven with what you're suggesting."

"Well, I didn't do it."

"Any thoughts on who might have done it, then?"

Amanda raised her shoulders before shaking her head. "No idea."

"Okay. Just a few more questions. Do you remember what you were wearing when you had that fight with her on Saturday in her house?"

"Not really. Is it important?"

"I'm just curious to know if you remember the house being particularly cold or hot while you were there?"

"Now that you mention it, it was hot. I had to take off my sweater, then nearly forgot it when I stormed out."

"Thank you for your time, Amanda."

CHAPTER NINETEEN

WHILE THOUGHTS about Amanda's and David's possible motives danced in her head, Kate couldn't pinpoint anything strong enough to get an arrest warrant for either of them. David had consented for the police to search his house and car and both had been a dead end.

Their DNA didn't match the DNA found on the murder weapon. David's DNA had matched the one swab for sexual intercourse, so their story held up, but that didn't bring Kate closer to finding Lori's killer.

They needed more leads. More evidence.

Everything else that could have been a lead had also been eliminated. Chainey had found the key hidden in the flower pot. The earth hadn't been disturbed, and no fingerprints had been lifted from the rusty mess. So the spare key had been a dead end, just like the call records on both her cellphone and the family's landline. The last call placed out had been on Saturday afternoon, to Amanda. After Saturday, Amanda, David, and various callers who were later identified as telemarketers had called the house or her cell, but all calls had gone unanswered.

Lori Davis hadn't spoken to anyone else over the phone, so who else could have heard of her lost virginity? Or was there another reason for her murder? Was Kate just reading too much into the religious theme? Why did the killer target Lori specifically?

And just as the thought entered her mind, Kate had a flash of genius.

"The confessionals!" she said aloud to the empty desks in the detectives' room. Everyone had left for the day, except for her.

She picked up her phone and dialed Rosebud's cell number. "You go to church sometimes, right?"

"Yeah. Why?"

"What type of stuff would you tell the priest in those confessionals at the back?"

"Whatever sin I've committed, I guess."

"Do you think the killer could have listened in on Lori's confession about losing her virginity before marriage? That's a sin, right?"

"Plausible."

"Do you think she could have confessed to it before mass on Sunday?"

"Confessions are received at various times. I don't see why not."

"I'm going to stay at the office a little longer. Get the paperwork going to search for bugs at the church where she went."

"Murphy! I know you're the lead, but you gotta listen to me on this one. Learn from your mistakes. You gotta take time off. You can't be on twenty-four seven and expect your mind to work its best. You're off until tomorrow. I took the afternoon so I'm coming in to work for a few hours tonight. I'll take care of it. Got it?"

She wanted to argue but knew he was right. "Fine. Thanks."

"Go home and do your best to think about something else. Anything else. Heck, try to have fun."

"Easier said than done."

"I know. I'll see you tomorrow."

She hung up feeling both grateful for having such a supportive partner and useless for not doing anything to solve the case faster. But she knew Rosebud was right. She needed to think about something else. Anything but the case and the dead woman.

Rubbing her palms against her cheeks and wiping her face

—a last ditch effort at keeping herself alert—she almost jumped when her phone rang.

Caller ID read *Luko*.

"Hey, baby! What's up?" she asked.

"Where are you?"

Surprised by the all-business attitude Luke had displayed, Kate began to worry. "At the precinct. Why?"

"You forgot your appointment, Katie!"

It took a split second for her to understand what he was referring to. "The hypnotherapist. It's today. Shit! Are you there?"

"Yes, and the doctor's here, too. The clock is ticking. Minutes aren't cheap in this part of the world."

"Shit!" Kate glanced at the clock on the wall. "Please ask her to wait. I'm on my way. Maybe fill her in on my past while you're waiting?"

~

WITH LESS THAN fifteen minutes left in the session, the hypnotherapist nonetheless agreed to take Kate back to her childhood.

"To make things easier on you, pick a happy time. Maybe when you were nine or ten years old, before your baby brother was born," the tall and slender brunette suggested, her legs crossed, a notepad resting on her lap.

"Okay."

"Can you remember a particular event? Perhaps a birthday party or summer camp?"

Kate tilted her head, daring to think back to her childhood, something she had purposely avoided for so many years. But with the therapist's recent prompt, she suddenly remembered one of her birthday parties having been quite cool. "My tenth birthday," she said.

"Okay. Can I assume you had a cake with candles on it and a bunch of friends?"

"Yeah," Kate said, nodding.

"Perfect. I want you to lie comfortably and close your eyes. I'm going to turn on some background music. Focus on my voice as I count down from ten to one. When I reach one, you will be at your birthday party. Think about the moment before you blew your candles and start there. When you hear the snap of my fingers, you'll instantly be brought back here."

Soft music began playing all around Kate as she closed her eyes. Surround sound had obviously been installed in the fancy office. But the music faded in the distance as Kate focused on the therapist's soothing voice.

"Three… Two… And one. You are now at your tenth birthday party. Can you see your cake?"

While Kate had her eyes closed, she could somehow hear faint laughter in the distance, as though some of her childhood friends were present in the room. She smiled but shook her head. "I can't see anything."

"That's okay. Breathe in and out slowly. Keep thinking about that birthday party. Think of your friends. Your parents. Your cake."

Kate obeyed, feeling her chest rise and fall along with her loud inhalations and exhalations, then suddenly she jerked.

"What is it?" the therapist prompted.

Kate crinkled her nose. "The smell!"

"What smell?"

"My mom's lasagna. I'd forgotten about that. She'd made me lasagna that day."

"What else can you smell?"

Kate inhaled deeper, letting her lungs fill up. "Vanilla from the cake."

"Can you see your cake now?"

Kate shook her head while shriveling her nose. "No, but I can smell my dad's cologne: Eternity for Men."

And just as the words left her lips, a wave of sadness came upon her, taking away the scents and trading them with tears. Kate's entire body began convulsing as memory after memory of her belated father flooded her mind. Although she couldn't see anything now, the image of his cologne bottle came to mind. She remembered it clearly, sitting among the other products hidden behind the bathroom mirror. She remembered her dad dotting her neck with it once, and how much fuss she'd made to try to get him to get the manly odor off of her. And then, clear as day, for just a split second, she saw him.

Snapping her fingers, the hypnotherapist brought Kate back to the present.

KATE SAT up and reached for her head, confused and sad.

"What the hell?" she asked the therapist, tears streaming down her face.

"Perhaps we didn't choose the safest time to go back to. You had a strong emotional reaction to something. What was it?"

"For a brief second, I saw my dad. Then…" Kate brought her fingers to her face, wiping off a new round of tears.

"Okay. Here, take some tissues," she said, holding up a box.

"So, what do you think?" Kate asked after composing herself.

"It's interesting that you couldn't see anything until the very end. But your sense of smell may help us revisit other times. I think we could unlock a few memories for you, but that would also mean reliving those very difficult moments. It's up to you."

A timer rang from behind the therapist's chair, indicating the session had come to an end.

"I'll let you think about it, perhaps discuss it with your husband—"

"We're not married."

"Your partner, whatever. If you decide to keep going, you'll need his support—or that of another friend or relative—after each session."

"Thanks, Doctor. I'll think about it and let you know." Kate stood and headed to the door.

"You can pay the receptionist out front," the doctor said as Kate reached for the door.

Luke ditched the magazine he was holding and got up from his chair the second she stepped back into the waiting room. "How did it go?" he asked, but he must have gotten his answer just by looking at her and her undoubtedly red, watery eyes.

He went to her and wrapped her up in his arms. "It'll be okay. You're safe," he whispered against her hair.

CHAPTER TWENTY

DETECTIVE ROSEBUD SAT at Lorraine Taylor's kitchen table, listening to yet another round of how wonderful their high school chastity club was.

"Even though high school ended quite a few years back for you, you're still part of that club?"

She lifted her left hand in the air in a move that reminded Rosebud of Beyoncé's *Single Ladies* video he may have watched a time or two. "You see a ring on that finger, Detective?"

Annoyed as he was by her reply, he let it slide. She was no Beyoncé. "No."

"Then I will remain chaste." She pursed her lips and nodded once.

He exhaled loudly, realizing the woman's lasting chastity had probably more to do with her looks and behavior than a vow she made with a bunch of friends. If he hadn't known better, he would have assumed the woman was a nun. A nun with an attitude, though. Her demeanor, combined with the medallion of the Virgin Mary pinned onto her gray turtle neck, was certainly not a strong mating call.

"Do you have a boyfriend?"

"Why would you need to know that?"

"Just trying to identify those associated with your chastity club, either directly or indirectly—as in girlfriend or boyfriend—so we can talk to everyone."

"Ah." She frowned. "Well, no. Not at the moment."

"And the same would have been true a few weeks ago?"

"Yes."

Rosebud refrained from smiling. It was definitely not his place, and she didn't need to hear his opinions as to why she was still single.

"Going back to the list of original members," he said.

"I have a photo of us if you'd like."

Her statement had made his ears prick up. "Yes! I'd like to see it, please."

While the photo in itself would be helpful, if only to post on the board in the conference room and give the other detectives a visual representation of every member of their club, a tiny part of him wanted to see who among that group had joined of their own merit—i.e., who would have been in a situation to *not* be chaste if they had chosen—versus those who'd followed the "cool" kids. Hair-dos, braces, and acne coverage would easily answer that.

"Here we are," she said, handing a portrait of twelve teenagers neatly lined up by height. The black sign with white lettering spelled out "Chastity Club 2013-14."

Rosebud took hold of it. "Can I keep it?"

"Sure. I have a few of them left."

None of the kids had been that bad looking, instantly shutting down the theory he had begun to build in his mind.

Was he the only one who looked like shit in all of his high school photos?

He flipped the picture and noted that names had been neatly printed in uppercase on the back.

"And that's everyone's name. In the order in which they appear in the photo."

"That's incredibly helpful. Thank you."

"I always did that right after I had my photos printed. Now Facebook tags people for me."

Her comment triggered a thought in Rosebud's mind. "Is there a Facebook group for your chastity club?"

"As a matter of fact, yes."

"Would you mind showing me?"

"No problem. I have nothing to hide." She dug out her phone.

"Any chance you have a desktop computer or laptop so we can see more information at once?"

"Sure, follow me."

They relocated to the living room where she kept her laptop.

A minute later, without having to enter a password anywhere—not to unlock her computer, not to enter Facebook—her fingers flew on the keyboard and she turned it toward Rosebud.

"Here it is."

"May I scroll through?"

"Do what you need, Detective."

Rosebud slowly went down the list of memes, animated GIFs, excerpts from the Bible, celebrity gossip (with lots of holier-than-thou comments from the group), and even posts about the odd celebrity like Selena Gomez who had also made chastity vows.

But what he had hoped to see was nowhere to be found. There was absolutely no slander toward Lori Davis.

"Can I see the list of members?" he asked, returning the laptop to her.

"Sure, but it's the same people from our group. We don't add or remove anyone." She slid her finger over the mouse, then tapped it to display the members. "Well, that's odd," she said.

"What is?" Rosebud asked, now looking over her shoulder.

"It says eleven members… Lori is missing. Does Facebook know she passed away? Maybe it removed her?"

"Unlikely," Rosebud said. "Can you look at her profile?"

She typed her name in the search box and her profile appeared, her timeline filled with condolence messages.

"Who are the admins for your chastity group?" Rosebud asked.

"Just me and Amanda."

ROSEBUD SPENT the rest of the afternoon interviewing more members of the chastity club. After sharing his latest discovery with Chainey, he split the rest of his interviews with him.

Unfortunately, none of the chastity members claimed to have noticed Lori had been removed from the group a couple of weeks ago. So much for his theory that another member could have had something to do with her death.

And he also confirmed David's and Amanda's comments about Lori's fiery temper. Everyone knew to avoid her for days when they had disagreements. It all added up. But that meant Amanda's motive was weak at best.

Now, sitting at his desk, he went over his notes, trying to make sense of what he'd learned.

Perhaps passive-aggressive behavior or jealousy had led Amanda to do that, but at least she hadn't posted publicly about one of their members being booted out of the group by breaking its only rule.

But that certainly didn't eliminate any of the other members who could have noticed. However, Rosebud's gut didn't think it was worth pushing.

He grabbed his jacket from the back of his chair and was putting it on when Murphy walked in, coffee and brown bag in hand.

"What's new?" he asked.

"Not much. Talked to neighbors and Amanda again. I'm still not finding enough for a warrant. With the wide berth on our time of death, it makes it near impossible to check for alibis."

"The forensic entomologist is still working on it," Rosebud said.

"I get that he can tell how many cycles of various insects hatched, but there's no way he'll be able to determine when those bugs got there. You know how chilly it was in that house. We don't know if the temperature stayed that cold the entire time or not."

"All we can do is go with the scene markers. Let the mail dictate the most probable date."

"Last seen on Sunday morning, on all accounts I got. Did anyone you speak to see her after that?"

Rosebud shook his head.

"The oldest mail on the porch was dated Wednesday. So

that means it arrived Thursday or later. That's a long time. I'll call that bug expert myself and ask. Do you have the number?"

Rosebud shook his head again. "The medical examiner will have it."

"Yeah."

"What do you have in there?" Rosebud asked, pointing to the bag.

"One of those chocolate muffins from across the street. Want half of it?"

"Do I?" He reached in while Murphy dialed a number.

He watched her write down a number as she talked on the phone. She soon dialed another one.

"Hi, this is Detective Murphy, is Dr. Mark there?"

She moved the receiver away from her mouth. "Break me off a chunk before you eat it all, will you?" Her hand extended, she waited.

Rosebud gave her a third of it, having already eaten half but wanting just a bit more.

Murphy had time to eat it before Dr. Mark came to the phone.

"Yes, thanks for taking my call. I just wanted to ask how you're doing with the timeline for Lori Davis's death. Our other evidence gives us a seventy-two-hour window. Is there any way you could narrow that down for us?"

She hummed and nodded as Rosebud finished off the crumbs from the inside of the bag. "No idea. No evidence to the contrary. Please assume the temperature remained constant." She moved the mouthpiece away for a second. "Hand me the calendar, would you?" She returned the receiver to her mouth. "And what would that be in days?"

Rosebud watched her pen count the days from the time Lori's body was discovered. She circled Sunday and Monday. "That's very helpful. Thank you."

She hung up. "He's not completed his calculations. But based on the cycles, it can't be as late as Tuesday or Wednesday." Kate lifted the bag and peered into it. "I should have known and bought two."

CHAPTER TWENTY-ONE

Wednesday, June 20th, 2018

"ST. Alban's, this is it. The church the Davises attend," Kate said as Rosebud slowed down to park.

"You have a plan?" Rosebud asked as they marched toward the large front entrance. Its white pillars made the building look more like a courthouse than a church to Kate.

"Let's wing it. Start with the priest, or the father, or whatever he's called."

"Seriously, Murphy. Let me do the talking if you're this clueless about Catholicism."

"Be my guest!" Kate said as she pulled open the large black door for her partner.

A stale scent of old books and candle wax reached Kate's nostrils as they entered. The clicks of her low heels made her self-conscious as they echoed against the pastel-colored walls. Only a handful of people were present, scattered along the front. Nobody was holding mass. The church was eerily quiet. Too quiet for her taste.

Kate took a few more steps then turned around to take in her surroundings. Various flags hung over the main area, perched along the edge of the two balconies that lined the main room. Above the entrance through which they'd just stepped reigned a large organ with long white and baby blue pipes. Although nobody was playing it now, she could easily imagine how beautiful the music would sound, echoing into this cavernous room.

She had to admit it was much plainer than she had expected, though. Nothing like the intricate churches she'd seen in movies... Then again, those had probably been cathedrals or some other larger places of worship built centuries ago.

"Come on, Murphy. Follow me. We'll head to the sacristy."

A minute later, Rosebud had found the man they had come to see: an older gentleman, probably in his early fifties, graying at the temples but still brown-haired everywhere else. He paced the floor, a loose sheet of paper in his hand as he talked aloud to himself. His round belly and short stature made Kate's gut doubt the man had anything to do with Lori's death—not to mention his profession as a man of God—but everyone was still a suspect as far as she was concerned. After all, hadn't many Catholic priests been found guilty of the most dreadful sin of all?

"Father Coffedy?"

"Yes?" He stopped in his tracks and looked up from his script.

"I'm Detective Rosebud, this is Detective Murphy. We're with the Boston PD. We'd like to ask a few questions if you have a minute."

His eyebrows lifted as he began nodding. "Of course, of course." Then he looked around him. "I'm afraid there isn't really a place for us to sit down, though."

"That's fine. We can stand. We won't take much of your time."

"All right. How may I help you?"

"Lori Davis, the daughter of Francine and Doug Davis, do you know her?"

"Of course! It's so horrible what happened to her."

The man kissed the cross that hung from around his neck and crossed himself with his right hand. His face looked solemn and somber, but Kate wondered if it was just a facade. "The Davises have been coming here forever. She was baptized here, first communion, confirmation, the whole lot."

"When did you last see her?"

Father Coffedy tilted his head and scratched his right temple with his index finger.

"I'm not sure, really. I want to say two or so weeks ago. It was while her parents were away. Do you know more? Why did this happen to such a lovely girl?"

"We don't know yet. We're trying to trace her last whereabouts. We're also trying to find a motive. Other people have reported seeing her here for mass on Sunday, June 3rd. Does that seem right to you?"

He brought his hand to cover his mouth, then peeled it away as he twisted the one end of his mustache. "I'm not sure she attended mass that day, but I remember hearing her confession."

"Care to share what she confessed?" Kate asked.

"I'm sorry, Detective. But her words were between the Lord and her. I cannot relay that information to you."

"I get that, Father," Kate said. "But she's dead now, and we're trying to find the killer. We don't know if he's currently looking for his next victim—"

"You don't think it was random? You think someone targeted this poor child?"

"Father," Rosebud interjected, "I understand your responsibility toward the church and the confidentiality of the confessions you hear, but if there's anything you remember that could help us identify her killer—and possibly prevent other murders—I'd greatly appreciate it if you shared that information with us. What you say will only be used to help the case. We won't share it with the media."

The man frowned at Rosebud. "Breaking the Seal of the Confession is grounds for excommunication."

"Are there security cameras on the premises? Something that would allow us to see who she may have talked to after mass or if she left with somebody?" Rosebud asked.

"I'm afraid not."

"Do you know a young man named David Dempsey?"

"Do you mean the son of Karen and Nate Dempsey? Over in the South End?"

Rosebud lifted his shoulders. "Maybe. He was dating Lori Davis."

"Yes, that's the one. I know him. Fine chap."

"Does he attend church here?"

"No, his family lives over by the cathedral. They go to mass there."

"And how do you know?" Kate asked.

"Lack of priests. We're no longer assigned to one specific parish anymore. We rotate to cover all the various masses and ceremonies that are needed of us."

"One more thing. Actually two more questions if you wouldn't mind," Kate asked.

"Of course, Detective."

Kate pulled a photo of the blue rosary and showed it the him. "We found this at the scene. Do you recognize it?"

The father nodded. "Yes, of course."

"That's what we'd like to ask you about. How many of those are around?"

He tilted his head once more. "I honestly have no idea, but I can give you the name and number of the volunteer who has been teaching people how to make them."

"Is this some sort of church program?" Rosebud asked.

"No, no." The father shook his head. "I'm afraid Catholics don't normally partake in any sort of fundraisers, other than the money we collect during mass to help with church maintenance. But our numbers are dropping faster than I can get new parishioners. Times have changed so the other priests and I decided to try new things. Be more forward-thinking. It wouldn't hurt to support those in need in the community. While they may not decide to join our church, at least we're doing something good for the neighborhood."

"I'm not sure I'm following," Rosebud added. "Your lessons on how to make rosaries help the community?"

"Oh no! That's just because we couldn't meet the demand. We sell the rosaries that our volunteers make. All profits go to those who need financial help. The only money we keep is to cover the costs of the thread. The rest goes to families in need."

"Any idea how many people actively produce those rosaries that you sell?"

He shook his head once more. "I'm afraid I'm out of the loop. Follow me. I'll get that information for you."

Rosebud and Kate followed him through a couple of

wooden doors and ended up in a small office where a man with a cast sat at a desk and typed with one hand.

"Anderson," the father said. "Could you print out Mary's contact information, please? And before I forget, there's some dry-cleaning I'll need your help with later today."

"Of course, Father," he said, smiling. He nodded at the detectives before moving his uninjured hand from the keyboard to the mouse and back.

"Must be tough to do office work with just one hand," Rosebud said.

"All I can do is my best. It may take a little extra time, but it's better my bones heal properly."

"What happened to you?" Rosebud asked, sitting on the corner of the man's desk.

Kate wanted to roll her eyes but refrained from it. As much as she despised small talk, she admired her partner's ability to do it. To stand it.

"Silly accident." He shook his head. "A friend convinced me to try roller skating. I was going really fast down a hill and fell. Badly."

"Ouch!" Rosebud grimaced.

"Wanna see my X-rays?" Anderson asked.

Kate cleared her throat, putting an end to the useless chatter. "Could you get that contact information first?"

"Of course."

A few seconds later, the intermittent sounds of an older dot-matrix printer echoed in the small room and a sheet of paper came out of the device just as a tall, broad-shouldered man entered the room.

"Should be on that piece of paper," Anderson said.

"Thanks, man," Rosebud said as he got up to retrieve it.

"Are you also a priest?" Kate asked, partly wanting to pin Rosebud for his lack of respect.

"No, not yet," he said.

"And you?" Kate asked the newly arrived man.

Father Coffedy chimed in. "This is Harold, a volunteer who helps us out. He's not a priest. This here is Candidate Anderson. He took time off during his last year of seminary for personal reasons. But he'll soon be returning to his studies. He should be ordained in the coming months."

Kate nodded. "So were all of you here after mass on Sunday, June 3rd?"

"Yes," Father Coffedy said while Anderson and Harold nodded.

Father Coffedy continued. "I try to stay for about an hour and mingle with parishioners. We have a core group that likes to hang out when the weather is nice. Then, if I recall correctly, I had to leave to perform a marriage ceremony at a different parish."

"And you?" Kate asked Anderson.

"I mingled for a while then probably came back here to catch up on my computer tasks. I'm not the fastest typist at the moment," he said, pointing to his arm.

"Harold?" Kate asked.

"Yeah. What they said. I, too, stick around after mass and help with whatever task I can help with."

"Do you want to see my X-rays?" Anderson asked Rosebud once more, his tone overly enthusiastic for this early in the morning.

But Rosebud took the bait. "Sure, I had a broken arm once. Let's see the damage."

Kate looked at her watch. Parts of her wished she could come across as friendly as Rosebud did. But then again, she didn't. *Oh, the boring discussions he gets into sometimes…*

Anderson opened a drawer and pulled out his phone, then swiped past a dozen photos before finding the one he was looking for.

"Look at that! Ain't I lucky the bone didn't pierce through the skin?"

Rosebud winced as he stared at the image. "Whoa! When did that happen?"

"A few weeks ago."

"Take care of yourself, man. Let it heal properly." Rosebud lifted the sheet of paper in the air. "Thanks, Father, Anderson, and Harold. You have a nice day now."

Rosebud started walking away when Kate pulled out one of her business cards and dropped it on the corner of Anderson's desk. "Father, Harold, or Anderson, if you remember anything that can help us solve Lori Davis's murder, do give us a call, please."

"Will do, Detective," Father Coffedy said.

"And Father," Kate said, stopping in her tracks. "Who are the other priests you referred to earlier? The ones from the area who are more forward thinking?"

"Oh, only one of them is the forward-thinking one: Father Matthews. He's new and very smart. Very educated as well. His breadth of knowledge on most subjects is nothing short of impressive. Father Miller and I are convinced he's onto something."

CHAPTER TWENTY-TWO

A GROUP of twenty kids sat quietly, their hands tying and twisting colorful bits of string. In the background, classical music played softly. In front of the room a stern-looking brunette in her late thirties or early forties sat in a wheelchair. Her hair was pulled back into a bun and her lack of a smile made Rosebud reconsider approaching her for a second.

She obviously wasn't their killer. No way would she be able to climb stairs with her wheelchair. But interrupting her evening class was his job. He had questions that needed answering, and time was of the utmost importance.

"Mrs. Mary Stuart?" he called out as he walked toward her.

"Yes?" she turned to look his way.

He opened the flap of his jacket, exposing the badge attached on his belt. "Do you have a minute?" He closed his jacket when he noticed several of the kids turning around.

"Finish your decade, then ask your partner to double-check your work. I'll be right back," she said to the class before wheeling herself and joining Rosebud at the back of the room.

"Can we step outside for just a minute? I don't want the kids to overhear my questions."

She frowned. "I can't leave them unattended for long. The church is holding me responsible for their wellbeing and safety."

"I'm sure they'll be fine. I doubt they'll figure out how to tie a noose on their own," he said before instantly regretting his words. "Sorry. My sense of humor isn't for everyone."

"I'd say. Please make it quick, Officer."

Rosebud held the door open for her as she rolled out of the room then spun around to face him.

"Detective, actually. I'm here to ask about those rosary classes. Do you teach how to make rosaries to adults?"

"Not normally. We've had a few mothers join their children here and there, but that was rare."

"What about Father Coffedy and Father Matthews?"

"Our priests? Of course not. And Father Miller either in case you were curious. They've got better things to do with their time."

"Okay then. Do you know if Amanda McCutcheon or David Dempsey have ever joined your classes?"

"The names don't ring a bell. Do they have children?"

"No, they're both in their early twenties. One attends St. Alban's, the other goes to the cathedral in the South End."

"Then no. I don't believe they've ever attended one of my classes."

"Okay, one last question. Could you tell me what happens to those rosaries that are put up for sale? Is there a large stash that you collect and store somewhere?"

"We don't *stash* them anywhere." Her tone indicated she found Rosebud's use of the term offensive.

"Where do they go, then?"

"At the back of our churches, there's a box of rosaries for sale, with a donation bin next to them. We also offer them at various fundraisers."

"The fundraisers that Father Matthews has begun holding throughout various parishes?"

"That's right. They've been very popular, you know? We've raised several hundreds of dollars."

A slight moan escaped Rosebud's lips. Perhaps the friendship bracelet craze of his youth had somehow been replicated with those handmade rosaries among the Catholic community in Boston. "Well, that's it for now. Thank you for your time." Rosebud put his notepad back in his jacket pocket. "Actually, one more question," he asked, pulling his notepad out again. "The fundraisers. Who's the one in charge of selling them at these events? You?"

"No! I'm afraid these wheels aren't allowed everywhere. You'd think public spaces would all be equipped for people like me, but that's not the case. There's a woman who volunteers for most of these fundraisers."

"Her name?"

"Adrianna Johnston. I think she normally goes with her son as well, if that makes a difference. Why are you asking me these questions?"

"I'm afraid I can't tell you. It's related to an ongoing investigation. You have a great evening, now. Let me get that door for you."

Her stern look morphed into that of curiosity and fear for a second but then she rolled her way back into the classroom.

Rosebud turned around and walked out.

Something didn't add up with these rosaries, but he couldn't quite figure it out. At least he had one more name to track, which could lead to another dead end.

Or maybe it would lead him to the killer.

CHAPTER TWENTY-THREE

Thursday, June 21st, 2018

"SO WHO IS SHE AGAIN?" Kate asked as she parked in front of a blue house.

"Adrianna Johnston. She's the woman who sells most of the rosaries at church fundraisers."

"That Mary woman who teaches how to make the rosaries gave you her name?"

"Yep."

"Did you look into her background, see if you could find a connection between Lori Davis and her?"

"I tried. Couldn't find anything, but that doesn't mean there isn't a link."

"Tell me more about her."

"DMV gave this as her home address. Looked into her some more. She's a single mother of a twenty-year-old named Jacob Johnston—still lives with her here."

"Maybe the boy…"

"Maybe. His age makes him more likely to have something in common with Lori Davis. Or to at least know of her."

"Let's find out, shall we?" Kate said as she opened the door and stepped out of their unmarked vehicle. "You keep your eyes on the mother, I'll keep mine on the son."

~

SITTING AT THE KITCHEN TABLE, Rosebud and Kate patiently waited for Adrianna Johnston to return. She'd promised to bring her son upstairs to join them for coffee.

That had been ten minutes ago.

"What do you think?" Kate asked, getting up and peering out through the kitchen curtain next to her.

"She said her son has behavioral issues. I don't think she's running away from us—"

"I'll be right there!" the woman yelled from downstairs.

Rosebud shrugged. "There you go."

"What a waste of our time," Kate muttered.

"I hear you. If only we had more leads to follow. I've had very little sleep these past few days. But no matter how I turn the situation around, I can't think of anything. There's no freaking DNA. No fingerprints. Nothing was found at the crime scene that didn't belong to either the vic, her family, her boyfriend, or her BFF."

"And our searches led to nothing on the last two."

"So here we are."

"Waiting for—"

"Sorry to have kept you waiting. Here's my son, Jacob."

Kate turned to look at the boy. His arms were crossed on his chest, his mouth stuck in a frown, his face red. "Say hi to the detectives, Son."

A grunt came out of him.

"I'm so sorry." She pushed him toward the table. "Have a seat, Jacob." She looked up to the detectives. "Can I offer you a cup of coffee or something?"

The boy didn't move. His mother moved the chair and then pushed his shoulders to guide him down toward his seat, then she pushed his chair closer to the table.

"Sure, coffee would be nice," Rosebud said before Kate could turn the woman down.

"Fine. Make that two." If the initial wait had anything to do with the upcoming interview, they could very well be here for hours.

"I have to apologize for my son. He's not very sociable. I do my best to bring him to church functions so he can interact with people, but he really doesn't enjoy socializing. All he wants to do is stay in the basement and play computer games. All day."

Anger—or perhaps impatience and stress—punctuated her speech. Kate looked at the young man but didn't dare ask aloud what disability he suffered from. The mother speaking not so kindly of her son in the third person while he was right there sure didn't make Kate feel comfortable about their household dynamics.

"So, while the coffee is brewing, why don't we start?" Adrianna suggested.

"Okay, then," Rosebud replied, retrieving his notepad and pen. "Lori Davis. Does the name mean anything to you?"

Kate paid attention to the son, but he didn't react any more than a brick wall would have. He hadn't moved a hair. His face hadn't twitched, he hadn't even blinked.

"Jacob," Kate asked, trying to get his attention.

Ms. Johnston exhaled loudly as she pressed a button. The first serving of coffee came out of the machine in front of her. "Please ignore him. He likes to stay in his head. Who's Lori Davis? The name rings a bell."

"She was found dead in her home last Sunday."

"Oh! The young blonde woman from the news."

Kate continued staring at the boy who remained motionless.

"Yeah. Her. Did you know her?" Rosebud pushed.

"No! But it's quite sad what happened to her. Do you know who did it?"

"That's what we're investigating."

"I don't understand. What do my son and I have to do with her murder?"

"Because of the rosaries you sell at the fundraisers."

"What? The church's rosaries?"

"Yeah. The colorful knotted pieces of strings, like the one your son is wearing," Kate noted, suddenly aware of the bright piece of yellow that was partly visible around the boy's neck.

"May I?" Kate asked, moving her hand forward toward the boy.

"No! Better not," Ms. Johnston said as she set the first cup of coffee on the table. "Let me get it for you."

She knelt next to her son and made eye contact with him.

"Jacob! Jacob. I need your rosary. I'm going to pull it over your head now. Okay?"

The boy began rocking back and forth on his chair, all the while shaking his head.

"I'm so sorry, Detective. Any chance I can give you another rosary? I've got a whole box worth. It's just…" She closed her eyes and exhaled loudly. "I can assure you that he and I have absolutely nothing to do with what happened to Lori Davis. But my son…" She crossed herself. "God bless his soul. He most certainly knows how to test my patience on a daily basis. Today's a bad day. It's like he's in his own little world."

"Where were you on Sunday, June 3rd?" Kate asked.

"I don't recall off hand. Give me a second to get my calendar."

The woman left the room, leaving Kate and Rosebud with the kid who'd finally stopped rocking and shaking his head.

"What do you think?" Rosebud asked.

Kate lifted her eyebrows. "I'm no doctor. Is he autistic?"

"No. I wasn't talking about that. Is this your coffee or mine?"

"All yours."

The woman's footsteps echoed as she got closer again. "Here it is," she said, holding a calendar filled with scribblings of various colors. "Oh, and where are my manners? I'm still missing one coffee. Coming right up. Have a look at my calendar. Everything's written down on it, otherwise I'd forget. Jacob keeps me busy with all of his doctor appointments."

"May I ask?" Kate started, not sure how to finish her sentence.

"About?"

"Your son," Kate said, her eyes directed at the young man.

She pressed a button on her coffee maker and black liquid started pouring out. "The doctors don't agree on what his condition really is. All we know is that the umbilical cord got wrapped around his neck at birth. He got some brain damage. The extent of which is yet to be determined. We're trying all sorts of programs to see if we can reverse the damage. He's not dangerous; he just requires a little extra care."

"Any chance Jacob would have known Lori from school or

some group activity they could have partaken in together?" Kate asked.

The mother shook her head. "No. I'm afraid his education has been lacking. Too many appointments with specialists. No time for group activities."

"So, the calendar says you attended a fundraiser at a school on June 3rd. Is that right?" Rosebud asked.

"If the calendar says so, then it's right."

"Then you had a bunch of appointments on the days that followed. Do you mind if I make note of these appointments to confirm your whereabouts?"

"I have nothing to hide. Do what you need to do."

"And your son?" Kate asked.

"I take him with me to all the fundraisers. And all of the doctor appointments are for him."

Kate glanced at the calendar. Not a single day was blank. "Do you mind if I ask how you can afford to pay for his medical bills?"

"Fortunately, Jacob's dad was a wealthy man." Ms. Johnston offered Kate her cup of coffee. "I'm sorry, where's my head? Do either of you take sugar or milk?"

"Black's fine," Kate said as she grabbed the cup before repeating the last four words she'd voiced before talking about coffee.

"Yes. He left us."

"For another woman?" Rosebud asked between sips.

"No. For the bearded man in the sky."

Kate looked at Rosebud while thinking of a possible motive the woman or her son could have had to kill Lori Davis.

"Sorry, that wasn't a very straight-forward answer, but Jacob reacts to certain words, so I've learned not to use them whenever I can."

"No problem," Kate said, half smiling as she considered where they stood. Asking the woman for her box of rosaries would result in days' worth of analysis with little to no possibility of getting anything out of it. They would be better off putting cameras at the back of every church and during each fundraiser to record who bought them. But that also had its flaws. They couldn't record the past.

"Do you remember one person buying several rosaries at once?" Kate asked.

"Yes. Quite a few, actually. We sell them for just two dollars each during fundraisers and they are pay-what-you-can at the back of the churches where they're sold."

"Thanks," Kate said.

"Do you mind if I ask you one question, Detective?" the woman asked Kate.

"Sure."

"Do you know Luke O'Brien? Marjorie's son?"

Kate hadn't seen that question coming. "Why would you ask that?" She felt her cheeks flush.

"So, *you*'re the competition."

"I'm not following," Rosebud said, his eyes going from one woman to the other.

"I met your guy a few days ago. At a fundraiser, actually. Good-looking man you have."

Kate didn't want to even acknowledge the woman's latest statement, so she got up and closed her notepad. "We got the answers we needed. Thanks so much for your time."

~

"WHAT THE HECK WAS THAT?" Rosebud said as they walked back to the car.

"Which part?"

"The abrupt end? You're the competition? The weird kid?"

"Whatever. None of my business," Kate said as she pulled open the driver's door.

Rosebud opened the passenger door and sat down.

"Well," Kate continued, "none of my business *if* her whereabouts and her son's check out. Can you look into those, please?" She inserted the key into the ignition.

"The two of them didn't strike me as a murderous duo, but I'll check everything."

"The thought of asking for her box of rosaries crossed my mind, but we don't have the time or budget to analyze them all. If you can't confirm their alibis, then we can reconsider."

"Agree."

"Let's hope Wang or Chainey made more progress than we did with the friends they spoke to."

CHAPTER TWENTY-FOUR

LUKE SAT ALONE, watching a re-run of *Friends*, his extended legs resting on the coffee table in front of him when he heard the front lock open. The beeps that echoed next told him it was Kate, and she was putting her gun away for the night.

The time on the TV read 10:38 p.m. He turned to face the hallway, hoping she'd join him on the couch for a few minutes but instead saw her silhouette sneak up the stairs.

"Katie, come in here!"

She backtracked then peeked her head into the living room.

"Hey, babe," she said.

"You made it home before midnight!" he said, earnestly pleased. But even he recognized the sarcasm that tinted his tone.

"I'm sorry. You know I want to spend more time with you. These past few days have been really bad. I feel awful. I mean… this case… I'm the lead. I've got to find the damn killer."

He tapped the couch next to him. "Come here for a sec."

"I should really take a shower. I reek."

"I don't mind. You know I love you *au naturel*. Sweat, stress, and everything else that makes your hair frizz."

She cocked her head, then smiled and walked into the room to join him on the couch. "I warned you."

"What are we going to do to get you a balanced life?" Luke asked rhetorically.

"You knew what you were getting yourself into when we started dating."

"I know, and I love you. And I love that you love your job."

She turned to look at him. "Why do I sense you want to add a 'but' to that statement?"

His brows went up. *The instinct is strong with this one*, he thought, refraining from laughing. He didn't dare share his geeky inner monologue with her, not knowing if she'd get the reference. Instead, he settled for a safe answer. "You know me so well."

"So what is it?"

"I'd like you to spend more time with me. With my mom. At home with us."

"There's a killer on the loose."

"I know. But you're my girlfriend, you live with me, yet I don't get to share more than an hour or two each day with you. Is that normal, you think?"

"Some people have it worse than us. What about long-distance relationships? Some people only see each other once a month!"

"I'm not one of those people. I need to see my girlfriend more than once a month. More than seven hours per week."

"I'll try my best. I want to spend time with you, too. But I also need to catch that killer."

"Didn't you tell me Fuller gave you hell for spending too many hours at work?"

"Yeah, but—"

"There's no but. Even your supervisor agrees with me. Share the load with the other detectives, even if you're the lead. Or else this job will drive you crazy."

"Can we talk about something else?"

"Sure. I sent you an email about June 24th. At 7:00 p.m. Mark your calendar. I'm doing something special just for you."

"What is it? You're not taking me to watch a play or something like that, are you?"

"Katie, I know you hate crowds as much as I do. I'm doing something special for you here, in the comfort of our home."

She straightened her back, her eyes glistening with anticipation. “Really? What for?”

He kissed her forehead as he realized June 24th didn’t mean anything to her. Even though it had meant the world to him: the day she’d reappeared in his life after decades of being away.

CHAPTER TWENTY-FIVE

Friday, June 22nd, 2018

SEATED IN CONFERENCE ROOM TWO, the team gathered around a large box of donuts and a tray of coffee from the coffee shop across the street.

After replenishing her sugar levels, Kate looked at the handful of portraits pinned to the cork board and addressed the other detectives. "No unmatched prints came back from the Bible, the thermostat, the front door, the night stand, the stupid blue rubber band on her hair, or the chair. Still no toxicology report. Nothing suspicious in terms of calls on either her cellphone or the family's landline. Everything adds up to a time of death after 10:00 a.m. on Sunday until possibly midnight on Monday. Several friends have confirmed the fact that she often screened calls, so we can't use unanswered calls. Her last public whereabouts were Sunday mass. Nobody saw her leave after church, but she obviously made it back home."

She took a sip from her coffee before continuing. "While we aren't positive on the actual motive behind the murder, the religious theme, her being a member of the chastity club, and her recent loss of virginity point toward that incident being important. As far as we know, the only people who had access to that information were the victim, the boyfriend, the BFF, and possibly Father Coffedy, the priest she confessed to. Who's to say whether or not gossiping would have spread out the news?"

She took another sip. "Wang, Chainey, based on the neighbors and other people you spoke with, can you narrow down the estimated time of death?"

Both shook their heads.

"Financial records? Does anyone stand to gain from an insurance policy on Lori Davis?"

"The parents, but we all know they weren't even in the country."

Kate exhaled loudly. "Did you look at the parents' financials? Anything suspicious? Could they have paid someone to kill their daughter?" As the words left her lips, she realized she didn't buy that scenario one bit. The parents had seemed truly devastated. Even if they had learned that their daughter had lost her virginity—a possibility she highly doubted—she didn't buy the possibility that they would have hired someone to kill her.

"Nothing."

"Chainey, give me something," Kate begged.

"I talked to the officers we had canvassing the neighbors, and nobody saw anything suspicious. I talked to friends from church, from work, from the school she last attended. Nothing."

Kate took another sip. "We considered the boyfriend, but he's been eliminated. He attended mass at a different location that Sunday, followed by a baseball game and an evening with friends. His whereabouts on Monday all day are also accounted for. His work supervisor confirmed his presence. Unless he did it in the middle of the night on Sunday night and somehow showed up looking sharp at work the next day, he's not our guy. Plus we found nothing in his house. No suspicious drugs, no rosaries."

"If I may…" Wang started.

"Go ahead," Kate said.

"I still think Amanda McCutcheon could have something to do with Lori's murder. She would have had access to rosaries through church. Amanda's part of the chastity club. She knew Lori had lost her virginity—and done so with the guy she likes, I think. When I saw her with the boyfriend, I sensed some sort of weird vibe between the two of them."

Kate straightened her back. "When did you see them together?"

"Tuesday morning. She came in to talk with you and Rosebud, but I met with David so he could sign his statement from the previous day. I had everything typed up and ready to go, as you asked me. I watched the two of them interact for a few seconds."

"Interesting," Kate said. "So you think she could have killed the vic because she was jealous? Love triangle?"

"Would she have the strength to pull it off? Lifting a passed-out woman isn't easy," Rosebud said.

"We're not sure that happened. She could have drugged the victim after getting her in her bedroom," Wang suggested.

Rosebud shook his head. "Undressing and redressing a body requires heavy lifting."

"Know that from experience?" Chainey chimed in.

"Ha-ha," Rosebud said, digging into the donut box once more.

Wang shrugged. "They could have played 'dress up' or whatever. She could have dared her to wear the awful nightgown."

"For what purpose?" Kate asked.

"No clue," Wang said, shaking her head. "Lost a bet or something silly? But we know Amanda and the vic were close. Amanda wouldn't have had to force her way into the house. They could have gone up to her bedroom to chat."

"There's only one chair and one desk," Rosebud said.

"One could have sat on the bed."

"Okay, I'll buy that," Kate said. "Except there's one tiny detail that doesn't add up. Lori was upset at Amanda. They had a fight. And based on everyone we talked to, all her friends knew to avoid her for days afterward. The vic needed a lot of time to calm down, or so it seems. Why would she have let a person she was angry with come into her home?"

"Maybe Amanda came with a big apology?"

Kate tilted her head. "Maybe."

"I can't think of anyone else," Wang said.

"Me neither. Wang, continue that scenario for me. Let's

assume Lori forgave Amanda, or at least had cooled off enough to let her in. Then what?"

"Then Amanda went up to Lori's room, somehow got her to dress up and then drugged her. She could have carried a drink with her that was already roofied—"

Kate interrupted her. "Amanda did mention that Lori's parents have quite the liquor cabinet. Wang, did you find anything in the garbage? A drink bottle or something we could test for drugs?"

"Nothing at all. The large bin just outside the house was empty. But so much time elapsed after the murder. Garbage would have been picked up. The small garbage cans in the house were almost all empty, except for one with nail polish-related trash and a few used tissues in one of the bathrooms. I'm having the contents analyzed for DNA. There was some stale bread in the kitchen garbage along with some granola bar wrappers, also in for fingerprint and DNA testing. Just in case someone licked the sucker. Unlikely, though."

"Get all bottles in the parents' liquor cabinet analyzed for drugs," Kate added. "Maybe it's been sitting there all along, under our nose. Wang?"

"On it. But maybe she had a pill or something that she slipped directly into her drink. Then she washed the glass. I'll canvas the neighborhood with Amanda's photo, ask neighbors if they saw her on Sunday or Monday."

"Good." Kate turned her attention to Chainey. "Any leads from the church friends or chastity members you spoke to?"

"Nope. Everyone says she was closest to Amanda. I asked—out of curiosity, I claimed—what would happen to a member of their club if they were to defy their one rule."

"And?" Kate asked, surprised.

Chainey muffled a laugh. "Every single one of them asked me to share who it was and swore they would keep the secret to themselves."

"What a gossipy bunch!" Wang said.

"Don't miss my school years for that exact reason," Rosebud added.

Chainey rammed his fist into Rosebud's plump shoulder. "Come on. I bet your curly hair, thick glasses, and love handles made you very popular with the ladies."

Kate watched Rosebud's nostrils flare. "Chainey, enough of your silly jokes. We're all exhausted. We've done as much as we can physically do this week, and I hate that we have nothing to show for it. Now I have to go and brief Fuller."

Rosebud grabbed one more donut before he spoke again. "Try to come out of it alive."

CHAPTER TWENTY-SIX

Saturday, June 23rd, 2018

KATE BEGAN the day like she did every twenty-third of June since 1996. Lying in bed with her eyes closed, thinking about her dead parents and baby brother. And about how lucky she was to still be alive.

She normally took the day off to head out of state, but she couldn't afford that luxury this year. Not with the murder of Lori Davis weighing heavily on her shoulders. Whoever her killer was, he or she was still out there. Since they hadn't found a single believable motive or a real suspect among her friends and relatives, Kate feared the worst: maybe Lori's killing had been random. Or part of a deranged person's larger plan.

Exhaling loudly, Kate forced herself out of bed, eager to do something else. To think of anything else but her family's cold case or Lori's murder.

After peering outside the bedroom window and seeing the sun shine, she decided to don her running gear and head out.

Pounding the pavement could lead to an unexpected stroke of genius. She could sure use one of those right now.

Her earbuds in and favorite selection of tunes lined up, she walked downstairs and stopped by the kitchen to greet Luke and his mom briefly before heading to the entrance to lace up her shoes and finally breathe in some fresh air.

The morning air was unseasonably crisp, but Kate hoped

the temperature would soar by the time the midday sun shone above the city, as it sometimes did this time of year when the air was clear. Dodging a dog walker and her five four-legged friends, Kate weaved her way around the pedestrians until she reached the closest park. She much preferred running in parks over the streets, even though she'd been badly beat up once, a few years ago.

But that was then. And this was now.

Her head was clear. The park was safe in the daytime and she was paying attention to her surroundings, even though music faintly reached her ears through her headphones. The sounds that surrounded her were much, much louder. She'd learned her lesson.

She ran loops around the small park, running on grass to take it easy on her joints, careful to avoid rocks and the treasures left behind by animals. By the time she finished her third loop, she realized no epiphany was coming.

The only thing that her gut told her was that she had to call the hypnotherapist and schedule another appointment. The doctor had been kind enough to offer some after-hour openings for her, considering the type of work she did. Of course, those slots came at a premium price, but her detective salary was enough to cover it and she'd have extra money coming in whenever she sold Kenny's house.

What better day than the anniversary of their death to go deep and figure this out?

She took out her phone and called the therapist, leaving her a message asking if she could fit her in later today, then headed back home to take a shower.

~

"...AND ONE," the hypnotherapist said to Kate. "You're at home, talking to your mom on the morning of June 23rd, 1995. Tell me what you see."

"I don't see anything, except for what I remember from my dreams."

"Forget about your dreams. Focus on what feels real right now. Maybe you smell something. Maybe you hear—"

"The mobile! I can hear the mobile over his crib."

"Good. Listen to it."

Kate hummed the melody. She tried to ignore the part of her mind that didn't understand how she could—clear as day—hear a melody she hadn't heard in decades. But the more she thought about it, the faster the notes faded, as though taken away from her.

"It's gone."

"That's fine. Try to listen to other noises. Perhaps your father is watching a game in the distance. Or listening to the radio."

"I hear the floor creaking." Kate focused on its sounds, half expecting the cadence to follow what she normally heard in her dreams, but it wasn't the repetitive cycle of creaks she'd associated with the rocking chair in her brother's bedroom. No. The creaks were uneven. Associated with someone pacing the floor. They weren't her footsteps. They weren't coming from behind her or downstairs. The noises echoed from the back of the room, where the window overlooked the street. Then she heard her mom's soft voice humming the melody of Bobby's mobile.

"She's holding him in her arms, pacing the floor next to the window."

"Good. What else can you sense?"

"I'm not sure, but something feels off. I can sense her fear. Or maybe it's my fear. I know what happens next."

"Don't read into what you're feeling. Just let yourself experience it, without judgment."

"No, no!" Kate shook her head. "Something's off. Really off. I… I can't…"

The therapist snapped her fingers and brought Kate to the here and now.

KATE INHALED, counting up to four, then pausing for two, and then counting back to four as she exhaled. She repeated the process several times, until she felt comfortable enough to open her eyes.

"Tell me. What was wrong?" the therapist asked, her inquisitive brown eyes staring at Kate.

At first unable to put words together to explain why it had

felt wrong, Kate shook her head. She sat up and glanced at the therapist, then she moved her eyes to Luke, who'd attended the session in the room this time, sitting in a spare chair along the back wall.

"It was *all* wrong," Kate said.

"Be more specific," the therapist prompted.

"If there's one thing I know it's what happened that day. For decades, I've had recurring nightmares. I see myself talking to my mom that morning, before heading out of the house to play. She rocks Bobby to sleep. I *know* that moment like the back of my hand."

"And?"

"And what I saw just now was all wrong!"

"Kate, you strike me as a smart person. There's no way you wouldn't be, considering your job. So what I'm about to say should, under no circumstances, be taken like a personal insult or anything like that."

Kate tilted her head, her curiosity piqued by the teaser. "Go on."

"You're probably aware of it as a police officer. Memories are unreliable. Testimonies from visual witnesses can often be proven wrong."

"Of course. The same event witnessed by ten people will result in ten slightly different stories. I know that. But I was there. I know what I saw."

"Maybe you do. Maybe you don't. Are you a gambling woman, Kate?" she asked as she put down her pen.

"Can't say that I am."

"Well, I like to indulge every now and then. And I'd be willing to bet that your subconscious has been so traumatized by what you witnessed over twenty years ago that it has filled in some of the gaps or replaced some of the painful details with other real memories as a way to ease the pain."

"What?"

"I'm saying that the recurring nightmare you've been having, the one where you see your mother rock your brother in her arms, could very well be a real memory—"

"It *is* a real memory!"

"Let me finish. A real memory, but from a different time. A different day. I'm sure you could have seen your mother rocking your brother to sleep several times before that fateful day. If you witnessed something odd that particular day, it's very plausible that your subconscious could have kept those 'real memories,'" she said with air quotes, "hidden from you. As protection to help you maintain your sanity. As a survival mechanism, if you wish."

Kate looked at Luke who shrugged, appearing puzzled. She'd taken a few psychology classes over the years. The idea didn't seem so far-fetched after all.

"Okay. Let's assume I buy that theory. You're telling me that, on that fateful morning, I saw my mother acting weird. She wasn't rocking Bobby to sleep, she was pacing the floor, worried."

"If that's what you saw or felt just now, then yes."

Kate looked down, staring mindlessly at the pattern in the carpet. "That could change everything."

A bell rang behind the therapist, indicating the end of their session.

"Well, I think it means you're making great progress. When do you want to meet next?"

"Hmm. It's tough for me to say. I could get called in anytime. Weekends are probably easier. Do you have time tomorrow?"

"I can fit you in at four o'clock. Would that work?"

After looking at Luke, who was nodding, she confirmed the appointment.

"You're doing great, Kate. But better come in prepared. We'll revisit your most painful memory tomorrow."

CHAPTER TWENTY-SEVEN

Sunday, June 24th, 2018

VOICING A SILENT PRAYER TO HER—SHE'D been on his mind a lot lately—he lit a votive candle. Among all the mistakes she'd made, he knew for a fact that the worst had been suicide.

She'd led a short life. A soiled and spoiled life scattered with sins of every kind.

He could still vividly remember her kneeling in front of their guardian. She had on the mini-skirt and spaghetti-string tank top he hated. The man's fingers were passed through her blonde hair as he moved her head back and forth. He could still hear the man's groans. His head had been tilted toward the sky. The guardian and he had never made eye contact that day. He'd simply walked out. Quietly. Stealthily, like he loved doing. It was always the best way to obtain information.

He crossed himself and closed his eyes. The disgusting man got what had been coming to him. He'd seen to that. Too late, perhaps, but he'd righted that wrong. It had taken him a while to work up the strength and willpower to act on it. Not to mention create the plan.

No more would that man take advantage of underage girls like her.

It had been nothing but painful to watch his smart, independent sister turn into… a stupid whore, a party animal, a drug and alcohol addict… And someone who'd go as far as commit the worst sin of all.

Even after all of the counseling he'd given her.

After all of the conversations they'd had. Day and night, he had tried different approaches to make her see the light. To help her right her wrongs. To steer her toward God. To stop her sleeping around, to stop her drug and alcohol habits. He'd even visited her and her horrible boyfriend, showing up unexpectedly to help them. For years, he'd done that.

But it had all been pointless.

Perhaps some souls couldn't be saved…

He reopened his eyes, as though a new surge of energy had come in from above.

He was in a position to save other young girls with potential. He could ensure they wouldn't follow in his sister's footsteps. He would not let them head down a path of sins that would lead them to their unredeemable downfalls. Not if he had a say or could act to save their souls while they were still pure enough.

He turned away from the rows of red votive candles and smiled at various members of the congregation who were slowly but surely dripping through the entrance and finding their seats for mass.

Perhaps it was their physical resemblance to his sister, but he spotted two young women he'd come to know better over the last few weeks. There was Amanda, who'd been gossiping a lot and exhibiting too much pride and greed for her own good. And there was also Jessica. She'd confessed to having done drugs and had sex out of marriage with someone inappropriate. With the confessions he'd heard, he had all of the puzzle pieces. It'd only taken him a week to figure out who the someone was: her dad's best friend—a married man and well-respected member of the community.

Perhaps saving her was more urgent.

CHAPTER TWENTY-EIGHT

DRESSED IN HER SUNDAY BEST, Kate accompanied Luke's mom to church. After days of endless interviews with neighbors, friends, and distant relatives, Kate and the rest of the detectives had yet to find a decent lead. But, after another sleepless night, she decided that following her gut and witnessing the fathers in their natural environment could spark a new idea.

Or perhaps enlighten her as to what the religious nature of the murder scene had been all about.

The drive over to St. Alban's church was done over the incessant jabber of Mrs. O'Brien, who couldn't get over her excitement at having Kate join her for mass. Nearly a year of begging had taken place, so Kate decided it was easier to let Mrs. O'Brien believe her offer had finally been accepted.

Mrs. O'Brien didn't need to know the grisly details going around in Kate's head. But then again, Kate didn't want to set the wrong expectations. No way she was going to make a habit of this. So she settled for a politically correct statement that would not affect her ongoing investigation.

"Mrs. O'Brien, I'm really doing this for work, so please don't expect me to join you every week."

"I'll take whatever I can get. Work or not. Maybe the words of the good Lord will reach your heart, and you'll decide to come back for more."

"Yeah," Kate said as she parked her Subaru, forcing

herself to keep the rest of her thoughts to herself. "Do you know Fathers Miller, Matthews, and Coffedy?"

"Father Coffedy's been around for decades. Lovely man. Wonderful baritone voice."

Kate thought back to her meeting with him, and she agreed. He did have a nice tone of voice. "What about Miller and Matthews?" Kate asked.

"Father Miller is a bit sterner. But his health has been declining a lot over the years. He rarely holds mass anymore. In fact, I haven't seen him in months."

"And Matthews?" she asked as they turned the corner, the church now appearing in the distance.

"Ah, swell young man. He's new to town. Too bad we're not going to mass at the cathedral in the South End. That's where he is these days. I think you'd like him. He's quite… hip."

Kate stopped walking and grabbed Mrs. O'Brien by the elbow. "Would you mind if we headed over there instead?"

"What?" She blinked faster than normal.

"I'd like to attend Father Matthews' mass."

"Oh!" Her brows furrowed, then she looked at the watch on her wrist. "By the time we get there, mass will have already started…"

Kate stood firm. "I can leave you here, then come back and get you after. Or you can join me there."

Mrs. O'Brien appeared to ponder her options. "As long as we're hearing the words of the Lord, it doesn't really matter where we go, I guess."

"Wonderful, I appreciate it very much. Let's go and see that *swell young priest*," Kate said, partly mocking Mrs. O'Brien and partly excited.

What better way to find potential suspects than to go where they congregated?

CHAPTER TWENTY-NINE

"THANK YOU FOR VOLUNTEERING," he said, his smile digging small dimples into his clean-shaven cheeks.

Too bad he's off the market, Jessica Stephenson thought, appreciating his good looks. He stood out among the group of well-dressed parishioners chatting on the front steps of the cathedral.

"Where should we talk about what you'll need me to do?" she asked.

He frowned for a second. "I'm afraid the office is busy at the moment. We can't really discuss anything inside. There are always parishioners coming in to pray in silence. I wouldn't dare invite you to my apartment. Some people could see it as inappropriate. What about your home?" he asked.

"Well…" Jessica thought about it for a second. She trusted the man. It wasn't as though she was inviting a stranger into her home. He was a man of God, after all. "Yeah, let's do that. Plus, I could show you some of the photos for the event I was telling you about. We'd do it differently, of course, but it would give you an idea of what I'm thinking."

He smiled and nodded. "That's a great idea! But then again, I wouldn't want to disturb the rest of your family as we chit-chat and plan the event. You live with your father, right?"

"You have a great memory!" She stretched out her hand and patted him on the arm. "Do you know this much about every parishioner?"

"Not everyone, but I do my best to learn a little bit about those I meet. I think caring and getting to know people is the best way to be involved with the community. Don't you agree?"

"Absolutely. My dad's working for another"—she lifted her phone up to check the time—"five hours or so."

"Okay. We shouldn't need more than an hour or two max."

"Do you want to start now?"

He bit his lips. "I do have to take care of something first, then I could meet you there in about an hour?"

"Sure."

"What's your address?"

CHAPTER THIRTY

JESSICA STEPHENSON WAS A HEAVIER girl than he'd assumed. She was short and thin, but quite muscular, as he noticed when he began undressing her with his gloved hands.

With efficient moves, he took everything off except for her underwear. He had no desire to see or touch what hid beyond those thin layers of fabric. In fact, he never understood the so-called common but lowly desires men had toward women. Sure, some had beautiful facial features, but the rest? Good thing he'd chosen a path toward God.

Of course, he understood that all creatures, men and women included, had been shaped by God. They were beautiful in that sense, but that didn't entice him in the least.

Whenever women approached him—and they did more often than he cared for—a single line had always sufficed to push them away: "My heart belongs to Him."

As he slid the green nightgown he'd lifted from the church's donation bin, he realized he could save the women that came onto him instead of turning them down.

Maybe…

He lifted her body so the fabric could slip underneath her, then let her be for now. She wasn't going anywhere. Not with the dose of cleansing solution she'd just ingested. He had a few hours ahead of him to clean up.

He headed down the hall and back to the kitchen to drink the rest of his wine. He found the garbage underneath the sink and thought about dumping the two travel-sized bottles he'd brought with him. He'd learned one thing from Lori's cleansing, the larger wine bottle wasn't very discreet. Either getting there or back. But putting two travel-size bottles in his pants was much easier. He put them back in his pockets for now, not wanting their existence to clue anyone in.

The sinner's father would be home shortly. He didn't have as much leeway as he'd had with the last soul he'd saved. Time had been on his side then. But now, he had to hurry if he wanted to keep his freedom.

He could dump the small bottles into someone else's garbage a few blocks away. Nobody would be the wiser for it.

But solving that one problem still left him with dishes to do. Opening the dishwasher, he noted it was nearly full. He popped in the two glasses, found the powder detergent under the sink, filled up the dispenser, and began the cycle with the hottest setting.

"Done," he said aloud before grabbing a handful of paper towels and a bottle of window cleaner.

Revisiting the living room where they'd sat minutes earlier, he proceeded to wipe every surface he could have touched before donning his gloves. He walked back to the door and wiped the handle as well.

Satisfied he'd left no trace there, he headed back to the bedroom to continue his cleaning ritual.

There were no chairs in her bedroom, but he could bless her soul while standing. After retrieving from his pocket a small container he'd filled with his concoction of olive and essential oils he'd consecrated at his private altar, he traced a small cross over her forehead with his gloved finger.

"God, accept this child into Heaven. Let her sit next to you, in your Kingdom. Welcome her with open arms so she can join you and forever rest in peace. Forgive all of her sins for she has already confessed to them. With the following words, I shall cleanse and bless her soul and grant her direct passage to your Kingdom."

He opened the Bible to the Second Epistle to the Corinthians and began reading aloud:

"Blessed be the God and Father of our Lord Jesus

Christ, the Father of mercies and God of all comfort; who comforts us in all our affliction, that we may be able to comfort those who are in any affliction, through the comfort with which we ourselves are comforted by God.

For as the sufferings of Christ abound to us, even so our comfort also abounds through Christ.

But if we are afflicted, it is for your comfort and salvation.

If we are comforted, it is for your comfort, which produces in you the patient enduring of the same sufferings which we also suffer.

Our hope for you is steadfast, knowing that, since you are partakers of the sufferings, so also are you of the comfort. For we don't desire to have you uninformed that we were weighed down exceedingly, beyond our power, so much that we despaired even of life.

Yes, we ourselves have had the sentence of death within ourselves, that we should not trust in ourselves, but in God who raises the dead, who delivered us out of so great a death, and does deliver; on whom we have set our hope that he will also still deliver us; you also helping together on our behalf by your supplication; that, for the gift given to us by means of many, thanks may be given by many persons on your behalf.

For our boasting is this: the testimony of our conscience, that in holiness and sincerity of God, not in fleshly wisdom but in the grace of God we behaved ourselves in the world, and more abundantly toward you.

For we write no other things to you, than what you read or even acknowledge, and I hope you will acknowledge to the end; as also you acknowledged us in part, that we are your boasting, even as you also are ours, in the day of our Lord Jesus."

He crossed himself then pulled three rosaries out of his pocket. Gently lifting her head, he passed the colorful strings between the pillow and her neck. Crossing the ends together, he tightened his grip and pulled as hard as he could.

"May you rest in peace. May you rest in peace. May you rest in peace." His voice had begun with a soft whisper but continued in a crescendo until he watched her life force escape from her eyes.

Remaining immobile for a few seconds, he took in her vacant stare then finally released the pressure around her neck. He watched her body, peaceful and cleansed, for a moment to confirm that her chest was no longer rising and to let his own heart slow down.

Somehow, her cleansing had given him a bigger high than the one he'd done weeks ago.

Was God sending him a sign? Was he being rewarded with a pleasant and powerful sensation because he'd freed another soul from the evil sins she no doubt would have continued committing?

He inhaled deeply, satisfied by his work, then pulled the rosaries away from her neck. Looking at the selection of colors he'd used this time, he settled on orange. Taking her arms away from her side and placing them on her chest in a prayer position, he then wrapped the chosen rosary around her hands.

The Bible she'd given him still lay on the nightstand. He debated which verse would be more appropriate, then settled on the First Epistle to the Corinthians. He placed the ribbon on that page, then left it open at Colossians 3:3 after reading one last passage aloud:

> *"For you died, and your life is hidden with Christ in God. When Christ, our life, is revealed, then you will also be revealed with him in glory."*

Minutes later, he let himself out after carefully ensuring nobody was coming into the building as he exited.

He lucked out. It was minutes before he encountered anyone. While he did his best to act normal, he concentrated on slowing down his racing heart. He resisted the urge to look around and see if anyone was looking at him for he knew that such behavior could attract unwanted attention. The more distance he placed between the apartment and himself, the closer his pulse got to its regular rhythm.

He thanked the Lord for not crossing anyone's path for five solid blocks, at which point he ran into a parishioner whose name escaped him.

A smile and a "good afternoon" were enough to look as though he belonged in the neighborhood. He continued his walk and stopped at a coffee shop.

Perfect alibi.

He ordered himself a cup of cappuccino and a slice of lemon pie, then sat down by the window, resting in his glory, reveling in his holy deed.

CHAPTER THIRTY-ONE

"SHIT! I FORGOT AGAIN," Tod Stephenson muttered as he pulled open the door to the apartment complex.

He retrieved his phone from his pocket, then dialed the landlord's number only to reach voicemail.

"Hey, Mr. Roberts. It's Tod from 5B. Could you do something about the broken lock on the building's front door? I don't like it. Doesn't feel safe for me and my girl. Appreciate it!"

Feeling a tad better—and very hungry due to the pizza box he'd brought back with him, its scent having lingered around his car for the past twenty minutes—he headed up the elevator and down the hall to his apartment.

Once again, his keys proved to be useless bits of metal as his daughter had apparently left it unlocked, again. He shook his head then pushed open the door. Muffled music could be heard from her room in the back of the apartment.

"Jess! I got pizza," he yelled after sliding it onto the kitchen table. "Come and eat while it's hot!"

He dropped his lunchbox by the sink, then opened the fridge to grab a cold one. The hissing sound of the gas escaping the can was music to his ears. Even though he could only afford budget brew, it tasted like the best thing on earth when he got home from work.

Beer in hand, he proceeded to prepare the table, adding a plate, knife, and fork for Jessica. Then he ripped a piece of paper towel for each of them. For whatever reason, she preferred to ignore his efficient method of folding the pizza and insisted on creating dishes that needed washing. But she took care of the wash, so he had nothing to complain about, really.

He sat down and opened the cardboard box, releasing an even more powerful scent of garlic, tomato, cheese, and bacon. "Jessica! I'm going to start without you!"

Without a peep from her still, he grabbed his first slice and smiled at it. "I've given her proper notice," he muttered before folding the thin wedge and inhaling half of it in one bite. Three more bites and the slice had disappeared.

He grabbed his second slice but paused before biting into it.

Something was odd. Jessica hadn't even turned off her music or lowered it. Maybe she hadn't heard him at all?

Slice in hand, he headed down the hall, the muffled music growing slightly louder with each step. He knocked on her door. "Jess!"

He rapped on it again. Louder. "Jessica! Cut that music off now!"

Holding his pizza slice with one hand, he turned the knob of her bedroom door and pushed it open with the other.

"Jessica?"

But what he saw on the bed made him lose more than his appetite.

CHAPTER THIRTY-TWO

"AND ONE..." the therapist said in her hypnotically soft voice. "You're now back to the time when you were thirteen years old on that fateful day. You're saying goodbye to Luke. Can you see it?"

"I can't see him, but I'm there."

"Good, now what did you do after you parted ways?"

"We raced home, as always."

"Do you remember what you wore that day?"

"Jeans and a T-shirt."

"Do you remember the color of your shirt?"

"Bright green."

"What about your shoes?"

"I wore white Adidas with the green patches at the back, just below the ankles. I had bright red socks on that day."

"That's good. You're doing great, Kate. So, start running back home. And pay attention to your surroundings. Is there anything you see, hear, feel, or smell?"

Kate's breathing accelerated as though reliving the memory of running back home was somehow part of her current reality. Her chest felt heavier than usual as it heaved up and down. The couch upon which she lay, her eyes closed, no longer seemed comfortable. She adjusted her position.

"Are you okay?" the therapist asked.

Kate nodded. "Yes."

"What are you seeing on your way back home?"

"It's hot. Humid. Muggy."

"Good. What else?"

"I'm worried. I'm running late."

"What are you worried about?"

"Disappointing my parents. My mom hated it when I arrived late and we ate dinner cold."

"Okay."

"And she made turkey that day."

The therapist stayed silent for a while. A very long while, allowing Kate to focus on her memories, those she'd purposely pushed to the very back of her subconscious. She could smell perspiration mixing in with her deodorant, coming out of her pores. Not the deodorant she wore today. The baby-powder kind her mom had bought for her when teenage hormones had kicked in. She inhaled deeply, as though unwilling to believe she was smelling it, but there it was, reaching her brain as though she were there.

"Are you smelling something?"

"Just a memory."

"Now try to focus on your sight. When you arrived home, what did you see? Try to use the smells to trigger images in your mind."

"Okay," Kate said, doing her best to force images to come, but they didn't. "I can't."

"Then stick to the smells or any other sensation you may remember."

Kate's arms suddenly flayed up in the air, and her breathing stopping for a few seconds before resuming at heart-racing speed.

"What's going on?" the therapist prompted.

"I saw the house. For a split second, then it disappeared."

"What did you see?"

"The front door. The white porch door, above the old wooden steps. It was slightly ajar."

"And?"

"Then nothing. I'm standing outside, worried. I know something's wrong. Dad always said doors kept the flies out. We never left the door ajar. Ever."

"Okay, Kate. Now's the time where you're going to need to be brave. You know you're safe here. Luke is here, sitting just a few feet away from you. I'm here, ready to pull you out if it gets too difficult. What you'll experience are just memories. They can't hurt you. Do you understand?"

"Yes." Kate brought her hands back together over her chest, as though the position could strengthen her mood, prepare her for returning to the raw emotions she'd previously sworn to forget.

"Now remember that while the experience may make you feel powerless, you're going through this to retrieve important clues. To ultimately take power again. So please focus on that. Focus on the things you've forgotten about. Are you ready?"

Kate took one long inhalation then replied in the affirmative.

"Now push open that door and walk into your house. What do you see, hear, or smell?"

Kate could feel her toes moving, even though she didn't do it on purpose, as though the heebie-jeebies were coming out through her socks. "It's totally silent. Eerily so."

"What do you see?"

"I can't see anything right now, but I remember the house was a mess."

"Just focus on your current experiences, whatever they are," the therapist said. "What room are you in?"

"The living room."

"But that's not where they were?"

"No."

"Where did you go after that?"

Kate felt dread building up in her chest. "I walked upstairs to check on my baby brother."

"Walk upstairs now. Is there anything you notice?"

"There's something in the air. It's faint."

"Can you describe it?"

As much as Kate tried to identify it, she couldn't. "Maybe it's just the stench of blood from a distance."

"Okay, are you in your brother's room now?"

"Yes." Kate fought the tears that came up, all the while trying to keep her face straight. An impossible task. She crossed her arms over her chest, as though pressing his body against her now.

Between tears, she mustered enough willpower to speak. "I

lifted his… little body… and brought it up to my chest… holding his head… like Mom had shown me how to… but he's cold… lifeless."

The pain in her chest was as sharp as that day, the understanding he was gone as troubling as the first time she'd felt it.

"You're safe, Kate. Take your time. Do you smell something different about him?"

The question took her out of the deepest emotions, and she inhaled deeply, as though the therapist's room somehow held the sensory answers she needed.

"His baby scent wasn't as strong. Dissipated somehow. And there's something else, it's faint."

"Do you see anything in his room?"

"No, I don't see anything. I don't hear anything either. The mobile is quiet. Complete silence in the house."

"What did you do with your brother?"

"I took him with me and headed downstairs to tell my parents something was wrong with him."

"Go downstairs."

Once again Kate's breathing increased rapidly. She held on to her chest, feeling her heart pounding within her body.

"Argggghhhh!" she yelled, before being overtaken with a tsunami of angst and sadness. Kate brought her hands up and covered her face.

"Where are you now, Kate?"

"In the kitchen."

"Is it where you found them?"

"Yes. I saw another flash, but not much. Not enough to know for sure."

"Are there sounds? Smells?"

"Blood. A thick stench. There's also roasted turkey. And garlic."

"Now, this is going to be difficult, but try to walk up to your parents. See if you can trigger another visual flash. Start with your dad."

Kate inhaled deeply while nodding. Her face was wet with tears, her nose snotty, her heart unsure what to feel.

She concentrated, focusing on the stench of blood, trying

to see something. Anything. One flash came back and disappeared.

"What did you see?"

"The blood pattern on the wall, his throat was slit while his heart was still beating. The pressure of the blood made it reach the wall."

"Anything else? His clothing?"

Kate shook her head.

"Try to have a look at your mom."

Kate began shaking. As though her body had uncontrollably taken a life of its own. Or perhaps her subconscious was doing its best to distract her. But she focused. She concentrated on her breathing, trying to remember the smells. As she moved closer to her mother, the scent of her perfume grew stronger. She tried to connect other memories to it. Then another scene flashed on her mental screen. Her mother's ripped dress, soaked with blood. The kitchen table had been set, the turkey left out in the middle of the table. One point puzzled her, though. Her ankles weren't bound to the chair like her dad had been. Like she'd remembered in her nightmares. And there hadn't been splashing on the wall around her.

Doing her very best to dissociate from her identity as the victim's daughter, she pushed away the tears and tried to see what her detective mind noticed.

Having seen so many crime scenes since that fateful day, she didn't doubt her mom had been raped by the killer. The ripped dress and torn panties tossed to the floor were clear indicators.

"My mom. Her throat was slit after her heart had stopped beating."

"What makes you say that?" the therapist asked. "Do you see other wounds?"

One last effort, Kate told herself. *One last push.* Then it would all be over. She'd return to the now.

Focusing on the scent of her mom's perfume again, she squeezed her jaw and willed her mind to see something. Anything.

But nothing came. The case file photos would have to

refresh her memories there. Then her nose twitched. She remembered something else.

"Cologne!" Kate exclaimed as a faint ringing sound reached her ears.

As agreed prior to the session, the hypnotherapist snapped her fingers and brought Kate back.

By the time Kate reopened her eyes, the therapist had grabbed her phone and brought it to her.

Fuller was calling, which only meant one thing: bad news.

~

"AND THEN THERE WERE TWO," Murphy said, shaking her head as she stepped into the bedroom where Jessica Stephenson lay. The sight was too familiar: a blonde woman in her early twenties, hair in a braid—this time tied with a proper hair band. She was dressed in a faded green gown, her hands in prayer position with an orange rosary, and a Bible resting on her chest.

For better or worse, this murder was recent. The stench of death had yet to emerge. Her skin had lost its pigmentation, the blood having begun to settle away from the surface, but no signs of decomposition yet. They'd, hopefully, be able to collect more evidence this time.

But that also meant they had a serial killer roaming the streets of Boston. A killer targeting innocent young women. They had to up their game and fast.

Her latest breakthrough with the therapist, as exciting, promising, and unsettling as it had been, would have to wait. She had to focus on the current cases and ignore her family's cold case for now.

But maybe they'd luck out now. With a new victim came new clues. Possible errors made by the killer. Possible leads for them to follow.

"Has she entered rigor already?" Kate asked the medical examiner who'd managed to once again make it to the scene before her.

"Yes, it's beginning with the smaller body parts: eyelids, neck, jaw. This one's really recent," Dr. Cooper stated, his gloved hands and eyes still on the victim. "A few hours at most."

"Strangulation again, right?"

"That would be my guess. I'll confirm tomorrow during the autopsy."

Murphy bent down to have a closer look at the vic's hands and nails. Their varnish impeccable, they showed no signs of struggle.

"What about the pupils and irises? Same as last time?"

George shone a light into the victim's lifeless eyes. "Afraid so."

"And we still don't have a match with anything from the toxicology report. If we could at least pinpoint what the killer used to drug them, it might give us a clue toward his or her identity."

"I'm here," Rosebud said behind her. "Another, eh?"

Kate inhaled deeply while shaking her head and turning to meet her partner.

"Three weeks apart," she said. "Our killer's acting fast. We have to catch this guy before he kills ag—"

"Got that right, Murphy!" Fuller barked. "This is *not* what I wanted to see today. What leads do you have?"

"Well, sir…" Kate exhaled loudly, fighting off her temptation to bark back and yell that she'd only arrived minutes ago. *What does he expect?* She was no psychic or miracle worker. "Not much. But connections between the two vics could prove helpful."

"Suspects?"

"The father is the one who found her. No boyfriend that he was aware of. He couldn't think of anyone who would have wanted to hurt his daughter. But he did say something about the building's front door having been broken for days. We'll look into all of this, but we'll prioritize any connections. This has to be the same killer. We never released the details. No way the two identical murders aren't connected."

Fuller's finger flew toward the vic's body. "I gotta go brief the district commander. The mayor wants to hold a press conference. This is going public tonight and Bostonians are going to freak out. You guys need to solve this ASAP."

"Yes, sir."

CHAPTER THIRTY-THREE

"MURPHY, FILL ME IN," Rosebud said after Fuller stormed out.

"Strangled. Looks like the same killer. We should bag every chemical product in the apartment in case she was drugged like the other. Maybe the killer just makes his potion from household products."

"Wouldn't hurt, I guess, but that's not going to help us fast. You know how long toxicology reports take. What about the Bible?"

"What about it?" Murphy asked as they both approached the body.

Rosebud thanked his lucky stars for the nearly absent stench. At least he wouldn't throw up so soon after his lack of gut control was last displayed.

After confirming that the photographer had already taken shots of it, he lifted the book off of her body with his gloved hands.

"Different Bible, but it's open to the same section: the book of Colossians," Rosebud said.

"So we need to study those passages. Figure out what message the killer is leaving us. Do you think..." Murphy walked away without finishing her sentence.

"What? Murphy?"

But she reappeared with her LED light and shone it on the open pages, using a different light spectrum.

"Nah. Nothing. I guess we could run more tests, but I was hoping he used invisible ink or something."

"There was none on the first Bible, either. The outside had been wiped clean and the only prints on the inside were those of the family. You watch too much TV," Rosebud said.

"But what else is there?" Murphy asked. "These murders are happening for a reason. The killer's got a motive. But what is it? Hand me that Bible, will you?"

Rosebud shrugged and passed it on.

A small line appeared between Murphy's brows as she began reading the passages aloud. Less than twenty seconds later, she stopped mid-sentence.

"Hey! The ribbon!" Murphy flipped to the page marker. "That has to be different."

"What do you mean?" Rosebud asked.

"With Lori Davis, the ribbon wasn't that far from the open pages. This one seems closer to the beginning of the book. If the killer's leaving us a message, that's where it is. Thoughts?" she asked, handing the Bible back to Rosebud.

The ribbon marked passages from the First Corinthians section. Glancing through the verses, he spotted a few possible themes.

"So?" Murphy asked.

He snapped a photo of it. "I'm heading back to the office to compare the two. You may be onto something."

"I'll look around the crime scene some more then take the vic's father to the station for his statement. Call me if you find something."

USING A PRINTED-OUT copy of the pages where both Bibles had been open, Rosebud re-read the one passage that made the most sense to him. He read it over and over again until Colossians 3:1-7 became ingrained in his head.

> *"If then you were raised together with Christ, seek the things that are above, where Christ is, seated on the right hand of God.*
> *Set your mind on the things that are above, not on the*

things that are on the earth. For you died, and your life is hidden with Christ in God.
When Christ, our life, is revealed, then you will also be revealed with him in glory.
Put to death therefore your members which are on the earth: sexual immorality, uncleanness, depraved passion, evil desire, and covetousness, which is idolatry; for which things' sake the wrath of God comes on the children of disobedience.
You also once walked in those, when you lived in them; but now you also put them all away: anger, wrath, malice, slander, and shameful speaking out of your mouth."

He highlighted the words "sexual immorality, uncleanness, depraved passion, evil desire, and covetousness."

Then he flipped to the ribbon-marked page and highlighted the First Corinthians 6:9 and 10:

"Or don't you know that the unrighteous will not inherit God's Kingdom?
Don't be deceived.
Neither the sexually immoral, nor idolaters, nor adulterers, nor male prostitutes, nor homosexuals, nor thieves, nor covetous, nor drunkards, nor slanderers, nor extortionists, will inherit God's Kingdom."

Then he looked at the photocopied pages from Lori's Bible where the ribbon had been placed and began highlighting from Galatians 5:19:

"Now the works of the flesh are manifest, which are these: fornication, uncleanness, lasciviousness, idolatry, sorcery, enmities, strife, jealousies, wraths, factions, divisions, parties, envyings, drunkenness, revellings, and such like; of which I forewarn you, even as I did forewarn you, that they who practise such things shall not inherit the kingdom of God."

Picking up his phone, he dialed Murphy's number. She picked up on the third ring.

"I figured out the Bibles. I think I've got the common thread."

"What is it?"

"Have you ever seen the movie *Seven* with Brad Pitt and Morgan Freeman?"

"I don't like where you're going."

"I think that's what our killer's doing. Selecting people based on their sins. I'm not exactly sure which ones yet. But I don't want it to end with someone's head in a box."

"You and I both. What do you have exactly?"

"I don't know for sure, but after reading and re-reading the pages marked by the ribbons and the open ones, I think the killer pointed to various lists of sins that prevent people from inheriting the kingdom of God."

"What's the list? Those seven deadly sins from the movie?"

"Not really. But common themes. Sexual immorality, idolatry, adultery, drunkenness, parties… There's a bunch. Different times, different views. I'm probably guilty of half of them, in a good week."

"We gotta figure this out. I'll try to dig into the vic's sexual history. Can you get one of the priests to give you his opinion on the meaning of those passages you found?"

"Can do."

"And could you ask all three of them? Just in case one is our killer. He may have a different reaction to those passages."

"Can't hurt, I guess."

"Listen, I know it's far-fetched. But let's cover all our bases, okay?"

"You're the lead, Murphy. It's already late. I'll get on that first thing tomorrow morning."

CHAPTER THIRTY-FOUR

LEANING AGAINST THE KITCHEN COUNTER, Luke watched his mother eat alone at the table. He checked his watch again, then pulled out his phone from his back pocket.

"You might as well leave it out," she said, shaking her head at him.

"I don't understand what's taking her so long."

"Really?"

"Well, I know she's working the biggest case of her career right now, but I also know the policies they have in place. She can't work twenty-four seven. They get some overtime, but they have to go home and sleep. That's just life. Their detectives will take turns and work different shifts if needed, but she should be here by now."

"Maybe she went to chat with Father Matthews again."

"What? Who's that?"

"A young priest. Quite dashing, really. I wonder if…"

Her unfinished sentence dangled over Luke's heart like an icicle threatening to split it in half. But his head wouldn't have any of it. He knew Kate too well to worry about that.

"Mom, that's just ridiculous."

"I don't know. She's a beautiful, smart woman. It wouldn't hurt if you showed her how much you care by proposing to her."

"Stop it! I've got a romantic dinner all set up for us here, but she's just not showing up!"

"It's not *that* romantic if your mother is here, is it?"

"What do you want, Mom? You'd rather I kick you out of the house?"

"I can always go to the theater and watch a movie. I may be older than you, but I can still walk and leave the house for a few hours, you know. I understand your need for privacy."

He checked his phone for the umpteenth time. Still no text message from Kate.

"I appreciate that, Mom, but it sure doesn't look as though my romantic evening will be happening tonight."

"What are you celebrating? Maybe she just forgot."

"It's the three-year anniversary of our reunion."

His mom pressed a hand against her chest and smiled at him. "Oh. You're as romantic as your dad, God bless his heart." She crossed herself and looked up to the sky.

"Yeah. I'm not sure my romantic gestures are always appreciated by Kate. I may be hopelessly romantic with a woman who doesn't seem to see it as a value worth having."

"Oh, Luke." She shook her head at him once more.

He shrugged but stayed silent.

"I used to think *your* job was quite dreary," she said. "Working in a lab, looking at samples that had nothing but horrible stories attached to them. Then I began thinking about poor little Katie. After what she witnessed decades ago… And now what she sees and deals with day in and day out… Can you really blame her for being a little emotionally detached?"

Luke poured himself a glass of wine as he let his mother's words sink in.

"I guess you're right. I can't imagine what her work days are really like."

"But keep the romance alive. She probably needs it more than you can imagine. Don't give up on her. I might even suggest you double down on it. Don't just be the most romantic of the two. Be romantic *for two*." She lifted her hands and pointed to her ring finger, which still displayed her wedding ring, even though his dad, her husband, had passed away years ago.

"Mom! Enough about the hints. You're not subtle at all. I get it."

Bringing his glass to his lips, he reflected on it, yet again.

The thought had crossed his mind more than once already. He'd even started putting money aside. Deep in his heart, he knew Kate was the one. If he was brutally honest with himself, he'd probably known back then, decades ago, when they were just children and she'd befriended him out of nowhere.

But did he really want to be married to someone who valued work more than family? Someone who prioritized criminals and murderers over those she loved?

CHAPTER THIRTY-FIVE

ALTHOUGH KATE HAD FANTASIZED about hitting the pavement the instant she got home, storm clouds had rolled in and the sky had opened up, making her look for an alternative. Yes, a late evening run would have cleared her mind, but she was exhausted, and the weather was obviously not on her side. Now was not the time to risk catching pneumonia. Not when the clock was ticking and she had a killer to find.

They'd made progress, though. She had to take the small victories where they came, even if they weren't the ones she wanted to win. Eliminating suspects did bring them closer to finding the real killer, but not fast enough. More lives were at stake, and she felt hopeless.

She exhaled, letting go of the anger that was bubbling in her chest as she secured her gun for the night. Her inability to fix the situation, or to put an end to the murderer's streak made her clench her fists.

Her run options discarded, she opted for a beer instead. Kate walked through the living room and headed to the kitchen to open the fridge, which lit up the darkened room. With its quiet ticking, the clock caught Kate's attention and explained why the house was so quiet.

Everyone had gone to bed, of course.

Luke…

She pulled out her phone and reread the string of messages he'd sent her. Messages she'd ignored while trying to find a killer, or a real motive, or a connection between the two victims.

She'd forgotten about Luke's romantic evening for the two of them. Tonight was the 24th. She'd forgotten that today marked their reunion. To be fair, as much as she'd enjoyed reconnecting with him, memorizing the date had never occurred to her. But it had occurred to Luke.

The date had meant that much to him.

How did she manage to find such a great guy? He was so much better at relationships than she was. Or was she subconsciously trying to ruin the one good relationship she'd ever been in?

As she took a swig of the cold amber liquid, her thoughts briefly turned to Matt, her ex-husband. She winced as she recalled how bad things had been. Matt and his manipulative lies, his double life, his… She forced him out of her mind. Such negative thoughts headed nowhere good.

Exhaling loudly, she took a second to be grateful for Luke. Her Luko. Being with him was just… easy. Easy and comfortable. Like an old pair of shoes. While the idea sure didn't sound romantic, she realized she desperately needed those figurative, worn-out shoes in her life. While work could be relied upon to bring in more than her daily share of chaos and violence, Luke could be counted on for grounding her, for bringing in the stability and comfort she needed to balance things out. He was the yang to her yin. He was her rainbow after the storm.

She took another swig knowing fair well that joining him in bed right that minute could lead to nothing but a night filled with twisted facts and gory images spinning in her head. She had to get work out of her mind, but she didn't want to make noise by turning on the TV.

Taking her beer into Luke's office, she decided she'd head down memory lane by going through the photo albums she'd brought back from Kenny's house. Looking at those photos could help make sense of the hypnotherapist session she'd gotten earlier today.

Now that she was detached from the urgency of the second murder, a swell of emotions came back to her. Even her nose played a trick on her and reminded her of that other cologne she'd smelled just before the therapist had taken her out. It hadn't been her dad's cologne, which meant it was more likely the killer's.

That and yesterday's discovery about how terrified her mom had been the morning of… It could only mean one thing. Her mom had known their killer. Or at least had been aware of the threat hanging over her head.

Perhaps she'd even invited him to dinner?

She took another swig of her beer then opened the first of the photo albums she found in the top box.

Hours passed by as she flipped through albums she'd never really seen before. Pictures of her as a baby. Pictures of baby Bobby. Pictures of the both of them with their parents. Back when life had been simpler. Before that fateful day…

She closed her eyes, pushing tears down her cheeks. Her identity and personality had been carved out of a horrible past. Those photos were just snapshots of her roots. One by one, she felt her tears drip onto her shirt, their cool presence seeping their way to her skin.

"Katie, baby. You all right?"

Luko's warm voice startled her. Wiping her tears, she opened her eyes and looked at the man she loved standing in the doorway.

She nodded.

"Come to bed."

"I'm sorry for tonight," Kate said.

He shook his head, a line splitting his brows. "Don't worry about it. I know you have lots on your plate right now."

Right there and then, she realized she'd never ever have an empty plate. There would always be serious crimes needing to be solved. That was her job, her life. There would never be a better moment to look into her family's murder cases. Getting the ball rolling now instead of later may make a difference.

"I'll do it," Kate said.

"You'll come to bed? I hope so, you look exhausted."

"No, yes. I mean, I'll talk to the sheriff. I need to do it. For them. For me."

Luke's lips curled into a faint smile and he walked to her and wrapped his arms around Kate.

"I'm proud of you."

CHAPTER THIRTY-SIX

Los Angeles, California
Monday, June 25th, 2018

PIXIE BROWNE WAS REMINISCING about her past and eating a bowl of clam chowder at her favorite Northeastern-themed hole-in-the-wall restaurant when her attention wandered to the news on the screen in front of her. Perhaps it had to do with the ambiance of the joint, but the owners always keep the TV tuned to the Northeastern news channels.

At first, the weather forecast showed nothing surprising. While sunshine and warm temperatures were the norm for L.A., the weather forecast for the Northeast had nothing going for it. The remnants of a tropical storm were hitting the coast and carrying loads of rain.

Suckers!

Pixie smiled, pleased with herself for having left that part of her life behind. She'd left her family, her name, her friends. She'd given up everything so she could start anew, away from *him*. The weather was just one tiny improvement, but oh, did sunshine make her new life more enjoyable!

Her mood changed when the screen flashed with a breaking news announcement.

The TV was muted but a caption scrolled across the bottom of the screen while random footage of a police cordon surrounding an apartment building repeated in a loop. Then the portraits of two young women appeared for a few seconds.

What the caption said next almost made her spit out her spoonful in surprise:

"Bostonians the target of a serial killer. Two confirmed murders in a few weeks. Both victims were blonde women in their early twenties. The mayor is urging the citizens to be overly cautious, even with people they know, and to report any suspicious behavior to the police."

That can't be him again, can it? Oh shit.

"Did you see that?" the man sitting next to her asked.

"Yes. Crazy, uh?"

"Hope you don't mind me saying, but you kind of look like those two chicks. Ain't you lucky to be living far away from there?"

"Yeah. Lucky me." Pixie dropped a handful of small bills next to her half-empty bowl, then darted out to the street, her stomach knotted and her heart pounding.

CHAPTER THIRTY-SEVEN

Boston, Massachusetts
Monday, June 25th, 2018

"SORRY, I'm late. What can you tell me, Doc?" Kate asked as she rushed into the examination room, wearing scrubs that matched those of Dr. Cooper, except hers were still clean.

"Same manner and cause of death. This one was just found sooner."

"Rape?"

"I don't believe so, although there were signs of recent sexual intercourse."

"How recent?" she asked while her eyes darted toward the bloody organs that had been taken out of the vic already.

"Hard to tell. Sperm can live for five days. But I collected a sample for you to compare with that of the other victim."

"What about stomach contents? Empty like last time?"

The doctor joined her by the side of the organs and lifted a plastic bag. "No, some pasty red stuff."

"Looks like grape juice and crackers in there. Drugs?"

"Hard to tell if the same poison or drug was used, but the irises and pupils point to that, as well as the clear lack of struggle."

"Whoever the killer is, he's not taking delight in being in charge or earning that kill. Is the rosary the murder weapon again?" Kate asked.

“The victim technically died of heart failure due to asphyxiation. Ligature strangulation with a few of those rosaries. Like the last victim, there are too many beads imprinted for just one rosary. The pattern is much clearer this time since the body isn’t bloated or discolored yet.”

“Did you bag the rosary for me?”

“Of course.”

“I’ll have the DNA analyzed. Thanks, Doc,” Kate said before grabbing the evidence bag he offered.

“One more thing,” the doctor said, holding another evidence bag with just a swab in it.

“What is it?”

“I didn’t notice this on the previous victim, but it may have been there as well. Decomposition and insects may have made it harder for me to notice. There was an oily residue on the middle of her forehead, shaped like a cross—”

“Someone performed a religious rite on her?”

“Possibly. That’s for you to determine.”

CHAPTER THIRTY-EIGHT

KNEELING in front of his altar, he lowered his head and began praying, his voice a soft whisper.

"Dear Lord in Heaven, give me the strength to carry on with Your plan. Allow me to save those young souls before they burn in the fires of Hell, destroying their only chance at being reunited with You in Heaven."

He paused as visions of flames engulfing a body came to mind.

Her. Again.

While their fraternal bond had never displayed the kind of connections some twins seemed to share while she was alive, he most certainly felt her burning pain these days. Perhaps it was because his connection with God had gotten stronger with each soul he'd saved.

Maybe watching her—and sometimes hearing her screams—as flames flickered around her body was his incentive. The vision of her body in Hell was clearly a sign sent by God to motivate him to move forward with His plan.

"Please ease her pain. I don't know if You can help since she's not in Your Kingdom, but…"

Before he could find the words to continue his prayer, his vision worsened. Suddenly, the fire swallowed his sister whole, her skin burning, melting, and exposing her bones, turning her beautiful face into a scene from a horror movie. But as unbelievable as it was, her blonde hair remained immune to the heat. As though his vision was becoming reality, he started sweating. His heart threatened to push its way out of his chest as it increased its cadence. He could hear the blood pounding in his head.

But suddenly, her blonde hair turned jet black and her terrified eyes stared directly into his soul, leaving a burning sensation in his chest.

He snapped out of it and blinked. Making the sign of the cross, he thanked the Lord for His vivid message then got up.

"I won't just save blonde women anymore. I'll expand my reach. Prevent other souls from burning in Hell. Thank You, Lord. Thank You for selecting me as Your servant in this very important mission."

CHAPTER THIRTY-NINE

SITTING AT HER DESK, Kate picked up the phone for the third time in less than a minute, then finally worked up the courage to dial the number she'd written down.

"Hey, Sheriff Ramsay. My name's Kate Murphy. I'm the daughter of Steve and Jocelyn Murphy."

Silence filled the air for a few seconds, then the man spoke up.

"Oh dear. I remember you. I'm so sorry we never tracked down the killer."

"Actually, that's what I'm calling about, Sheriff. I'm now a homicide detective with the Boston PD."

"Oh! Congrats on that!"

"Thanks."

"I saw on the news. You guys seem to have your hands full these days. Are you involved with that investigation?"

"I am."

"I hope you find him fast."

"Yeah. You and me both. We don't have much to go on, but listen, I'm not calling to discuss that."

"Obviously," he said, even though Kate wondered what was so obvious about it. Perhaps just a pattern of speech.

"I'm calling about my family's case."

"What about it?"

"My partner—" hearing her own word to refer to Luke

made her realize how odd it sounded "—convinced me to look at the case files. He seems to think that, with what I know now, and perhaps with a bit of luck, I may be able to find something. Now, I'm not saying you weren't thorough with the case back then. Far from it—"

"I understand. No need to apologize or explain why you'd want to have a look. I've got nothing to hide. As a fellow law enforcement officer, you're more than welcome to look at our case files."

"How would I go about that?" Kate asked.

"It's been a cold case for nearly two decades. We got very little room here, so the files were moved to a secure facility out of town."

"Any chance you can hook me up with the address and permission form so I could go and access those files?"

"I can take care of that. No problem. Why don't you give me your badge number, phone number, and email? I'll see what I can arrange."

Kate provided all the information he needed, then added, "It most likely won't happen until we find our serial killer here, but I thought I'd touch base and get the ball rolling sooner rather than later."

"I get it. Those homicide scenes really mess up one's mind, don't they? I still think of your parents nearly every day. I never really got over their case, you know? Their bodies—"

"Sheriff," Kate interrupted. "Can I ask one question about the case?"

"Shoot."

"How would you describe the stab wounds on each of my parents?"

Quite a few seconds passed, then a loud exhalation reached Kate's ears. The sheriff cleared his throat.

"Your dad wasn't stabbed. His throat was slit. That takes a lot of work, or knowledge, to do right."

"And my mom?" Kate prompted.

"She was stabbed. Multiple times in the chest. Her throat was slit as well, but nothing like your dad's. I don't know why, but I'm sorry for describing it to you like that. It was horrible. And you poor thing found them like that. I'm amazed that the sight of those wounds didn't ingrain itself in your mind forever."

"The mind is a funny thing. I think it filled in some blanks for me over time. I really gotta go, but thanks again for your help, and I'll be in touch."

"Hope you catch your killer soon."

CHAPTER FORTY

WHEN ROSEBUD WALKED into their shared office, he saw Murphy hanging up the phone and grabbing her jacket.

"Any of the priests react oddly?" she asked when she saw him.

"Nope." Rosebud dropped his body into the old chair and tested the strength of its support as he leaned way back. He loosened his tie and exhaled loudly while retrieving his notebook. "Their personal takes were all slightly different but nothing major."

"What do they think?"

He began scanning his notes. "Some boring stuff. Colossians is the twelfth book in the New Testament, written by Paul, although that wasn't globally agreed upon—"

"Who cares who wrote it? That was centuries ago. What does it mean?"

He scanned through more text, his finger sliding down past his scribbles. He then flipped a page. And another.

"Father Miller, the older priest, talked lots about the history behind it. Let me get to the good parts." He flipped one more page. "Here. This particular 3:17 section is about the rules for Holy Living."

"What do you mean? Like what constitutes a sin?"

"That's pretty much how I understood it. But one of them, Father Matthews, went on about the Old Self and the New Self. I honestly didn't get that part."

"So, we're back to square one."

"Except we know the killer's targeting sinners."

"Are the sins identical between the two passages? Lori's and Jessica's ribbon marks?"

"Similar but not identical. How was the autopsy? Did I miss anything important?"

"I missed a big chunk of it myself. Fucking paparazzi and journalists have been following me around. They were at my house this morning! Can you believe it?"

"Since when do the press care about detectives investigating homicide cases?"

"I know, right? The questions they yelled all implied I was to blame for our lack of progress since I was the lead. The world's going crazy. Anyways, they eventually understood my 'no comment' and left me alone. The M.E. confirms it's pretty much the same as with the first vic. Recent sexual intercourse, no rape. And there was some dark red paste in her stomach."

Rosebud shivered as he imagined that. "Glad to have missed it."

"One new thing, though: some oily residue was used on her forehead."

"What oil?"

"I sent it to the lab to get it analyzed. I bumped it up in the queue. Anyways, I'm heading out to meet our second vic's BFF, a woman named Lucy Hamilton. She has a strong alibi, she was attending a race, and it checked out; she won third place. I was just on the phone with the organizers. But she could know more about where Jessica was prior to her death. I'm heading out to talk to her now. Want to come with?" Murphy asked.

"Sure. Beats doing paperwork. But could we grab a coffee and donut first?"

"I'll do you one better. She works at an Italian coffee shop. Why don't we grab something to eat there? We should have enough time before my meeting with the profiler."

"Great!"

CHAPTER FORTY-ONE

AS ROSEBUD DROVE to Lucy's place of employment, Kate sat in the passenger seat, going through her notes from the interviews she'd conducted already. The father and one of their neighbors had stated that Jessica wasn't seeing anyone that they knew of (nobody came to the apartment on a regular basis).

The medical examiner's findings sure didn't add up with what those two had said.

Jessica had obviously been seeing someone. Or perhaps the killer had left his DNA and was indeed raping his victims. The lack of struggle… But with unprotected sex, fluids would have oozed out of her if sexual intercourse had occurred just prior to or post death. It would have been a mess to clean up. Leaving blatant DNA behind like that when all of the prints had been wiped clean? Nope.

That scenario didn't make sense.

Not for the killer. And not for Jessica.

"Jessica had to have been seeing someone. And not a woman, obviously. So this removes homosexuality from the list—or at least makes it much less likely. Who knows? She could have been bi, but she had obviously had sex with a man recently. What else did you have on that list again?"

"What list?" Rosebud asked, taking his eyes off of the road for a second.

"The list of sins from the Bible. For Jessica."

Rosebud tilted his head. "Idolatry, sexual immorality, moral impurity, promiscuity, hatred, anger, jealousy, selfishness, envy, drunkenness, sorcery—"

"Sorcery?"

"Yeah, that one's on the list. Ri-di-cu-lous. I don't think it applies here. I think our killer has to get his kicks from one particular sin."

"But why the two passages then?"

"Damned if I know. But let's start with giving Jessica the facts, and we'll see where things go from there."

~

AFTER FINDING a parking spot near the Italian coffee shop where Lucy worked, Kate and Rosebud headed in.

The aroma of freshly baked pizza and the delighted faces on various patrons made Kate turn to Rosebud. "What do you think? A pizza to go?"

"I thought you'd never ask, you slave driver!"

"Let's find Lucy and see if we can have our questions answered and get an order ready to go in time."

The order ended up being the easiest of both tasks, the chef insisting on Lucy being absolutely essential for the next five minutes. After the detectives showed their badges, Caesar salads appeared. "On the house," a short man said as he delivered the plates.

"We can't accept free food," Kate explained, "we just need to talk with Lucy for a few minutes."

"Ah, come on. It's not a big deal," Rosebud said.

"Accepting free food is clearly against our department's policy."

He'd already stuffed two forkfuls down his throat. "In your world. But fine. We'll leave a generous tip that covers the cost of those salads. How about that?"

"It blows my mind. How you can navigate through shades of gray like this when the policies are black and white."

"It gets easier with time. I promise. I've got a solid decade of detective work over you, so—"

"Detectives, you wanted to see me?" Lucy said.

Kate turned away from Rosebud to stare at the woman

wearing white from head to toe—except for various orange stains on her apron. Her eyes were hollow and heavy, as though she hadn't slept much the previous night.

"I assume this has to do with Jessica. Her dad called me last night. It's so horrible what happened to her—"

"Lucy!" someone yelled from the kitchen.

"That's the chef. I really don't have much time. We're understaffed and have lots of orders to fill."

"We'll make it quick. I attended the autopsy earlier today. Turns out that Jessica was seeing a special someone."

"Well, she was seeing someone. But it was very secretive. Nobody but me knew about it."

"You, Jessica, and him," Rosebud said, his mouth not fully empty yet.

Kate resisted the urge to elbow him. "Who's he?" she asked Lucy instead.

"If I tell you, will it stay private?"

"We'll have to look into him. He could be a suspect."

"No, I don't think so. Plus, he's married. Nobody can find out."

Rosebud cleared his throat. "Perhaps the man's wife found out. We need to know."

"Well—"

"Lucy!" the chef yelled again from the kitchen.

"Give us a name and you can get back to work," Kate prompted, noticing the hesitation in the brunette's eyes.

She exhaled deeply. "All I know is that his first initial is A, he's married, and he's friends with her dad. That's it. I'm sorry I can't give you any more because I don't know anything else. Please don't smear her name. Or his."

"Thanks, Lucy," Kate said as she finished noting things down.

A pizza box arrived just as Lucy returned to the kitchen. The waiter insisted on transferring Kate's untouched salad to a to-go container, then they covered their meal—all of it at Kate's insistence—and headed to the station.

With heavenly smelling pizza in their hands, a solid lead, and their upcoming meeting with the profiler, things were starting to look up.

CHAPTER FORTY-TWO

Tuesday, June 26th, 2018

AMANDA MCCUTCHEON TRIED to stare at herself in the mirror but couldn't meet the reflection of her own eyes.

Was it my stupid tongue that got her killed?

Who am I to judge her for getting it on with David? He's freaking hot. I probably wouldn't have stayed a virgin as long as she did.

Am I responsible for her death?

Digging a hand down into her pocket she pulled out a little baggie with two pieces of candy her friend Joshua had given her. "To ease the painful memories," he'd said.

She'd never taken any drugs before, but if she was to blame for her friend's death, she might as well check out. The gaping hole in her heart was unbearable, and the more she thought about Lori, the larger that hole got, as though widening with her surge of pain and guilt.

She popped one in her mouth and waited. As she sucked on the slightly-odd tasting candy, she considered calling David.

No. I can't do that. Not with the police still considering me a suspect.

She walked to the kitchen, slightly anxious to have the chemicals kick in. Would she pass out? Or start giggling for no reason? She had no idea how it would work.

All she knew is that nothing was happening right now.

Desperate for something—anything—to kick in, Amanda pulled the cork from the wine bottle she'd opened the night before and took a swig right from it. She didn't particularly enjoy the taste of wine, but at least she was *doing something* to numb the pain. She downed another swig then returned the bottle to the counter before corking it once more.

Checking the time on the kitchen wall, she wondered how long it had been already. Five, ten minutes?

She returned to the living room, crashed on the couch, turned on the TV, and set it to a music channel. Halfway through the second song, she finally began to feel something other than pain and guilt.

The corners of her lips lifted just as the weight on her shoulders faded away. Her thoughts fled to a land of happiness. Her surroundings suddenly began to look and feel different. Even the texture of the couch's fabric was different. Softer, plusher.

Music seemed to transcend space and enter her pores instead of just her ears. She got up and began to sway her hips, unable to resist the rhythm of the song. Amanda's eyes were glued on the barely-dressed woman dancing on the screen in front of her, singing lyrics that made very little sense, when the sudden urge to eat came over her.

She nearly ran to the kitchen. Opening the fridge door didn't reveal anything particularly good, so she opened the pantry instead. The bag of salt and vinegar chips called out to her like she needed it to survive.

She tore it open and her hand dove into the bag, scooping up a large handful which she stuffed down her mouth a second later.

The salt was heavenly. The vinegar stung the insides of her cheeks with just the right bitterness.

Then she spotted the wine bottle again and carried it back to the living room with her. Feeling happy for the first time in over a week, she wondered if taking the second edible would amplify her happiness. She craved more of it.

Did he say I was supposed to take both at the same time?

She went and grabbed her phone from her room and was debating if she should even bother with it. Deciding that it wasn't worth the trouble of calling her friend to ask, she popped the other in her mouth.

Tossing her phone on the coffee table, she returned her

attention to the latest music video, this one more cinematographic, showing a young woman longing for her lover. The lyrical notes of the singer brought tears to Amanda's eyes.

Whether the edibles were to blame was debatable. The video had just reminded her of Lori. Her best friend who she'd no longer be able to see or talk to ever again.

She crumbled onto the couch, her face buried in her hands, her eyes gushing tears faster than she thought possible when the doorbell buzzed.

"What?" she asked aloud, surprised by the sound. It was late. She wasn't expecting any company.

After wiping her face with her hands, she mustered her strength and headed to the door.

Maybe it was David…

CHAPTER FORTY-THREE

AMANDA'S brown hair was a mess when she greeted him. Her lipstick stretched past the confines of where her lips ended, and crumbs specked her fitted shirt.

"What are you doing here?" she asked, her eyes puffy, watery, and red.

"I thought you could use some company. Or something to get your mind off of her," he said, lifting two tiny wine bottles up in the air.

Her eyes darted to them, then she stepped aside to make room for him to enter. "Why the hell not?" she asked. "Oh! Sorry. I probably shouldn't use that word around you."

"It's all good. Don't worry. I know young people use that term to sound cool."

He walked into the living room and noted another bottle of wine on the coffee table, but no glasses.

"Young people. You don't seem much older than me. But wait," she said after closing the door. "How did you find my address?"

"Remember that petition you signed? That info is now in the church's database. Do you have glasses?" he asked.

"Of course. Just… Just take a seat. I'll bring some back."

Something felt a little off.

He grabbed the remote control and lowered the volume a tad. He cringed, glancing at the singer exposing her body in such a shameful manner. *She's spreading evil thoughts.* Then he decided to switch the channel to something else. Anything else.

By the time Amanda came back with two wine glasses, he'd settled on a channel that aired classical music while displaying a slideshow of lovely landscapes.

"How have you been?" he asked, accepting the glasses she offered before taking a seat on the couch.

She exhaled loudly, then blinked several times. "To be bluntly honest, I've been better. I…" She shook her head, then tears began pouring out of her.

He hesitated, unsure how to react. But then he realized it would be easier for him to cleanse her soul if she first trusted him. So he extended his arm and wrapped her shoulders, bringing her closer to his chest. Tapping her arm gently, he added, "There, there. Let it all out."

While she cried her little heart out, he analyzed his surroundings. No signs of a roommate, as he had guessed based on her Facebook posts. By the door hung only two jackets, which he'd seen on her before. Three pairs of shoes, all around the same size. No manly presence here. The photos spread around the living room only showed Amanda with some of her friends.

"So, you don't have anyone here with you to comfort you during this tough time?" he asked, just to double-check.

She pulled herself away from him and he refrained from letting out a sigh of relief.

"No. I…" She rubbed her face. "I'm feeling guilty. I didn't want to be with other people."

"Not even your friend David?" he asked, reaching for one of the small bottles he'd brought.

"Why don't we finish off the bottle I've already started?"

He felt his left eye twitch as the first part of his plan got slightly derailed, but knew she was right. He grabbed the other bottle and pulled on the barely re-inserted cork.

"Did you want to talk about her? Or would you like us to pray together?" He poured wine into each of the glasses as he spoke.

She exhaled loudly, then grabbed the bag of chips. "To be honest, I don't know what I want."

Anger and impatience spread in his chest like a virus. He

didn't have all day. Twisting thoughts in his mind, he finally settled on something that could get her out of the room so he could resume his plan. "Do you have a photo of you and Lori together?" he asked.

"Yes, in my bedroom."

"I'd love to see it."

She paused and frowned at him. "I don't want to take you to my bedroom."

"No, that's not what I meant! Obviously, I'm not that kind of a man." He placed his hand on the crucifix that hung around his neck. "Could you bring it here?"

Her brows furrowed some more as she tilted her head left and right, then left. Something appeared *off* with her.

Then she finally nodded and got up. "Be right back," she said.

Digging into his sleeve, he retrieved the tiny vial and dumped its contents into the glass that was closest to where she'd sat, then he added just a bit more wine to both glasses to mix his cleansing medicine.

She returned just as he put the bottle down.

"What did you do? Did you drink some while I was away, then topped your glass back up?"

He smiled and shook his head, all the while thinking this wasn't going well at all. "No, I just thought I'd try to finish that bottle off. There was very little left in it," he said.

"Here you go." She handed him a small frame that showed the two women wearing fancy red dresses and grinning at the camera.

"When was it taken?"

"High school graduation," she said, once again digging her hand into the bag of chips. "Want some?" she offered, holding the bag toward him.

"No, thank you. Shall we toast in memory of your friend?" he suggested, grabbing his own glass.

"Or just get wasted and forget all of this ever happened," she said, reaching for her glass, clinking it against his so suddenly that some of its content splashed into his own glass, then she downed it all in one go.

He didn't dare drink from his own glass now, but he

pretended, bringing the glass up and tilting the glass so its contents barely touched his closed lips.

She brought down her glass so hard it nearly broke, then she grimaced. "Argh! Wine doesn't go well with salt and vinegar! I need to wash this down with something." She got up, nearly tumbling over herself and headed to the kitchen.

She came back a minute later, her face pale, holding a tall glass of water.

"I don't feel so good," she said, wavering as she made her way back toward him.

He watched her grab ahold of the wall.

"What's WRROONNG with me?" she yelled.

"Shhh! Quiet! Everything's good," he whispered.

"No! I'm NOOOTTT good!"

He prayed that her walls were well insulated, that nobody had heard her, that his medicine would soon kick in and silence her.

And it finally did, just as she crumbled to the floor, her glass shooting out of her grasp and landing in a loud crash, a few feet away on the kitchen floor.

He fumed, annoyed beyond belief.

Then three consecutive bangs echoed from underneath the floor.

"Are you all right?" a man's muffled voice shouted from below.

He considered his options. Staying was risky. But then again, she was now passed out, she wouldn't air a peep anymore. If he didn't act now, he may never have the chance to do it again. She would not let him into her home another time.

Should he clean up his prints? He began wiping the coffee table and thought about bringing the glasses to the sink, then realized there was no time for that.

Plus he hadn't really done anything that could get him in trouble. Yet. Someone banged on the door.

His fast pulse echoed in his head. He fidgeted, rubbing his thumb and forefinger against each other. He needed to give himself a reason for being here. He knew she'd forget a big chunk of time when she awoke, but he wasn't sure how much she'd still recall.

Seeing her cellphone on the table, he grabbed it to dial his own number. He had left his phone behind, in case he ever was suspected. He knew that GPS tracking could end his holy mission.

But now, since he hadn't saved her, he'd just cover his tracks.

The banging on the door repeated. "Amanda! Open up!"

He grabbed his unopened bottles of wine, hid them back into this pants pockets then headed to the door to meet an angry-looking man. The man stood in front of him, his fist up in the air, as though he was about to bang on the door again.

CHAPTER FORTY-FOUR

Los Angeles, California
Tuesday, June 26th, 2018

WHAT PIXIE HAD SEEN on TV wouldn't leave her mind, so she scoured the Internet looking for more information.

Online papers and video snippets from TV channels only offered a handful of details, the police likely keeping the rest away from the public while the investigation was still ongoing.

But she did find a strange conspiracy blog of sorts, with several photos of police perimeters. Whether or not the caption was true was up for debate, but the cop cars in the shots displayed the Boston PD logo she was familiar with.

Pixie scrolled down some more until she saw a photo of a gurney with a black body bag. She glanced at the wall of text that followed, making her head spin. Swallowing suddenly became a chore. The anonymous blogger hadn't bothered to include paragraph breaks, making the never ending stream of words uninviting, to say the least.

She hit CTRL + F on her keyboard, and a little search field appeared. After entering the word "blonde," she was rewarded with a handful of highlighted words within the never-ending paragraph. Her eyes jumped to a couple of lines prior to the first instance of the word, and she began reading:

"The victim is blonde, in her early twenties. Lori Davis, according to the neighbors. The news later confirmed her name. Most of the neighbors were crying around me as we watched her body being taken out of the house, saying things like 'such a lovely girl!' 'She lived with God in her heart. Who would do such thing?' and 'While her parents were away!'"

Pixie hit the arrow to find the next instance.

"A second blonde woman was found yesterday. My source at the police department hinted at something religious about the crimes and a weird way to pose the bodies."

That last bit piqued her interest, so she kept reading, hoping to learn more, but the blogger had gone off on a tangent about some other murders he'd heard about while growing up.

She hit the arrow again to find the next "blonde" instance.

"In both cases, the blonde hair was tied in a braid, and the victims wore clothes that weren't theirs, but I couldn't get my source to spill the beans here. And both scenes featured a religious theme, but once again I wasn't able to obtain more precise information."

Fuck! she thought.

It could be him. Was she certain? No. But it added up.

She clicked to see where the other two instances of the word "blonde" appeared and read inane details about the blogger's first girlfriend and how he still missed how her hair looked while the sun shone on it.

"Pixie, sweetie! I'm back!" John said from the front door.

"I'm in the bedroom!" Pixie yelled back, glancing at the rest of the article and deciding she'd wasted enough time on this.

She closed her laptop.

Why did she care so much? Even *if* it was him, she was safe now. John and she were far, far away from his deranged mind. Their plan had gone off without a hitch.

John grinned at her as she moved her laptop over to the nightstand and tossed her legs over to the side of the bed.

His arms wrapped around her and their lips met.

"You had a good day?" he asked.

"Yeah. You?"

"Boring work, but it's over now. I'm ready to celebrate! What did you want to do?"

She looked up to him, her heart swimming in gratitude for

having met the perfect man for her. Not only had he tamed the crazy out of her—looking back, she was embarrassed at the things she'd done, the *people* she'd done—but he'd forgiven her and showed her what it was like to really love someone.

And oh! did she love the man he was.

Not every boyfriend would have uprooted their entire life and cut all ties—not to mention broken a few laws—to up and move to California without notice.

"A full year of Californian freedom… I'd love to go to the Santa Monica Pier and get on that Ferris wheel. What do you say?"

"Or we could head down memory lane. You could make more of those X-rated photos like you used to when we first met. Remember?"

She punched him lightly on the shoulder, a big grin on her face. "Hey! They worked, didn't they?"

"I still remember those dial-up days… Watching the images fill my screen line by line… Those photos you shared…" His hands went to her breasts, groping her through her shirt. "You had—and still have—the tits of an angel."

"I thought you preferred my other shots? From behind, with my mini-skirt riding up, exposing myself."

"I loved every single one of your photos… You must have driven someone mad with desire where you had your photos developed."

"I did," she said, undoing her shirt. "Alan Black, his name was. I still remember him like it was yesterday. He got to see a lot of failed shots, though. Oh, the money I spent on film back in those days."

"Developing them couldn't have been cheap."

She peeled off her sleeves and tossed her shirt aside, propping her chest forward as she moved her arms behind her back to unclasp her bra. "That's where you're wrong. After the first roll, Alan and I came to an agreement. He got to keep some of the shots for himself and developed my films for free."

"Is it all he did?"

"Well," she started as she lasciviously stripped the bra off of her, watching the hungry grin grow on his face. "You know how horny I was back in those days. How about I show you what Alan and I did in his darkroom before you managed to tame my wild ways?"

CHAPTER FORTY-FIVE

"WHO ARE YOU?" the angry-looking man asked as he lowered his arm.

"I'm a friend of Amanda. And you are?"

"Her downstairs neighbor." The big man eyed the other up and down for a few seconds before speaking again. "How come I've never seen you here before?"

"We're friends from church. I just came by to see how she was doing. You know… Considering that her best friend recently died."

"Hmm," the big man said, frowning. "And what was that noise I heard? Why was she screaming?" He pushed his way into the apartment. "What the fuck?" He ran to her body lying on the floor, a tiny pile of vomit had somehow come out of her since he'd left her a mere minute ago. The broken glass and spilled water still littered the kitchen floor.

"What happened here?" the big man asked as he rotated around.

"She was already buzzed when I got here. She offered me a glass of wine, then next thing I knew, she started to freak out, and she fell."

The man looked at the two wine glasses on the table, one full, one empty.

"And you were going to leave her like this?"

He did what he excelled at and came up with an excuse on

the fly. "No! I was going to knock on the neighbor's door. Ask for help. Possibly get her to the hospital. I don't have a car."

"Why should I believe you? What tells me you didn't come in here to get her drunk, then take advantage of her?"

"Because I'm still here, talking to you."

The big man proceeded to move her body to the side, placing her legs in such a way as to prevent her from rolling over. "I'm a paramedic. I'll take care of her. Get out. And I don't want to see you here ever again."

He nodded then left the apartment, part relieved his lies had worked, but also perplexed as to what to do now.

Amanda wouldn't be saved. Not today. Not ever.

He had a goal, but he wasn't stupid. The risk of running into that big man again far outweighed the satisfaction of saving her soul. Plus he had plenty more souls to choose from.

He used the staircase, out of habit to avoid the elevator cameras, but then realized halfway down that he could have used it this time since he'd left a much, much more condemning piece of evidence on her phone.

Incriminating or exonerating.

Only time would tell.

As he continued walking away from the building, one detail wouldn't leave his head: Where exactly had his plan derailed?

Why did she puke?

Was there something wrong with his latest batch of cleansing solution?

He needed to figure this out and soon. His inner itch to save another soul roared within him, making his eye twitch as he sped up his pace.

His mind began homing in on the next person worth saving.

CHAPTER FORTY-SIX

Wednesday, June 27th, 2018

AMANDA WOKE up dazed and confused. Fully dressed, she lay in her bed. Big Danny, her neighbor, was sitting in the corner of her room, cross-legged on the carpet, his head resting where the walls met.

"B… Big Danny?" she called out.

He blinked a few times then looked up to her. "Hey! How you feeling?"

She tried to sit up, then decided against it. Her head felt like it was about to explode.

"What? … Why… Why are you here?"

"I had to keep an eye on you. You passed out in your vomit. Lucky I saw you and had the evening off so I could look after you."

"What? What are you talking about?" But as she aired the words, she tasted bile in her mouth. She'd indeed been sick.

"Who was that man that came to visit you yesterday?" he asked, rubbing his hands up and down his face.

"What? What man?"

Big Danny got to his feet. "I'm gonna splash some water on my face. Want a glass?"

"Sure," Amanda said.

"Be right back."

In the few minutes that passed, she racked her brain as to

what had actually happened. She tried to rewind her memories. Last night she…

Last evening she…

Her heart began beating faster, suddenly aware that several hours were unaccounted for.

Yesterday she… She took those edibles!

"Shit!" she yelled, folding her body up in bed, then suddenly hating herself for it.

Bringing a hand to her forehead, she forced her eyelids down, hiding daylight and hoping that it would decrease the intensity of her pounding headache.

Big Danny put one of his big-bear hands on her back. "Here, Amanda. Drink up."

She opened her eyes, grabbed the glass and downed all of its contents.

"You said there was a man in here yesterday?" she asked.

"Yeah."

"Who was he?"

"Are you okay?" he asked her. "You should remember who your guest was, shouldn't you?" With his index finger and thumb, he forced one of her eyes to open some more, then the other. "Were you high on something yesterday?"

She winced, then realized Big Danny was a friend. He wouldn't judge her.

"Well, yes. One of my friends gave me some edibles. Said it'd help me forget about what happened to Lori."

"Shit, Amanda! You shouldn't do drugs. And you most definitely shouldn't do drugs alone! What if I hadn't shown up?"

"Why did you show up? Why are you here?"

"You really don't remember anything?"

She shook her head.

"That's messed up." He exhaled deeply then sat on the edge of her bed. "I heard you scream, then something crashed on the floor, so I ran up. I was knocking on your door when this young guy was about to leave."

"Who was it?"

"Beats me. He said he was a friend from church."

"A friend from church?"

Amanda frowned and rubbed her forehead, but it wasn't a

magical lamp. Nobody came to mind, and no memories came back.

"Well, the mystery man left, and I stayed. You had already begun vomiting, so I placed you in the recovery position and I kept an eye on you. Once the vomiting stopped, I moved you to your bed, but I wanted to stay to make sure you were going to be all right."

"Thanks, Big Danny," she said leaning forward to hug him.

"You should really get in the shower now. And I've got to get ready for work. Don't do anymore of those edibles, okay? Promise me?" he asked as he got up.

"Yes, I swear. Thanks for taking care of me. I owe you, big time."

CHAPTER FORTY-SEVEN

"MURPHY, tell me something good. Where are you at with those cases?" Fuller asked from behind his desk, his suit and tie disheveled and the bags under his eyes a deep shade of purple. "They're riding my ass. I can't buy us any more time. The mayor and the media want answers. We need to give them something. Anything."

"The rosary from the second victim showed DNA from both the first and second victim, confirming our theory that several rosaries are used, but only one left behind. But the killer's DNA isn't on there and we couldn't lift any fingerprints due to the small size of the thread."

"What else?" Fuller asked.

"The profiler we met with on Monday came back with new information," Murphy said.

"Shoot," Fuller ordered as he leaned back into his chair and waited for the information.

Murphy retrieved her notepad and referred to it as she replied. "He thinks we're dealing with a person who's suffered a very deep wound that altered their moral compass. Someone for whom religion is very important but someone who kept disappointing their parents or someone who never received the love they wanted from them, so they developed a strong intolerance toward certain behavior. Mostly behavior that would go against the Church's preaching. Possibly to match the behavior the killer himself received or witnessed."

"The killer is hyper religious and intolerant toward what exactly?" Fuller asked.

"Witness statements and the medical examiner's reports confirm that both victims had sexual intercourse before their death," Murphy said.

Fuller frowned. "You're saying he's intolerant about people having sex?"

Murphy put her notepad away. "Outside-of-marriage sex or inappropriate sex in general, whatever that definition would be, according to his beliefs. We just heard that the second vic was having an affair with a married man."

"Married man?" Fuller repeated. "Could the wife have found out? Or could the married man be our killer for both victims?"

Rosebud interjected. "All we had was a first initial and a relation with the victim's dad, but Wang worked her magic, and it paid off. We identified him: Alex Redford, a wealthy businessman who dabbles in politics. His alibi—and that of his wife—were solid. They both attended a live TV program when Jessica was killed. The man even offered to show us his bank account statements if we agreed to keep his affair away from his wife and the media."

"And?" Fuller asked. "No signs that he would have paid someone off to get rid of the mistress?"

"Absolutely none," Murphy said. "And we couldn't find any evidence that he or his wife would have known Lori Davis."

"Okay. Go back to the profiler," Fuller ordered. "Did he state anything in terms of physical description? Gender? Something tangible, please."

Murphy shook her head. "We still can't narrow it down. Either the killer knew the victims or impersonated a trustworthy figure to gain access to their households. The fact that the victims were drugged first removes the necessity for the person to be physically strong to strangle them. We still think the killer has to be able to lift a body from point A to point B, but the lack of rape almost prevents us from knowing for sure if it's a man we're dealing with. And the combined use of drugs with strangulation indicates this person doesn't seek power over the victims. That's not typical. But the killer is obviously very thorough and careful about not leaving any DNA behind."

"But if we stick to statistical probability, it's more than likely a man," Rosebud added.

"Yeah, yeah," Fuller said, wiping the side of his nose with his hand. "White male, Caucasian, charismatic, good-looking… We've all read those studies, but who are your best leads or suspects?"

"David Dempsey's story checks out," Murphy said. "He had no plausible motive to kill his girlfriend. No financial gain. No jealousy. They had a fight, sure, but he passively waited for her to contact him again. Victim's friends all confirm he's a pushover. Plus, he had alibis for both murders."

"And?" Fuller prompted.

"The father was at work. Phone records back up his story for the broken lock being reported to the landlord. He's not a suspect."

Fuller exhaled loudly as he let those facts sink in. "Rosebud. Talk to me. Anything else?"

"Amanda McCutcheon," Rosebud said. "First vic's BFF. They had a fight the night after she had sex with the boyfriend."

"Lover's triangle?" Fuller asked.

"Chastity club feud. But lover's triangle is not out of the question. Wang thinks there's something brewing between the first vic's boyfriend and her BFF."

Fuller leaned forward on his desk. "Does she look strong enough to lift a person?"

Murphy tilted her head to the side. "Possibly."

"Alibis for both murders?"

"We checked. It's weak, but Netflix confirmed she was watching movies *and* pressed the button to continue streaming every hour or so on Sunday afternoon and evening."

"Someone else could have pressed that button," Fuller stated. "Where was she during the second murder?"

"Same. Netflix binging. No parents, siblings, or roommates living with her."

"What do you think, Rosebud?" Fuller asked while stroking his salt-and-pepper mustache.

"Our search warrant led us nowhere. We don't have enough to arrest her."

"Did she know the second victim?" Fuller asked.

Murphy spoke up. "We asked, and Chainey looked into it. He couldn't find any links."

"Doesn't mean there isn't one."

"We still don't have a real motive, though. Lover's triangle wouldn't explain the second murder."

"The district commander wants to see something. We'll get eyes on her twenty-four seven. I'll approve the extra manpower."

"There's more, though," Murphy said.

Fuller leaned back in his chair again. "Speak!"

"Father Matthews. He's a new priest in town. Young, bright, forward-thinking, handsome, charismatic. Through confessions, he may have had knowledge of what was going on and targeted his victims based on the sins that triggered him. A priest could match what the profiler described. It would make him a trustworthy figure. Someone with easy access to someone's home."

"Alibi?"

"We haven't officially questioned him yet. I attended part of his mass this past Sunday, then met up with him afterwards. He looked truly sorry for what happened to the first vic. I asked where he was after mass on June 3rd and on June 4th. He answered he was either surrounded by parishioners in church, alone in the sacristy of the cathedral, or at home. No witnesses. I know for a fact he was working Sunday morning, but he could have headed to the second vic's house after I finished talking to him. I'll get him to come down here to get an interview on the record."

Fuller played with the end of his bushy mustache. "*Catholic* priest?"

Murphy nodded.

"They'll never share their confessions with us, so…" He rocked back and forth in his chair and began tapping the desk with a pen.

"Don't priests have to pass some sort of psychological exam? I don't think he's our guy," Rosebud chimed in.

"That's your Catholic side speaking," Murphy said. "Just think like a cop—"

"Fuck you, Murphy!"

Kate winced then swallowed hard, realizing her mistake. "Rosebud, you know, I didn't mean it that way—"

"Enough!" Fuller barked. "We're all tired. You're sorry. He's sorry. Moving on."

Rosebud shook his head and swatted Kate's excuse with his hand. "I know," Rosebud said. "But Father Matthews has been helping the community, raising funds, helping the poorest families—"

"And listening to confessions and collecting names and addresses, which he could then use to find his—"

Fuller slapped his desk. "I've heard enough! I don't care if he's a priest. His profession doesn't put him above our laws. We'll surveil them both. Let's hope the killer is one of them so we can stop the next murder before it happens. And one more thing."

"What's that?" Murphy asked, her tired face giving away her cards. Being the lead was taxing her. Just like it did every one of his detectives. The system and the evil in the world—in Boston—had begun to break her, just like it had the rest of them.

"This case began nearly a month ago. I've seen you guys in the office around the clock. This can't go on. As of today, I'm implementing a forced rotation. Murphy, I need you here during the day. One other detective will be working days with you. The other two will split the other sixteen hours, one eight-hour shift each, catching up on office work and interviewing people in the early evening if needed. That means Rosebud, Chainey, and Wang will rotate until we finally catch the killer. But that won't happen if you guys don't go home, clear your heads, and rest between shifts."

Murphy and Rosebud looked at each other but stayed put.

"Now get out of my office!"

CHAPTER FORTY-EIGHT

AS HE STARED at his lye pellets, pH strips, distilled water, paint stripper, and tiny vials of finished product, he couldn't shake the thought that had been on his mind the entire walk home from Amanda's house the previous evening. The sight of that sinful woman puking on the floor had haunted him like a buzzing fly that wouldn't go away.

He raised one hand and dug his nails into his fist, thinking about hitting the wall for a second but resisting the urge.

What good would that do?

He'd lose his safety deposit.

Closing his eyes, he reconsidered where he stood. He'd been put on this earth to cleanse souls, not floors. He could either ditch his latest batch or test it on himself.

Hesitation hovered over him like a black cloud as he pondered his options. If he had in fact messed up his recipe, he could die. Suicide, even by mistake, was the worst sin of all. He knew that all too well.

Inhaling deeply, he knelt, brought his hands together, and began praying for her soul even though it was damned. Then he tried to clear his mind so he could hear God's voice coming to him.

Focusing on his breath was his gateway to a trance. Three. Four. Five sets of deep inhalations and exhalations were enough for his worries to dissipate and morph into hope.

Hope for salvation. Hope for God reuniting with His misguided souls.

Through his hands, following His voice and guidance, he could save the sinners around him and make them join Him by His side while they still could.

Looking at his vials and raw ingredients—and knowing he couldn't afford the expensive drugs they sold on street corners—he emptied the mixture down the kitchen drain and got ready to start a fresh batch.

Grabbing his container of paint stripper, he measured the appropriate volume he'd printed from the Internet. Then he used his kitchen scale to weigh his lye pellets. He took out the stainless steel pot he used solely for that purpose then began preparing a new batch of cleansing solution.

As he double-checked the measurement of the first ingredient, he couldn't help but reflect on how different he was from the other people in his field. He believed in God, of course. Faith led his life and directed all of his decisions, but he always wanted to understand everyone else's views. Educating oneself never hurt anyone, and it was also wonderfully helpful when bridging the gap between people of various faiths. Converting someone was much easier once you knew where they came from.

So he'd taken quite a few extra-curricular classes online while attending seminary. He had grown quite fond of chemistry and physics in particular. He liked to think that faith was the missing variable in quantum mechanics. His beliefs were, of course, not the most popular among those he worked with, so he kept them to himself. But chemistry had most definitely proven useful over the past few months. Very useful indeed. Science and faith had always enhanced each other in his hands, guided by Him.

Another flash of Amanda puking on her floor came to mind, which made him triple-check the measurements.

He had to focus.

No more distraction.

As he added the right quantity of distilled water to his pot, he committed to carefully adhering to the correct timing and temperatures to make his latest batch the greatest one yet.

CHAPTER FORTY-NINE

AFTER REFILLING his and Kate's wine glasses, Luke loaded the dishwasher, then joined her back at the kitchen table, aware that the long stems on his favorite glasses didn't fit in the top rack. First-world problem. But he liked how they looked. A little hand-washing had never hurt anyone.

He watched Kate trace the rim of her glass with her index finger, her stare aimed at a tomato stain on their white table cloth.

"You know that cologne you smelled on your mother?" he asked.

"Yeah?" She looked up and squinted at him, her head tilted.

"That had me thinking."

"Please don't change your cologne."

He smiled at her, amazed at her ability to diverge from subjects as painful as the death of her parents. The *murders* of her parents.

He, too, had experienced the events that had ensued—and rocked their entire small town. He'd been disturbed by it for years. How she'd managed to remain sane was nothing short of amazing to him.

She was quite the woman. Different from the others he'd dated before. Far less dramatic. Far less crazy. But he still worried that he might have done something that could trigger her to snap at him. They'd only lived together for a year.

Although he enjoyed getting to know her little quirks and tics, he'd probably just seen the tip of the iceberg. He was waiting for the figurative *other shoe* to drop—if it was ever going to.

So he twisted a few options in his mind about how best to broach the topic and settled on what seemed more natural: the truth. Just re-arranged in time, assuming she'd go down the path he expected her to take.

"Do you remember what you told me in the car on Sunday, after your session?"

A line appeared between her brows. "I'm not sure I do. I was pretty emotional." She brought her glass to her lips.

"About your dad's wounds being less personal than your mom's?"

"Oh! That part. Yeah. And the sheriff confirmed she was stabbed several times in the chest. My dad wasn't. Whoever killed them knew my mother."

He inhaled deeply, pushing his luck as he voiced his original plan. "So… This had me thinking that perhaps we could go through the boxes you brought back. You know? The photo albums and such? Maybe we could find a lead there."

Kate shook her head. "I *so* don't have time for this right now, Luko. We've got that serial killer on the loose. I need to focus on him." She took another sip of her wine.

Luke smiled as he stared at his own glass, still full.

She'd answered just as he'd expected. He didn't bother to remind her of her department's policies or the conversation she'd shared with him about what her supervisor had already stated about her spending too much time at work.

He just had to push his luck a tad more.

"Would you be okay if *I* did?"

"What?" she asked, one eyebrow higher than the other before downing the rest of her glass.

"If I went through your boxes?"

"Be my guest!" Kate said before standing up to rinse her glass off in the sink. "I'm going to bed—"

"Good, because I already did," Luke confessed, about to find out whether begging for forgiveness would be easier than asking for permission. Or was he about to see a new side of Kate? He stood tall and watched her slowly rotate to face him.

"You did *what*?"

Not sure if her brows were slanted due to anger, misbelief, or just exhaustion, he voiced the safest words that came to mind as he bridged the gap that separated her from him.

"Don't get upset." He wrapped his arms around her. "I was sitting in my office the other night. Out of curiosity—or boredom perhaps—I opened the top box. I found an old photo album. Some cute photos of you as a kid. Before I met you."

"Okay…" Kate returned to her glass, squirted a bit of liquid soap onto the sponge and proceeded to wash her glass by hand.

He stepped away from her. "I also found other things."

"What things?" Kate dried her glass then returned it to the cupboard.

"Letters. Unopened letters. Addressed to your mom."

"What? Where?" She unplugged the sink, the sucking noises of the liquid draining down the pipe covering her words.

"Underneath those photo albums. Didn't you pack those boxes?" Luke asked.

"Some I found in the attic. I brought them as-is after peeking in and finding photos. Others I packed myself, going through the stuff on the shelves, in dressers, on walls… You found unopened letters. Addressed to my mom?"

Luke nodded.

"Did you open them?"

"No! I wanted to talk to you first. See what you thought."

"What was the date on them?"

"That's the thing. They weren't stamped by the post office. No paid postage. No return address. But your mom's full name and mailing address is hand-written on those envelopes. The address where you lived as a child."

"Someone other than the mailman could have put them in the mailbox. I'm gonna get my evidence kit out of my car. I want to see them. Now!"

CHAPTER FIFTY

BY THE TIME Kate walked back into the house with a pair of disposable gloves, her LED flashlight, and a roll of plastic evidence bags and tape, Luke was already in his office, leaning against the wall and sipping his wine as she sat behind his desk in silence.

Her mind had been so focused on catching their serial killer that she never for a minute considered the boxes she'd brought back from Kenny's house could hold new information about her parents' case.

But how could that be? Wouldn't the sheriff and his team have seen those letters decades ago?

That unexpected bit of news had perked her up more than a cup of the district's potent brew would have. She donned her gloves. Perhaps the letters meant nothing, but if they could help find the killer, she didn't want to contaminate what was left of the evidence.

"What box were those letters in?"

Luke put his glass down and got up.

"Second one from the top. Under two or three photo albums."

Kate lifted the first box and set it aside, then opened the crossed flaps on the second box, definitely one of the boxes she'd gotten from the attic, her belated uncle's handwriting marking it with the words *Steve and Jo's attic*.

After putting the albums aside, she retrieved the bundle of letters Luke had described.

"Those are the ones," he said.

Shining her light on the envelopes, Kate saw several prints, but they were more than likely Luke's.

"Sorry, Kate. I wasn't thinking."

"That's all right. His prints could be inside. Heck, the saliva that sealed those envelopes…"

For a split second, she debated whether she should just send the envelopes to the sheriff. Let him determine if they were relevant to the case. But her curiosity had the upper hand.

"Letter opener?" She put out her hand, like a surgeon waiting for a scalpel as she examined the handwriting.

Luke riffled through his desk drawer, the clinks of various pens rolling around as she focused on the angularity and sharpness of the strokes, the open loops, the angle at which the letters slanted. Kate knew graphology could tell a lot about the person, but unfortunately, she wasn't trained to read into it. All she could say was that the handwriting was unfamiliar to her. It wasn't her belated mom's or dad's. It wasn't that of her belated uncle or aunt, either.

She felt the weight of a metal object landing in her extended hand, then realized she'd unknowingly been holding her breath. "Thanks, Luke."

With palpitations, she ripped open the top of the first letter, then carefully pulled it out of the envelope, barely touching its edges.

The yellowed paper released a faint smell as she unfolded it. Or was it just her mind playing tricks on her?

Those hypnotherapy sessions had confused her a little too much lately. The aromas that had reached her nose had felt absolutely real. As real as Luke's Irish Spring scent right now.

"Here goes," she said as she prepared to read the very short note in the same handwriting as what covered the envelope.

Dear Jocelyn,

I wish things were less complicated.

But I still appreciate watching you from a

distance. Your smile, your hair, your eyes. You beam and radiate, like a beacon calling to my heart.

She has your smile and your eyes.

E xox

Kate lowered the note, a shiver going down her spine as she re-read the last line. "I hate that. Mom had a stalker?"

"I don't know, Katie," Luke said, leaving the back of his desk and joining Kate as she carefully returned the note to its envelope.

She ripped open the second one.

Dear Jocelyn,

I haven't heard from you, even though I gave you my address. Maybe your husband makes it hard for you to communicate with me.

Rest assured that I'll stick around, waiting for you to come to me when you're ready.

E xox

"I don't like these letters," Kate said as she reinserted the second note into its envelope.

"Are you sure you want to keep reading them?" Luke asked, his hands massaging her shoulders, working on a knot at the base on her neck.

Dear Jocelyn,

I heard a rumor that your husband will be out of town next week? Is that true? I'll try and swing by, discreetly. Leave the back door open like before.

E xox

A stabbing pain poked her in the chest as the unspoken nature of her mom's and E's relationship suddenly became clear.

Dear Jocelyn,

Seeing you last weekend was the best gift I've ever gotten. Even though you said you didn't open

any of my letters, I'll keep sending you my notes, so you know I keep thinking of you.

The way our bodies meshed together, can't you see we were meant for each other?

I can still smell your perfume on me, and I love that feeling. I'll be dreaming of you tonight, as always.

E xox

Dear Jocelyn,

Are you avoiding me? You changed your schedule. What's going on? I always look forward to running into you at the grocery store on Monday mornings, the flower shop on Friday, and the baker on Sunday. But I haven't crossed paths with you in over two weeks.

What's going on? Are you okay?

E xox

Kate tossed the most recent letter onto the desk, unable to take any more of it. Unable to bear the harsh reality of what they meant. A dozen more envelopes had yet to be unsealed, but the world around Kate shrank, making her dizzy and weak.

She ran to the bathroom and locked herself in. Leaning against the sink, she stared at herself in the mirror.

Do marriage vows not mean anything to anyone?

"Mom?" she whispered, her lips shaking. "How could you do this to Dad? How could you… cheat on him?"

She watched her eyes fill with tears as the old wounds from her ex-husband's unfaithful ways stabbed her in the chest. Her eyelids became heavy as though they alone bore the consequences of what she'd just learned, pushing out her silent tears and letting them drip into the sink below.

CHAPTER FIFTY-ONE

"I'M SORRY, KATIE," Luke said, his hand resting on the door to the bathroom where Kate had gone to hide. As though hiding was even possible.

There was nothing but silence now. No water running, no throwing things, no talking.

They'd been there before. Many times. Sometimes in reversed positions, with him locking himself up and her begging to be let in. That was just something they did. Something she did a lot as a way to cope with the difficulties of her job.

But he recognized his error this time.

He shouldn't have mentioned the letters. Heck, he shouldn't have looked inside those boxes in the first place.

But he had no way of knowing the letters would reveal such unbearable things. How could he have known?

"Katie, baby. Let me in."

Nothing.

Turning around, he slumped his body against the closed door, and let himself drop to a sitting position. He knew they could be here for hours.

"I was an ass. I shouldn't have mentioned those letters. I'm sorry."

This time he thought he heard her sigh, but he wasn't sure.

"I can't even imagine the pressure you're under with work. I get it. I'm *sooo* sorry, but I can't travel back in time."

His thump on the door made it vibrate.

"I love you, Katie. But it's not my fault those letters exist. Can you please open the door?"

Nothing. Not a word. Not a sigh.

Bringing his hands to cover his face, he spoke aloud to himself. "I'm such an ass sometimes. I really shouldn't have pushed you to look into your parents' old case. You already have too much on your plate. I don't understand how you deal with me and my countless—"

He fell backward, his head landing on the tiled floor before he could finish his sentence. "Ow!" he yelped.

"Oh no!" Kate said, dropping to her knees next to him. "Are you okay?"

He smiled at her, even though he had no doubt he'd get a bump out of this.

"I'm sorry, Kate."

"It's not your fault," she said before leaning down to kiss him. She slid her hand underneath his head then lifted it right back up, as though checking for blood.

"I just… I just needed to shut the world away for a minute. Are you really okay? Should we go to the hospital to have your head checked out?"

"I'll be fine, Kate," he said before sitting back up and hugging her. "But let me in from time to time, okay? I'm on *your* team."

CHAPTER FIFTY-TWO

Friday, June 29th, 2018

PIXIE JERKED HERSELF AWAKE, her body covered in sweat, her heart beating out of control.

"Are you all right?" John mumbled next to her, his voice sleepy and coarse.

"I'm fine." Going online to re-watch some of the Boston news footage and read new articles had been a bad idea. As though the victims' headshots had been imprinted in her mind, she couldn't shake off the possibility that *he* had had something to do with the poor women's demise.

Focusing on her breathing, Pixie finally managed to slow down her heartbeat.

She got out of bed, grabbed her laptop from the nightstand, then went to the kitchen to make herself a cup of herbal tea, to soothe herself and somehow try to return to sleep, but she found it unlikely.

What if it was *him?*

She remembered his fingers braiding her long blonde hair. He'd always been fascinated by it. He'd even kept a piece of her hair when she'd shaved it off in her rebellious years. How he loved braids.

Her hair had long since regrown; that was the way John liked it. That was why she'd posed with a braid like that in the final photo they'd sent him.

Had her plan for freedom backfired in the worst possible way?

Well, she already suspected it had backfired, but she'd assumed it had started and ended with Mr. Thompson.

But what if it hadn't?

Had her lies and deception turned him into a monster?

And if so, what could she do about it now?

She opened her laptop and Googled her way to the Boston PD website. She quickly found the phone number to their anonymous tip line.

A quick glance at the clock followed by some mental math told her the sun had already risen in Boston.

She got up and dove her hand into her purse, retrieving her phone, which she stared at for what had to have been ten minutes, minimum. Calling the tip line was anonymous, so they said, but they probably received all sorts of tips through that line. Who knew how long the police took before acting on them? Chances were, all sorts of crazies called to report shit, right?

No, she needed to talk to the detectives. But doing so wouldn't be anonymous. She wrote down the detectives' number for the Roxbury district, which she'd remember hearing on the news.

If Pixie called—and if her gut was right—she could put an end to this. She could potentially save innocent lives.

But if she called, she'd also potentially get both John and her into trouble. They'd broken the law.

Was their hard-earned freedom more important than the lives of women she didn't even know?

Maybe there was a way to have her cake and eat it too. Calling from her cellphone would be too risky. She had to find a public phone. Where the heck would she find one of those nowadays?

"Hey, babe. What's going on?" John asked as he walked into the kitchen, rubbing his eyes. "It's four in the morning. Come back to bed."

"I gotta go and run an errand."

"Now? Nothing's open."

"There's just something I gotta take care of."

"Come on, you can do it later. Come back to bed."

"No, I need to get this done. It's about… *him.*"

"What?" He rubbed his forehead and blinked. "Don't tell me he found you, after all we did to get away."

"No. We're still safe. But to keep everyone safe I just need to make one phone call. An anonymous one to the Boston police."

"Can't you just file a report online?"

"I need to talk to the detectives, but I don't want to call or email from my devices."

"Whatever you say. You're the genius. But if you're going anywhere at this time of night, I'm going with you."

AFTER THEY DROVE AROUND AIMLESSLY for an hour, Pixie spotted a phone booth, and John stopped to park their car. She had absolutely no idea how much calls cost these days—her last call from a booth had to have been at least a decade earlier—she grabbed a handful of coins and the piece of paper where she'd written the BPD number.

Pushing the folding door to enter the booth, a concentrated smell of urine reached her nostrils.

What the fuck?

She stepped right out.

Staring at the phone through its glass surroundings—the scent still present but much less potent—she debated whether making the call would be worth it. The black machine looked different from those she remembered. It had a slot for credit cards. It also had quite a few pieces of faded, chewed-up gum stuck to its side, and some snotty-looking residue dangling on the cord.

"What's wrong, Pixie?" he yelled after rolling down his window.

"It's fucking gross in there."

She turned away from the booth and looked at her surroundings. The phone had been placed near a strip mall for those with dwindling budgets: Western Union, a pawn shop, and a dollar store. A liquor store and diner were the other two businesses, and only the latter appeared to be open.

Would they have a phone?

"I'm going to try the diner. Wanna go in with me?"

"Sure," John said before getting out of the car.

They walked there together while Pixie pondered giving up if they didn't have a phone. Perhaps it was just the universe telling her *not* to bother with the police.

But she also knew guilt would tear her apart if her gut turned out to be correct.

A bell tinkled as she pulled open the door, letting the scent of frying oil and coffee replace the remnants of what she'd smelled in the booth. Only a handful of patrons were in. All of them sitting alone, tables away from each other, as though they needed their own private areas for rummaging through their thoughts.

Pixie headed to the bar, John followed. If they had a phone, she'd best be positioned to see it from there. And spending money in the diner would most likely help her get permission to use their phone.

"Morning, dear!" a woman standing behind the bar said. Her graying hair was tied in a bun and then wrapped with a black hairnet. She placed a porcelain mug on the paper placemat in front of Pixie. "Coffee?"

"Sure," Pixie said.

"Please," John said.

"Decaf or regular?"

"Regular please."

"Same."

The woman reached out to the nearby pot, then filled their cups before handing them menus and various types of sugar packets and individual cream servings.

Pixie wasn't hungry but seeing pancakes on the menu made her salivate a little. She and John never made pancakes at home. *Why not?*

"I'll have some pancakes with real maple syrup if you have it."

"Afraid not. Maple-flavored syrup all right?"

Pixie shrugged. What could she do? "Fine."

"And you, sir?"

"Just coffee."

The waitress disappeared into the kitchen, granting Pixie more room to—not so discreetly—stand and stretch her legs, her feet on the footrest of her stool so she could look at the counter across the bar from where she sat. Glasses, coffee mugs, a sink, and other kitchen things one would expect. Turning her head to the other side, she spotted a screen, which she assumed was used for keeping track of orders or printing bills.

"Watcha looking for?" the waitress asked, making Pixie's heart skip a beat.

She was a paying patron. The worst the waitress could say was no.

"Any chance you have a phone I could use?"

"No cellphone, eh?"

Pixie shook her head, hoping her eyes didn't give her away.

"Sure, as long as you're not calling China."

"No, it's a local number," she said, tacking one more lie to her conversation. Toll-free was as good as local in her head, and the same was most likely true for all phone companies.

"Let me get it for you."

A few seconds later, the waitress handed Pixie a cordless phone, which relieved her beyond belief.

"If it's all right, I'll just go in between the entrance doors. For a little privacy."

"Whatever. I'm not sure the signal reaches that far, but maybe."

"Thanks!" She told the woman before addressing John. "I'll be right back."

Fidgeting with the piece of paper in her hand she made her way to the entrance, then dialed the number.

Several rings echoed before a woman picked up. "Detective Wang."

The name didn't seem like the one she'd heard on the news, but now wasn't the time to back pedal. "Hi, I'm calling about the man killing women in Boston."

A slight paused occurred before the detective spoke again. "What's your name?"

"I'd rather not say."

"Do you have any information for us?"

"I think so. You need to look into the murder of Mr. Eliah Thompson."

"Pixie," John said as he pushed the entrance door open.

She brought her index finger to her lips while widening her eyes.

"Your food's here," John whispered before returning into the diner.

"And how are these murders connected?"

"I think the same man killed them all."

"And what makes you believe that?"

"I gotta go. Follow the clues. Look for a Caucasian man. Twenty-six years old."

She pressed the button to hang up and exhaled loudly, feeling better about having given the detectives a useful tip. The ball was in their court now.

And she had not risked their hard-earned freedom. As long as they paid cash for breakfast, the police would have no way of tracking them down, even if they traced the phone call.

She headed back in, eager to bite into her pancakes.

CHAPTER FIFTY-THREE

SITTING ALONE in conference room number two with a large cup of district coffee, Kate blinked to try to get back on task.

Had she picked the worst timing or what? She shouldn't have wasted her downtime going through those letters. Now was not the time to stir up the past or relive painful memories. Not when their serial killer was still on the loose.

And Kate hated herself for not having caught him (or her) yet, or even having caught a break with the case.

"Time to grab a coffee?" Rosebud asked from behind her.

"Only from the lunchroom, I'm afraid. No time for fancy snacks from across the street."

"You look like shit, Murphy," Rosebud said.

"What everyone wants to hear first thing in the morning."

"Come on! Isn't there always time for a decent cup of joe that won't pierce a hole in your stomach? I don't know how you can drink that awful shit."

"I'm immune to it by now, maybe." Kate rubbed her face, trying to somehow make up for the serious deficit in her sleep.

"Didn't you go home early last night? You were supposed to spend time with your guy, forget about the case for a few hours. We're not machines."

"Yeah, yeah."

"What did you do? Get run over by a Zamboni?"

"I…" Kate poked the side of her cheek with her tongue, debating whether she should share her worries with Rosebud.

"Come on. You don't have to. But I'm here. We've got"—he stretched his arm to look at his watch—"ten minutes before Wang gets here to brief us."

What harm could come of it? She was too tired to come up with an excuse for keeping a secret from her partner. "Promise to keep it between you and me?"

"Sure." Rosebud pulled a chair and turned it around, straddling the back of the chair as he sat.

Summarizing the discoveries she'd first made through hypnotherapy and then the unopened letters in a way that would make CliffNotes feel inadequate, Kate explained why she hadn't managed to sleep a single minute the previous night. "As though our serial killer wasn't enough. Now I'm haunted by new revelations about my family's murders. I think I should get sleeping—"

"Morning!" Wang said as she entered the room, coffee in one hand and her notepad in the other. Her hair was disheveled but she otherwise looked fine. She'd had a better night than Kate.

"Anything interesting happen last night?" Kate asked as she forced her eyes to open wide.

"Toxicology report is still not ready, but we just got an interesting tip," Wang chimed in, notebook in the air, as though ready to share.

"Please make it good," Kate said, lifting her cup of coffee to her lips.

"We've gotten loads of anonymous tips. Want them all or just this latest one?"

"We're all exhausted. Just share the helpful stuff."

"Anonymous woman. Said our killer may be related to an unsolved case for the murder of Mr. Eliah Thompson. Also said the killer was male, Caucasian, and twenty-six years old."

"Very specific," Rosebud said, echoing what Kate was thinking.

"Who knows if it's a good lead or not, but I tracked down and retrieved the case file number. Eliah Thompson died nine months ago, in New Bedford. They never found the killer. But we can revisit their case and see if there were any twenty-five-

or twenty-six-year-old males involved, possibly as a witness or suspect who got eliminated."

"Isn't Father Matthews around that age? Check the records for his DOB and talk to whoever was on that New Bedford case. Drive over there if you need to. Shit, you're off." Kate turned to Rosebud. "You wanna drive there, or should I? I've got Father Matthews coming in shortly."

"No! Let's talk to Fuller. Tell him that we may finally be onto something. He'll call in Chainey. I don't want you to interview Matthews alone. Not today."

"Fine," Kate said before he got a chance to expand and tell Wang stuff that was only meant for his ears. "We'll do that, but we'll send Chainey with photos of all our male suspects, especially Father Matthews."

"Wang, before you go home and get some rest, anything else about the call or things that happened last night?"

"The call… I don't know why she didn't call the anonymous tip line, but as soon as she said she was calling about the case, I tapped the record button on my phone. Want to hear it word for word, in case it makes a difference?"

"You did! That's freaking awesome! Can you put it on speakerphone?"

Wang placed the device in the center of their group, hit *Play* followed by the speakerphone icon.

Kate sat with her eyes closed, doing her best to absorb all of it. The recording was put on loop and everyone listened in about half a dozen times.

"Is it me, or is a man talking to her in the background?"

Rosebud shook his head. "I didn't hear. But let me get my earbuds," he said before digging into the breast pocket of his jacket.

"You carry this with you at all times?" Kate asked.

"Two minutes of guided meditation can be squeezed in any time."

"What?" Wang said.

"Ignore him," Kate said before donning the earbuds and tapping play. The now familiar lines began again. "Trixie! Listen for it, near the end. The noises change in the background. I think a man says 'Trixie.' That has to be her name. Rosebud, listen to it." Kate offered the earbuds. "See what you make of it."

Rosebud got ready and tapped the play button. Once. Twice. Three times.

"Maybe. But how does that help?"

"We could track down that number from our phone records, look for a Trixie. Then maybe she could provide more information. It sounds to me like this woman knows the killer. She could be someone who got away from him. Why didn't she give us her name?"

WITH CHAINEY freshly recalled and dispatched to New Bedford, Kate sat next to Rosebud in the interview room, across the table from Father Matthews, who'd agreed to answer their questions as long as he could return to his duties within the hour. The father had even agreed to provide his prints and DNA after acknowledging that he didn't have an alibi for either murder.

"Lord is on my side. I have nothing to hide," he said, as smug as the Pope. The way he sat, his perfect posture, the dimples in his clean-shaven cheeks, and his clerical collar made Kate want to slap the smile off of his face. Her gut was telling her—no, it was screaming—that the handsome priest had something to do with the murders.

DNA will eventually be his downfall, she thought as she glanced at the list of questions she had prepared for him. She skipped the wine-related questions for now. "Jessica had an oily cross drawn on her forehead," Kate said.

Father Matthews raised his brows as he shrugged. "I don't know what to tell you. Do you have a question? I have things to take care of. As I said before, I'm a busy man."

"You'd have access to such oils at church, wouldn't you?" Rosebud asked.

"We have holy oils, of course, but their usage is reserved for priests and deacons under very specific circumstances."

"Enlighten us," Kate said, straightening her back and matching the posture of the father in front of her.

"The Church typically uses three types of holy oils: the oil of the sick, the oil of the catechumens, and the holy chrism oil."

"What's the difference?" Kate asked, writing down those names before they escaped her short-term memory.

"The first is used according to its name. Priests can anoint sick people either during a mass or privately through a sacrament that involves laying hands on the sick, saying a special prayer, and tracing a cross with the oil on the sick person's forehead and hands."

"And hands?" Kate made a note to ask the medical examiner if he'd spotted such oil residue on either victim.

"Yes," Father Matthews stated in a flat tone. He smiled, but Kate recognized it for the facade that it was. Genuine smiles involved the eyes. His smile was purely for show; his eyes shot icy stares her way. A perfect picture of practiced charisma.

Kate met his glance. "And what ingredients would be used in the oil of the sick?"

He didn't blink before answering, his eyes daring Kate to a staring contest of sorts. "Olive oil."

"That's it?" she asked, incredulous and doing her best not to blink, but her bodily instincts were too strong.

"And the blessings of our bishop."

Kate resisted the urge to roll her eyes, realizing that the placebo effect could very well extend beyond medicine and work its magic with religious oils, if people's faith or belief were strong enough. "Tell me about the second oil you mentioned, cate…" Kate glanced at her pad.

"Catechumens," Rosebud finished. "It means people who haven't been baptized yet," he added, for Kate's benefit, obviously.

"Priests or deacons can anoint catechumens as they pray for God to instill in them the strength and wisdom necessary to discern and avoid evil, in preparation of their future life with Christ, our Lord. They use the oil to draw a cross on their forehead before blessing the child with the waters of baptism."

"And what's in that catechumen oil?"

"Same as the other."

Kate wanted to ask why they categorized the two differently if the oil was one and the same but kept her question to herself. She was exhausted and had already displayed too much ignorance in front of Rosebud and the smug priest. And she didn't want Father Matthews to think he could outwit her with his good looks, charming smile, and snappy answers.

"And the third oil?" she asked but then changed her mind. "No. Tell you what. Just tell me if any of your oils would have frankincense and sage mixed into them."

"No," he said, shaking his head. "Not a chance."

"What's in the third oil?"

"Olive oil, balsam, and the bishop consecrates it."

"Balsam," Kate repeated. "Is that hard to come by?" she asked Rosebud who held his phone in his hand.

"I'll look into it," he said as his finger touched his screen.

"We don't purchase the ingredients. The bishop blesses the oils on Holy Thursday each year, just before Easter, then each parish receives enough to last them throughout the year."

"Readily available online. Cheap as well," Rosebud said.

"Do Frankincense and sage have any meanings to you?" Kate asked the priest.

"Not as an oil, but Frankincense is an important ingredient in the incense we burn during certain ceremonies."

Kate flipped to a new page on her notepad. "Meaning of those ceremonies?"

"They're normally part of a ritual having to do with cleansing and purifying."

Rosebud chimed in next, reading from his phone. "Google mentions antiseptic and disinfectant properties."

"And what about sage? Is it used at all in any ritual?"

Father Matthews shook his head. "No. In fact, we recommend against it. Centuries ago, sage was used to bless homes as part of an ancient pagan tradition. Catholics are strongly urged to part ways with any sort of superstition or non-Christian traditions."

Kate thought about the oil and the potential meaning for using a different blend.

"Would it be hard for someone to gain access to the holy oils? Are they left unattended anywhere in the church?"

"They are kept in an ambry, near the baptismal font."

Kate stared at the father, but he didn't clarify. "In plain English?"

"In a recess near the receptacle we use for baptisms."

"So anyone could go and steal those oils if they wanted?"

The father's nostrils flared as a darker shade of red reached his cheeks. "I don't know what you have against me or my church, but our parishioners are not thieves who'd steal the holy oils!"

"All yours, Rosebud," Kate said as she decided to step out of the interview room.

Her exhaustion was affecting her work. No way she'd be able to make friends and work her magic with Father Matthews. But maybe Rosebud could play good cop and build rapport for a change.

She headed into the small observation room that oversaw the interrogation she'd just exited and hoped he could get something out of the man.

"Father Matthews, please accept my apologies for my partner. She's obviously not religious."

A groan escaped the father's lips as he readjusted in his chair.

"You know why I became a cop?" Rosebud asked as he closed his notepad.

"I have no idea." Father Matthews leaned against the back of his chair, crossing his arms on his chest.

He's closing off… Come on, Rosebud. Work your magic.

"My dad. My granddad. It's a family tradition. I'm just following in their footsteps."

"Okay."

A few seconds of uncomfortable silence followed.

The priest glanced at his watch. "Do you have more questions for me? I really have to get back."

"Why did you become a priest?"

"It's my calling. I heard Him tell me loud and clear."

"Like you hear my voice right now?"

The father flipped his palms up in the air, a confused look on his face. "I'm not crazy!"

"What do you mean then?"

"During my prayers. In my head. And he kept showing me signs. I only followed the path he'd already lined up for me."

Kate rubbed her face as she added up their facts to see if she could tally up enough elements to reach probable cause: no alibi for both murders, he knew of various rituals (but that was part of his job, and the oils used didn't match), his use of sage went against his faith (but it could have been done to throw them off his scent). So, other than the man being a priest and not having an alibi, she had nothing.

No judge would ever approve an arrest warrant for him. But Kate could fill out the required paperwork for a search warrant and gain samples of those holy oils.

That she could do.

CHAPTER FIFTY-FOUR

Saturday, June 30th, 2018

THEY SPENT DINNER IN SILENCE, and Luke had to admit it was probably better that way.

He'd watched the latest press conference by the mayor. Bostonians were angry. They wanted the killer caught, and he, too, wanted nothing more. That would mean Kate could relax a bit. Having the entire city scrutinize her lack of progress hadn't been easy on her.

He watched her tired eyes as she moved peas back and forth on her plate. Maybe she'd also lost her appetite.

Why did the Boston PD Public Relations person have to go and mention their lead detective by name? Rookie mistake. Their household was paying the price for it. And now some nosy reporter had made a connection between his job at the DNA lab for the Massachusetts State Police and Kate as the lead investigator, exposing something any defense attorney would have a feast with.

But that was neither here nor there. They still had to find a killer first before they would worry about that. Luke knew they'd done everything by the book, but he couldn't help but worry nonetheless. Their relationship had been disclosed to all who needed to know. He had personally avoided involvement with any evidence brought in by Kate and her team for any and all cases she worked on. But he was still the lab supervisor in charge of the DNA analysis the Boston PD needed done. A greedy defense attorney could probably make some connection somewhere that could get them in trouble.

But there was nothing he could do about it now. Nothing but keep the house's curtains closed. Those reporters would eventually go away, like they had around twenty-four hours after the last time Kate had been mentioned by name on the news.

The doorbell rang yet again. Luke looked at the clock on the wall. A good twenty minutes had elapsed since their last attempt.

"Should I go this time?" Mrs. O'Brien offered.

"No, Mom. They'll go away if we keep ignoring them."

But he knew the only way they'd go away for sure was if Kate and her team found the killer.

Not having personally examined the evidence the detectives had brought in hadn't prevented Luke from keeping an eye on the results. Everything the detectives had examined had been proven useless. Even those oils they sampled from five different churches around town and the oil on the second victim's forehead. They'd all been made from the same batch. Whether or not that had helped the detectives, Luke had no idea. All he knew was that unless they had more evidence to point them to one specific church, they'd only expanded their scope instead of narrowing it down as they had probably hoped.

Perhaps they'd have more luck trying to trace where the frankincense and sage had come from.

"How about we watch a comedy after dinner?" Luke suggested to his mom and Kate. They could all use a laugh.

Kate got up and shook her head.

"Sorry, I'm not in the mood for it."

Exactly my point, he thought, but he knew better than to voice those words.

As she scraped a few untouched bites into the garbage, Kate spoke up. "It was delicious, Mrs. O'Brien, as always."

"My pleasure, dear. Glad you liked it." She got up, grabbing her dirty dishes and taking them to the sink.

"You guys watch something. I'll just go back to those boxes

in your office," Kate said to Luke, not even bothering to look at him while she spoke.

Luke inhaled deeply as he pondered what he should do. Then, hearing his mom turn on the faucet, he re-opened his eyes and got to his feet.

"Mom, please don't bother with the dishes! I'll take care of them. Why don't you go and find something to watch? I'll be right with you."

She turned off the water but left her hand on the faucet as her stern eyes met his.

"You're going to ignore your old mom and take care of her. That poor child—"

"She's not a poor child. She's one of the strongest women I know."

"You know that's not what I meant. Not only is she dealing with the stress of every Bostonian blaming her for the lack of progress on those murder cases, she's also decided to reopen her old wounds from decades ago?"

Luke cleared his throat, knowing fair well that he was to blame for that, not Kate.

"Mom—"

"No." She grabbed Luke's dishes from his hands and added them to the sink in front of her.

"Do your best to ignore me. Go and make her think of something else. Anything other than those murder cases."

Luke considered refusing but knew better. "Fine."

He refilled his glass of wine and headed to his office, but instead of walking in, he just leaned against the frame of the open door, staring at Kate, sitting in his chair, her gloved hands carefully opening more envelopes.

Her nose twitched, then she looked up and he realized she was fighting back tears. Again.

"Smell this!" she said, offering a yellowed Christmas card.

He walked toward his desk and leaned down to do just that. "Is that… cologne?" His nose twitched as well. "Old Spice?"

"Is that what it is? Old Spice?"

"I'm pretty sure. Dad used to have some back in the day."

Kate smelled the card again, then closed her eyes. "That's

what I smelled around my mom when the hypnotherapist took me back."

"That means…"

She dropped the card and her hands dug themselves into her hair, scratching her scalp as her face contorted in pain.

"After all these years! I don't understand why nobody ever found these letters! Why didn't the police see them when they searched the house? Why didn't Mom open them? Why did she keep them? Who's this E guy?"

"And how is the smell still in there?"

But she shook her head and got up instead, reaching for Luke's glass and then downing half of it in one large sip.

"I'm no detective, but I know this isn't your handwriting on the box. Who wrote that?" Luke asked, pointing to the words *Steve and Jo's attic*.

"That's Kenny's handwriting. He must have found it in Mom and Dad's attic when they cleared it. That's the only reason why the sheriff and his team wouldn't have found it. But why did he never show it to me? Why didn't he unpack what it contained?" She finished the rest of Luke's wine.

"Maybe it was too difficult for him as well. Wasn't your dad his only brother?"

"Yeah," Kate said, wrapping her arms around Luke's waist and letting her head rest against his chest.

"That's one thing we'll never know. Kenny took that information with him to the grave, but you can do something about those letters now."

"But I still don't understand why she kept the letters and never opened them. And why did she keep them in the attic?"

"I don't think she wanted your dad to find them."

"But why not throw them away? Why keep them?" she asked, her green eyes looking up to him. From the sadness that shone from them, he knew Kate had connected the dots, but acknowledging those facts had to be painful.

His chest tightened at his inability to make her feel better. No matter what he said or did, there was nothing he could do to ease her suffering. Those damned letters had soiled whatever memories she'd kept of her belated, beloved mother.

And it was his fault she'd opened them.

But there was no point beating himself up over it. He'd

already apologized for that, and she'd have eventually found them on her own.

"So what do you want to do?" He rubbed her back as she inhaled deeply.

"I'll send them to Sheriff Ramsay. He can have them analyzed for prints, maybe find some DNA in the envelopes' glue. Come on, let's go watch a movie. But nothing about cheating spouses, please."

CHAPTER FIFTY-FIVE

Sunday, July 1st, 2018

THE SUNDAY HYMNS didn't sound as heartfelt as they normally did. Or perhaps he wasn't standing in the exact spot where he normally stood, where the echo bounced off the floor and walls in such a way that it made his soul surge, as though trying to leap toward God with each breath he took.

No, today felt different. Hollow, somehow.

Maybe it was the growing anticipation building up inside of him. Maybe it was a sign that he had to save more souls. And he had to do it soon. Perhaps God wasn't happy with his performance.

Had he disappointed Him when he'd failed to save Amanda?

He bowed his head and prayed in silence while the congregation in front of him continued chanting.

"Lord, my savior,
Lord, my liberator,
Guide me toward your light,
Together our souls will unite.
Your spirit calls, through the dark times it beckons,
With open arms, you'll greet me in the heavens.
Glorious is your name,
Glorious is your flame.

Lord, while I walk with shame,
My sins you forgive the same,
I look up to you and your name I'll forever proclaim."

And as he repositioned himself for the next portion of the service, he silently promised to God that he'd get back to his duties. He would be the proud servant he'd been born to be. And he would no longer let someone's gender or hair color dictate whether or not their soul deserved saving.

Hope and pride boomed in his chest as he silently made a promise to God: he'd save another soul, and he'd take care of it right after mass.

THE AFTERNOON OFFERED the best alibi he could ever need: today's fundraiser was hosted right in the middle of the parish. The sunny weather had allowed them to proceed with their plan A, which meant that dozens of sinners would be gathered near their residences. Nobody would notice him disappearing for a short while.

He'd already grabbed a couple of vials from his latest batch and snuck them into church in the pocket of his pants. While bringing a bottle of wine—even a travel-size one—would look suspicious, the fundraiser also came with a built-in solution: punch. He had to time it correctly, but punch would do just fine. He would offer a cup of it—with his cleansing agent added in—just before walking away from the crowd, into the sinner's home.

But whose turn was it now?

Whose soul needed saving the most urgently?

Relieved that he no longer had to oblige by the blonde-only rule—having heard and recalled his Lord's message very clearly—he began perusing the church's database, this time starting his search with the addresses first.

A handful of people who had signed up to attend the event lived less than a block away. That was perfect.

With sinning so commonplace these days, he knew several sinners would be in attendance.

He paused as he browsed his list, trying to remember what

each of them had confessed to recently: light drug usage, cheating on an exam, cheating on a boyfriend, lying to parents, masturbating, stealing someone else's lunch at work, lying on their taxes, having sex with the neighbor, and getting an abortion.

His choice was clear.

He turned off the computer, voiced a quick prayer, grabbed a handful of rosaries, then headed out to find her among the mingling sinners.

CHAPTER FIFTY-SIX

IT HAD BEEN days since her blackout and Amanda couldn't believe her mind hadn't recovered a single memory from it. And she hadn't been able to fill in more blanks since Big Danny had headed out of town. Gambling trip with his buddies, he'd said.

But whether her stomach harbored queasiness or just worries was still unclear. Ever since that day, she felt as though someone had been following her. Spying on her.

Or perhaps it was just paranoia after what Big Danny had told her.

What friend from church? Had David come over? She pulled out her phone, hesitant to call him, wondering if the police would read something into that. Lori's death was still so recent…

Deciding against it, she returned her phone to her purse and headed into a coffee shop instead.

Caffeine could make her even more antsy, she thought while waiting in line. When she reached the barista, she opted for an herbal tea and a granola bar. Something to soothe her nerves instead of feeding the paranoia that already inhabited her.

She sat at an empty table in the shop, staring out the window for a while, pondering while glancing around, when she noticed a dark gray sedan a block and a half from where she sat.

Hadn't the same car been parked by her apartment this morning when she'd left?

She shook the thought away. She just needed to sleep it off.

That edible experiment had been an epic fail. She really had to give Joshua hell when she ran into him next.

Had he been the friend from church who'd showed up?

Why couldn't she identify that man? Wouldn't he have contacted her again?

This whole week had been a nightmare, she realized as she once again forced herself to put aside those negative thoughts.

Ditching her empty cup and wrapper in the garbage on her way out, she walked home.

But as though a tiny voice spoke up in her mind, she turned around. The sedan was leaving its spot. She continued marching down the sidewalk, then turned into a random street, curious to see if the car would follow her.

Sure enough, it did.

Whether it was the anger she felt at her inability to fill in her blackout or the adrenaline from something else, she pointed straight at the car, then dashed toward it, her elbows pumping at her sides. No way in hell was she going to be followed by some creep.

She wouldn't be stalked. It was broad daylight. She risked nothing. She could scream her heart out if that sedan driver was the killer coming after her.

Someone would hear her.

CHAPTER FIFTY-SEVEN

OFFICER ALESSANDRO AGOSTINO-PERSICHETTI, aka Smitty, sat in his unmarked vehicle, his third cup of coffee in hand, his eyes locked onto the community get-together organized by the church. In a wide-open space in front of him, behind a foot-high hedge of flowery bushes, people who were dressed to the nines chitchatted loudly.

How times had changed!

Sure, he hadn't been to church in years—perhaps getting to see the worst of humanity had contributed to that a little.

Well, a lot.

His faith in God had ended around the time he stumbled onto his fourth body, a woman he knew. A pretty awful sight, which he still remembered in vivid detail. The discovery of her body had followed a domestic disturbance call. He and Mansbridge, his regular partner, had shown up as fast as they could, but it had been minutes too late for the poor woman who'd been stabbed in the chest by her violent husband.

They'd first seen the pool of blood ooze out and stain the carpet in the hallway, the dark liquid soaking into the fibers from the other side of the apartment door. The stench of her fresh blood had haunted him for about a year, enough to prevent him from buying fresh meat.

His mind flooded with images from that awful day. They'd managed to force their way into the apartment, only to find a very confused and sobbing man hunched over his wife, his hands joined, his arms anxiously pressing his full force onto her chest, as though attempting to resuscitate a woman who'd just bled to death.

His breath had reeked of alcohol and smoke. Another stench that Smitty disliked.

Yeah. As he watched various members of the congregation chatting among themselves, he recognized a few familiar faces. People he hadn't spoken with for years. He had last talked to them… Well, around the time he stopped going to church. Around the time his faith dissipated into the abyss of corruption, violence, and the evils of what humans could do when facing bad situations.

His phone rang, and he looked at the caller ID: Vanessa. He ignored the call, which stopped the ringing. But not a minute elapsed before it rang again.

"Damn it!"

Peeling his eyes off of Father Matthews for a second, he sent her a text message:

Can't talk right now!

He tossed his device onto the empty passenger seat next to him. Mansbridge had received an emergency call about his family an hour earlier, so he'd headed to the hospital. Something wrong with one of his kids. So Smitty was short a partner—and free of the voice of reason he'd come to depend on.

Staking out a homicide suspect alone sucked. Smitty certainly couldn't blame the man for taking care of his kid, but having his partner here would have made the rest of the afternoon more enjoyable. Maybe Mansbridge could have offered advice or helped Smitty get out of the mess he was in with Vanessa.

Smitty's phone rang yet again just as he watched Father Matthews relocating to a different group of people. That young new priest certainly looked like he enjoyed chatting and mingling with his parishioners.

Smitty debated whether he should pick up. He didn't want to. His job certainly made it clear he wasn't supposed to. Especially when his partner had gone and left him as the solo surveillance officer. But he sure as hell knew the woman wasn't going to stop calling until she'd said whatever she needed to say.

Silencing his phone was an option, but not a great one if important calls were to come in.

His eyes went from the community in front of him back to his phone, then back to the priest.

What harm would there be in having a quick chat? Then he'd be able to fully focus on his surveillance task.

"Make it quick, Vanessa. I'm at work and I can't talk right now."

"I didn't want to leave you a text message. I had to tell you."

"Can't this wait until tonight? After I come home?"

"It'll be too late by then."

He put the phone on speaker and set it on his dashboard. He rubbed his temples, struggling to follow along while doing his best to keep an eye on the father.

That woman had grabbed his attention with her fiery attitude—both on the dance floor and in bed—but he'd never managed to have an easy conversation with her. If he were honest with himself, he'd have to say they shared intense chemistry. But that was it. She wasn't the sharpest tool in the shed, and that little tidbit made for difficult conversations. He knew he wasn't a rocket scientist either, so he'd let it slide, enjoying the perks that came with their relationship.

"What? Why?" he asked.

"I'll be gone. My bags are packed. I'm leaving."

"What? Why?"

"You sound like a broken record. I told you last night. But then you fell asleep halfway through our conversation."

Smitty made fists with his hands and stared at his car roof. The woman drove him crazy. Not even a month ago, she'd begged to move in with him, saying it would be good for their relationship. "Vanessa, what are you saying, baby? Why do you want to leave now?"

"See, I've been thinking about it all day. When I told you I was pregnant, the only thing I heard from you was a snore. That's not—"

"What? You're pregnant?"

"Yes, I told you last night, Smitty! You never listen to me, that's the problem!"

As though a kaleidoscope had burst open in his brain, he suddenly couldn't think straight. Images of a screaming baby fought with those of Vanessa microwaving breast milk or dipping a pacifier into whisky. His life as a sleepless cop flashed to mind. While Vanessa went on and on about whatever she was going on about, he couldn't register the words she spoke.

Then he thought of his partner, the voice of reason, and finally spoke.

"Vanessa, baby! I didn't hear any of that last night. I'm sorry you've been freaking out about it. I've been exhausted. I told you I wasn't in the mood for a discussion. I wasn't kidding. I just fell asleep."

"But I told you it was important!" Her voice had reached new levels both in terms of how nasally she sounded and how close she was to tears.

But then Smitty looked up, trying to see if Father Matthews was still where he'd last seen him, but he could no longer see the man. "Shit!"

"What?"

"Vanessa. I'm so sorry I have to hang up on you, but I'm at work. I've got to run. Please, I'm begging you, stay home until I get back from work. Then we'll talk about this, okay?"

"Promise?"

"Yes!" He hung up then rubbed a hand over his face, as though the motion could somehow make him forget about what he'd just learned in the past few minutes. He had to focus on work.

Where the fuck had the father gone to?

He looked over to where he'd parked his vehicle. It was still there.

Relief washed over him as he realized he could most likely recover from this stupid mistake. How did he let his personal shit get in the way of an important case? His one chance to make a difference in a fucking serial killer case. The sergeant had thrown them a bone and assigned them to surveil one of the suspects in a major crime, and this was how he was paying him back?

He'd really messed up this time.

Smitty had never hated himself as much as he did at that moment.

Then Vanessa's latest bomb came back to haunt him, not helping his case.

He got out of his unmarked vehicle and headed to the meetup. He'd just follow the breadcrumbs. He'd ask around. It would likely raise more questions than anything, but at least he'd get his eyes back on the suspect.

As he marched toward the crowd of old friends, dressed in his cheap gray suit, he realized he kind of looked like he belonged. He headed to the cluster of people where he'd last seen him.

"Hi, have you seen Father Matthews?" Smitty asked a red-headed woman in a green sundress, one of the handful of women holding on to red Solo cups or tiny cardboard plates.

"He was just here a few minutes ago. I don't know where he went."

"I saw him head inside the building," a blonde said, her hand pointing toward the back entrance of the six-story building.

"Thank you," he said, although he really meant to swear, but knew it wasn't the proper time or venue.

He'd messed up. It was his own fault. Well, Vanessa shouldn't have called him. *No! My fault for picking up. Shit, shit, shit.*

Holding tight to his phone, he thought about calling the detectives and admitting he'd messed up. Then, he didn't want to. How bad would that look?

He made a pact with himself. *Ten minutes. If I don't find him by then, I'll call it in.* He looked at his phone, surprised by the time on his clock.

"How long was I on the phone with her?" he muttered as he headed toward the elevator doors.

For ten minutes, he surveyed every floor. But it was all in vain. No way he'd knock on every door. He just hoped he'd somehow run into the man.

But that was dumb. The stupidest plan he'd ever had.

Why did he have to go and answer Vanessa's call?

He fucking messed up and messed up bad.

The worst mistake of his career!

Smitty was calling himself all sorts of names by the time he stepped outside again, ready to admit defeat. But then he spotted Father Matthews smiling and nodding at a young woman near the punch bowl.

He let out a long exhalation and closed his eyes. “Thank, God!”

CHAPTER FIFTY-EIGHT

LUKE SAT ON THE COUCH, his sock-covered feet resting on the coffee table, a folded newspaper in front of him, pen in hand.

How he loved the complexity of those Sunday crossword puzzles. He had yet to finish one, but using a pen did increase their difficulty level. Pure challenge and fun for his morning alone in the house.

The sound of a key in the lock had him look up to the clock below the TV. Had Kate returned from the precinct already? But when he didn't hear the beeps from the safe, he realized it was his mom.

Mass ended late today, he thought.

His mom walked into the living room a few seconds later. Her slippers clashed with her outfit, but he knew she would head to her room and change soon. She only wore her best outfits for church.

But she put her hands on her hips and frowned the instant their glances met. "Luke Stewart O'Brien! Get your feet off that table!"

As a reflex, he obeyed. Then he put them back on there. "Mom, this is *my* house. I get to do as I wish."

She pursed her lips and shook her head. "I raised you better than that."

"My house, my rules, Mom. That was the deal when I invited you to live with me."

"Well, I don't care for this particular rule. It's not proper."

"We're not hosting a fancy dinner with company. I'm just working on my crossword puzzle and I want to relax." Not wanting to hear or say another word about such a trivial topic, he turned the tables on her. "What took the priest so long today? Aren't you home a good twenty minutes later than usual? Did your friend have car troubles?"

"As a matter of fact, I stayed behind to chat with Father Coffedy."

He frowned, exhaled, then put his pen down. "Dare I ask why?"

She smiled. "Let me get my purse. I'll show you."

A few seconds later, she was back in the living room, taking a seat next to Luke on the couch, staring at his socks.

"Fine!" He moved his feet to the floor and straightened his back. "What do you want to show me?"

"Well…" She smacked her lips, a sound she only made when she was about to say something that would upset him. "I was waiting to talk with Father Coffedy after mass. But you know, he was busy, chatting with other parishioners who wanted to share some news with him, so I got to talking with Candidate Anderson. The young man is so helpful—"

"Get to the point, Mom."

She frowned at him, her head tilted. "Anyways, I finally got my turn with Father Coffedy and I asked about the church's marriage preparation course. For you and Kate, of course. Not for me."

He dropped his newspaper onto his lap. "Mom! Why did you go and do that?"

"There's no reason to get upset. I didn't book a date for a ceremony or anything. You know it's the right thing to do. Make it right under the eye of God!"

"Mom, we've been through this before. Kate and I have something that works. I don't want to mess it up. The status quo is perfect. I don't want to ruin the best thing I've ever had."

"Asking someone for their hand in marriage is the furthest thing from ruining a relationship!"

"But Kate doesn't care about marriage! She's never brought it up."

"Then here's your chance to broach the topic." Her hand reached into the purse that had been resting on her lap, then she pulled out a leaflet. "Have a look. Share the information with Kate. Leave it on her pillow tonight if you prefer. That will get the conversation going."

"Mom, Kate isn't religious. She'd be annoyed if I did that."

"Nonsense. She prays before meals with us."

"If you weren't here, she wouldn't."

One of her eyebrows had raised above the other as her lips pursed. "What are you saying?"

"She's only praying with us before the meals because it means something to *you*. She doesn't want *anything* to do with the church or religion in general."

She shook her head. "You're wrong there. She came to church with me the other morning. She was really interested in that young priest, Father Matthews. In fact, I don't think she's the cheating kind, but I'd be careful if I were you."

"Mom! Come on! You're being ridiculous now. I trust Kate. And if she were to cheat on me, she would most definitely not do it with a priest! You watched too much of *The Thorn Birds*. Seriously."

"Well, why else would she be so interested in him? We missed half the mass so we could go see him instead of Father Coffedy."

Luke shrugged. "It probably had something to do with her work. The news was pretty clear about it. There's a religious theme to the latest strings of murders. She was probably scoping out the crowd, wanting to talk to him to get some information about certain parishioners."

His mom shook her head before exhaling loudly.

"You know what, Mom?" Luke asked, tapping his mother's lap briefly. "There is something that would make me feel a lot better, now that we're kind of on the topic."

"Reading the leaflet?" she suggested, once again pushing her unwanted literature into Luke's hand.

"No. I want you to hold off on going to church for a little while. Just to be safe, you know?"

"Luke." She got up but continued shaking her head at him.

"I'm not saying to abandon your faith. I'm just saying to skip your religious functions until they catch the killer."

"That's where you're so wrong. Out of all times, *now*'s the time for me to strengthen my faith and spend more time at church. Only by praying will light overcome the darkness."

CHAPTER FIFTY-NINE

KATE STOOD in the center of conference room two, soaking in the photos, maps, and clues their team had pinned all around the room. She knew she was disobeying Fuller's direct order by coming into work today, but she couldn't help herself. Her brain wouldn't magically switch off, so she might as well put it to good use.

Instead of pretending to listen to Luke and his mom—something she'd shamefully caught herself doing too many times over the past few days—she was better off wasting time rehashing the same clues over again at work instead of at home.

There had to be something they'd missed.

The killer couldn't have gotten away with murder twice without leaving a single clue. She looked at the map and added one pin: Father Matthews' apartment, whose address she'd just looked up. Its location didn't jump at her as anything overly convenient for either of the two victims.

Using one of the blank whiteboards, she turned to the mental game she played when she was really stuck: brainstorming. She began by selecting two words that had appeared at both crime scenes, then she let her mind make whatever mental associations it felt like making. No time for second guessing or political correctness.

Rosary: religion, church, choir, hymn, prayer, father, amen, cross, oil, blessing

Used nightgown: beggar, poor, donation, charity, non-profit

Out of words for now, she stopped and stared at the board. Then she stepped forward and circled two words: donation and choir.

A while back, Luke had mentioned to her in passing that the church had been collecting used clothing. In fact, he'd suggested it as a way for her to get rid of Kenny's clothes instead of just throwing them away. The nightgowns. The detectives hadn't bothered with tracking those down. While some DNA had been found on them, it hadn't matched anyone in their databases or on their list of suspects. Not even Father Matthews.

For a few seconds, Kate wondered if they should try to contact second-hand stores, see if they could have sold or given those two articles away, but she couldn't picture anyone spending money—not even a dollar—for those really worn-out pieces of clothing. They had to have come out of the back of someone's closet, trash can, or donation bin.

But which? There was no real way to tell unless a volunteer would recall those specific items. Kate had no idea how many donation bins existed, either formally or informally, within the city, but she guessed the number to be too high for the time they had. Not worth the effort.

She turned to her other brainstormed option: the choir. That majestic organ she'd seen… Could the killer be part of the church's choir? Would one choir rotate through several parishes?

But before answers could come to her, her phone rang with the tone she'd assigned Fuller.

"Detective Murphy," she said, bringing the device to her ear while hoping he hadn't just driven by the station and seen her car in the parking lot.

"We've got a third one."

"What's the address?" she asked, marker in hand, ready to add to her board.

He gave it to her. "I'm heading there now, but I need you to contact our surveillance guys right away. Confirm where your two main suspects were for the past few hours. First officer on the scene talked about a rosary. He said the vic hadn't cooled off yet."

"On it."

"Call me back right away."

She ended the call then dialed the shift supervisor's number who promptly provided the names and numbers of those currently surveilling. Next, she called one of the officers with eyes on Amanda McCutcheon.

"Officer Lofland, this is Detective Murphy."

"I was just about to call you guys," he said.

"Why?"

"We're bringing her in. She spotted us and went ape-shit!"

"What?"

"It appears she may have been a target of your murderer. Long story, from what I gathered. We're heading back to the precinct with her now."

"Fine."

Kate smiled as she dialed Smitty's number. She'd shared a few shifts with him before. He'd even pulled a favor and helped her out with her uncle's case a few years back. Perhaps he'd have helpful info for her once more.

"Smitty, it's Murphy. I need a status update on Father Matthews."

"Hey, hey! Good afternoon, blondie!"

"No time for small talk. Where was he during the past few hours?"

A small pause, then he spoke. "He's been at the church's fundraiser for at least an hour."

"What does that mean. Where was he the hour before now?"

"Is it really important?"

"Smitty, we just got a third victim. It happened within the last few hours. Tell me you guys had eyes on Matthews the whole afternoon."

"…"

"Smitty!"

"Mansbridge had to leave, and I may have lost him for about thirty minutes."

"Fu—" Her nails digging into her palms, Kate swallowed letters she didn't voice. Could this be good news instead? Was that enough for probable cause? "Tell me exactly where he was before and after you lost him."

"At the fundraiser."

"Address?" Kate asked as she walked toward the map.

She added a pin to mark the fundraiser's location and another for the third murder. They were a stone's throw from each other. The man could have gone from one to the other and killed the person within thirty minutes.

"Man, Smitty, you should have called it in when you lost eyes. I'm gonna ask for another unit to take over for you. The minute you're relieved, I need you to report to Detective Lieutenant Fuller." She gave him the crime scene address and hung up, mixed feelings brewing in the pit of her stomach.

Is this it?

She grabbed her jacket and headed downstairs, phone cradled against her shoulder as she stepped out of the elevator, waiting for Fuller to pick up.

"Sir, we've had developments on both sides. Officer Smitty, our eyes on Matthews, lost him briefly this after—"

"What the fuck?"

"I know. I'm just about to call the patrol supervisor. I'll get a replacement for him so he can brief both of us in person. His fuck-up may be our opportunity for probable cause. Matthews was a block away!"

"What's the other development?"

"Amanda McCutcheon spotted our surveillance team. She freaked out and has something to report to us. She's here now," Kate said, recognizing the brunette walking into the precinct's lobby.

"Here, where? Are you at the precinct?"

There was no point lying to him now. "Yes."

A groan echoed on the line.

"I'm heading out to meet you now." Kate hung up.

"Detective, I need to speak with you," Amanda said as Kate dialed the shift supervisor's number once more.

"One minute!" Kate raised her index finger in the air before leaving a message for the supervisor. "We got a new development, Sergeant. Detective Lieutenant Fuller and I need Smitty to report to us urgently. Could you get someone to replace him ASAP?"

Kate hung up the phone and turned to Amanda before speaking. "What did you need to tell us?"

"Hmm. Here?" she asked, looking around at the handful of police officers and civilians hanging around.

"Can you identify the killer?" Kate asked Amanda.

"Right now, no."

"What does that mean?"

"It's complicated."

Officer Lofland nodded next to her. "I'd say so."

"Okay, I'm sorry but I can't stay to get your statement right this minute. It's not that I don't care. Something major just happened." She turned to Officer Lofland. "Please call Detective Wang. She'll come in and grab her statement. I've really gotta go!"

KATE ARRIVED at the scene just as Smitty did. She recognized his tall, good looks from a distance, but she didn't know how to feel about him right this minute. What kind of a rookie error was that? He knew better. His only task had been to keep eyes on one person.

How had he lost Father Matthews?

Well, she would soon find out.

"He's with me," she said to the officer manning the perimeter, holding two sterile suits in one hand and flashing her badge with the other. She tossed one suit over to Smitty while she filled out the crime scene log. "Dress up, Smitty."

Bodies covered in their paper suits, they headed into the multi-tenant residence.

"What's her name?" Kate asked as she found Fuller. Another young woman, a brunette this time, lay on the bed, a bright red rosary wrapped around her praying hands. She wore an oversized Christmas themed nightgown.

"Mariana Gomez Alvarez. Talk to me, Murphy," Fuller said.

"Sir, this is Smitty, he had eyes on Matthews."

"What is it I heard? You lost him?"

Smitty brought his gloved hand to his mask-covered face,

as though he was going to scratch his cheek but obviously couldn't. "I'm sorry, sir. I lost him for about thirty minutes."

"Didn't you stalk our suspect with a partner? Where he is?"

"He got called off. It was just me."

"We'll deal with that and the *why* later. But *when* did you lose him exactly?"

"Between about one thirty and two o'clock this afternoon."

Kate and Fuller turned to look at the medical examiner who was hunched over their latest victim. "What do you say, Doc?" Kate asked. "Could the murder have occurred between one thirty and two?"

"Body temperature is 94F, so yes. Most plausible."

"And where was Matthews when you lost sight of him?" Fuller asked.

"At the community fundraiser, a block away."

"And where is he now?" Kate asked Smitty.

"The event was winding down. Tough to say, but Benz took over from me. He's watching him now."

"Sure hope he's gonna do a better job at it," Fuller said, a deep line clearly visible between his brows.

"We've got his proximity and unknown whereabouts during the murder. We've got the easy access to the rosaries, donated clothes at church, no alibis for the first two murders, easy access to the holy oils. Do we have an oily substance on the forehead?" she asked.

"That's affirmative," Dr. Cooper said.

"Anything oily on the hands?" Kate asked.

"Negative."

"Profiler's description could match," Kate said.

Fuller cleared his throat. "We've got probable cause. Go get him, Murphy, and if he doesn't want to come voluntarily, arrest him."

"And me?" Smitty asked.

"You fucked up. Expect consequences," Fuller snapped.

"Now?"

"Get out of here!"

~

ROSEBUD MATCHED Kate's broad strides as they marched down the aisle of the cathedral, ignoring the parishioners peppered on various seats, some kneeling, some seated.

Although Kate's mind was on the impending arrest, she couldn't help but be amazed at the grandeur of the place. The roof arched so high up above them, intricate carvings and pillars surrounded them, colorful stained-glass windows let in daylight several stories above.

They found their suspect in the sacristy, donning his robe for what had to be an upcoming ceremony. One he'd most definitely miss now.

"Father Matthews," Kate said, making him turn toward her, Rosebud, and the two uniformed officers who accompanied them in.

"Detectives, I don't have much time to talk right now. I've got a mass to get ready for."

"I'm afraid that's no longer the case. You are a suspect in a homicide investigation, so we need you to come down to the station to provide a statement. Now."

He lifted his chin and scoffed at Kate. "You can't make me."

Kate beamed at the cocky priest. "I'm afraid I can. Father Gabriel Matthews, you're under arrest for the murder of Mariana Gomez Alvarez."

The uniformed officers proceeded to handcuff and search him.

"But—"

"Officers, could you please convey the father to the district. We will meet you there."

"I've got mass!"

"Your parishioners will have to miss it. Justice can't wait."

His icy blue stare met her glance. "I want to call a lawyer. I won't say a word until then."

"Fine by me!" Kate said as she and her coworkers followed their suspect out of the sacristy.

CHAPTER SIXTY

SINCE FATHER MATTHEWS' legal representation hadn't arrived yet—and had an ETA of about five hours—Kate and Rosebud agreed to part ways and get more ammunition for the upcoming interview. The clock had begun ticking and they had to finish building their case. They had to collect more evidence.

Kate had never typed so fast. She filled out line after line of the affidavit describing her training and experience and listing the case's facts and how they related to her basis for probable cause to get a search warrant for Father Matthews.

Two hours later, she ran out of her meeting with the judge and DA, a signed warrant in hand. The judge had agreed with Kate's recommendation. Perhaps he, too, was getting desperate for some relief in a case that had kept Bostonians scared for weeks.

Rosebud took that warrant and headed to search the father's apartment with a few uniformed officers while Kate tracked down Detective Wang who was still interviewing Amanda McCutcheon.

Instead of interrupting them—Kate knew too well how unsettling those interruptions were—she walked into the small room that overlooked theirs.

Wang sat next to Amanda instead of across the table from her. Both wore stern expressions. Amanda's swollen eyes and pale face hinted at some recent tears.

Kate pressed the button to overhear their conversation.

"So, you don't remember who, but you think someone came into your apartment to drug you and then possibly kill you?"

"Yeah."

Wang looked at her notepad. "And that Danny guy from downstairs saw the man in question."

"Yes, he found me passed out in my apartment. He said he saw a man leave. Someone he'd never seen before."

"And you don't remember passing out or having a visitor over?"

"No."

Kate's hopes escalated faster than a geyser sprouting his powerful burst. *She was drugged, like the other victims.* Kate eyed Amanda up and down again. While she wasn't blonde, their latest victim hadn't been either. She was a young, practicing Catholic. Her virginity (and that of the third victim) were unknowns, though.

"Forgive me for asking such a blunt question, but…"

Kate leaned forward, hoping her fellow detective would ask what she herself was thinking.

"What?" Amanda asked, her upper lip quivering, her eyes overflowing with fear.

"Are you still a virgin?"

"What?" Amanda's back straightened.

"I'm sorry, Amanda. I'm only asking because we believe the killer targets women who are *sexually active*, let's say."

"No! Never!"

Kate shook her head and decided to walk into the interview room. There was no harm interrupting them now.

She knocked and immediately let herself in.

"Wang?" Kate traded a nod with her partner and sat on the vacant chair across from them both.

"All yours," Wang said, getting up from her chair.

"Your neighbor saw him?"

"Yes, that's what he told me."

"Let's get him in here, then. Show him photos."

Amanda shook her head. "I'm afraid that's impossible."

"Why's that?" Kate asked.

"He's out of town."

"Where?"

"Vegas, I think."

"Thanks, Amanda." Kate turned to Wang. "We need to find that Danny guy ASAP. Our clock is ticking with the main suspect. Your number one priority is tracking him down. Talk to the Vegas police. Time is of the essence! Do we have his full name?"

Wang shook her head, so Kate faced Amanda once more.

"Big Danny is what I call him. I don't actually know his last name. Isn't that weird? I've lived in the same building for over two years. I've known him since day one. He offered to help me move my furniture in. Something Irish sounding. O'Neill maybe? Or O'Leary? I don't know. He lives in the same building as me. He's a paramedic. All around good guy."

"Do you have his phone number?" Kate asked, hopefully they could track him down that way.

"No. I've never called him."

"Email?" Wang asked.

Amanda shook her head. "He lives just below me. We just knock on each other's door if we need to speak. He heard me yelling and then a loud crashing sound, that's why he came up, and that's when he saw that man who claimed to be a friend from church."

"A friend from church?" Kate repeated, getting to her feet. She was more and more convinced that they had something real on Father Matthews.

"Wang, we'll get the landlord to give us Danny's full name." Turning to Amanda, she continued. "Please repeat the exact details of what you remember, either directly or from what your friend Big Danny said, and start with the date."

"Okay," she finished swallowing, all the while nodding. "It happened last Wednesday. He spent the night with me—not in that way!" she said, as though anticipating another question by the detectives. "He was keeping an eye on me because I was throwing up when he found me."

"Okay. Do you remember eating or drinking something specific that would have caused you to throw up? Either quantity or specific things?"

She shook her head. "I honestly do not recall eating or drinking, but when I got up the following morning, I looked into my garbage can… to … fill in some of the blanks, I guess."

"And?" Wang asked.

"A bag of salt and vinegar chips and an empty bottle of wine."

Kate opened up her pad. "Just that?"

"I'd recently emptied my garbage."

"Just the one bottle?"

"Yes, and it wasn't a full bottle because it had been open for a few days. I think only half the bottle remained last time I drank—or remember drinking from it."

"Okay, it's not the best combination of flavors, but that's not a reason for anyone to pass out drunk and throw up. Forgive me for what I'm about to say, but any chance some of your vomit hasn't been cleaned up?"

"Gross!"

"I mean, did you wipe it down with a towel that's now sitting in a washing machine or something? We could try to analyze it. To identify the substance you ingested."

"No. I… Big Danny cleaned up after me. I don't know what he did." Amanda reached toward the crucifix that hung around her neck.

Fidgeting. Kate had seen her do that before.

"There's something else you're not telling me," Kate said.

Amanda swallowed hard, the movement of her throat betraying her. *What is she hiding?*

Putting two and two together, Kate voiced her theory. "Amanda, did you by any chance smoke, inject, eat, or drink anything not approved by our legal system?"

Her eyes widened.

Bullseye.

"What if I did?" Amanda said, sheepishly looking at the table instead of meeting Kate's glance.

"Listen. I don't want to pin you for possession if you still have any. But we need to know what you took so we could determine whether or not it would have made you pass out on your own. Maybe that friend from church was just a friend. Our job is to find the real killer. It's also to ensure we don't pin that crime on the wrong person and have him rot in jail while the real killer is on the loose. Do you understand?"

Amanda nodded in silence.

"Do you have more of whatever you took?"

"No, I'm afraid not."

"What was it?"

"Edibles. My friend told me they'd make me forget about Lori for a while. I'm not sure if they also made me forget my entire evening."

"Does this friend have a name?"

CHAPTER SIXTY-ONE

DETECTIVE ROSEBUD RETURNED to the precinct just as Father Matthew's church-assigned legal representation arrived, a man who appeared to be in his seventies. His gray hair matched his suit. He walked into the interview room where the father sat.

"Give me some good news," Murphy said as Rosebud joined her just outside the interview room.

"I'm afraid his home was a dud," Rosebud said. "Austerity has officially been redefined for me. Absolutely nothing in there. A bed, a few canned goods, a crucifix, and a wobbly kitchen set for two. No signs of drugs. No handmade rosaries."

"Could be stashing those elsewhere. We still have a handful of rosaries and a small container of oil from his pants pockets when we picked him up," Murphy said, holding photos of the evidence they'd collected, bagged, and already dropped off at the lab.

Rosebud lifted his glasses up on his nose. "Did you make any progress?"

"Wang's following another tip. Amanda may have been targeted. Her neighbor found her passed out with a 'man from church,'" Murphy said with air quotes. "She's trying to track that neighbor down. If we can get his statement. If we can show him photos and get him to point to Father Matthews being at her house—"

"Security camera? Was that before we had surveillance on her?"

"The evening before. Wang should have already tracked down the landlord by now. She'll also look for security footage around the area."

Through the small window in the interview room door, they watched the defense attorney approach the door. "We're up," Murphy said.

Fuller arrived just as they were about to enter the interview room.

"I'll be listening in with the prosecutor," Fuller said, holding open the door to the overseeing room. "He's going to be here any minute. Any leads they give, I'll dispatch to follow up on. You guys nail him now."

"CAN you tell us where you were between one thirty and two o'clock this afternoon?" Murphy asked.

The attorney and the father exchanged a nod before the father spoke. "I went to see a parishioner in the privacy of his apartment."

"Which parishioner. What's the address of the apartment?"

The father once again looked at his lawyer who nodded.

"Mr. Patterson. I don't know the exact address, but the apartment was in the tall building right next to where the fundraiser was held this afternoon."

"What's the apartment number?"

"I believe it was 6A, or maybe it was 6B. His name is probably on a lease somewhere."

"Why did you go see him? How did you get to his apartment if you aren't certain which it was?" Murphy prompted.

"I accompanied his wife. She wanted me to anoint him. Not that it's any of your business, but he hasn't been able to attend mass for several weeks now. And his wife feared for the worst. He'd been told he had three weeks to live. That was six months ago."

Rosebud stayed silent, admiring the father's demeanor. He seemed poised. Perhaps too poised. Was he just overly cocky?

"It's easy enough for us to send officers to check on that."

"Please do. I have nothing to hide."

"Well, you wanted to hide and not speak until your legal representation got here—"

"Detectives," the gray-haired lawyer said. "My client was well within his rights to remain silent. He told me you Mirandized him already."

"Can you explain why you had these items on your person this afternoon?" Murphy asked, putting two photos on the table between them: the rosaries and the small vial of oil.

The lawyer once again exchanged a nod with his client.

"I bought those at the fundraiser this afternoon. I wanted to hand them to a few homeless people I see in our neighborhood sometimes."

"We'll see if the DNA on them tells a different story. What about the oil?"

"Don't you people recall any of the conversations you have with innocent people who help you? This is the holy oil of the sick."

"Why did you have that oil with you?"

The father clenched his fist. His nostrils widened. "I'm a priest! This oil is used to anoint the sick! Exactly what I did this afternoon with Mr. Patterson! Don't you listen to what people say?"

"Didn't you yourself state to us that the holy oils are kept in some recess near the baptismal font?" Murphy asked, snark oozing out of her like pus from an infected wound.

"You illiterate, agnostic idio—"

"Father!" The lawyer slammed his hand on the table. "Don't say a word more!" Turning to the detectives, in a soft voice, he overarticulated every syllable as he answered for his client. "I believe that Father Matthews meant to say that, he, as an ordained priest, is allowed to carry a small sample of the holy oil with him, so he can provide the Last Rites, if needed."

Murphy turned to Rosebud, and he nodded. He should have thought about it. Sure, Murphy had no idea, but he knew that. He'd just forgotten. Sleep deprivation probably had something to do with that.

But they still had the rosaries.

"I'll go and follow up with the lab," Rosebud said as he got up.

ROSEBUD POKED his head into the room where Fuller and the prosecutor stood. A light creaking made them both turn toward him.

"Not looking so good," Fuller said, shaking his head. "Better hope the lab finds the victim's DNA on those rosaries. Because the probable cause we had is quickly evaporating."

"The Patterson story?" Rosebud asked.

"I dispatched officers and they can't get anyone to answer the door at either 6A or 6B. We're following up with the landlord and 911 dispatch. If the father's not lying, then Patterson could have been taken out by ambulance."

"Murphy said something about Wang trying to track down a man who may be able to prove Matthews was at Amanda McCutcheon's house earlier this week."

"Well, she'd better act quickly on that," said the prosecutor. "We're running out of time."

CHAPTER SIXTY-TWO

HER GUT HAD BEEN WRONG.

Kate stewed in silence as she watched Rosebud address Father Matthews. "You're in the clear. Sorry about the confusion, Father. Hope you won't hold it against us. We were just following our leads, trying our best to catch our killer."

"I appreciate your working hard to catch this evil, evil man. But I can assure you that I am not *him*. A man of faith doesn't kill in the name of God!"

Kate was nothing short of flabbergasted. Had he really said that?

"I'll drive you back to the cathedral, Father," Rosebud said, sending an evil eye toward Kate.

She clenched her fist and exhaled loudly. Rosebud knew her too well. But she had managed to keep her mouth shut, to *not* tell the father that most religions, Christianity included, had collectively been responsible for countless deaths since the beginning of mankind.

As Kate watched them walk away, she racked her brain. Where had they gone wrong? If not Father Matthews? Then who?

The security footage in the Pattersons' apartment building, and Mr. Patterson's admittance to the hospital, had given him a bulletproof alibi.

But they still had a few leads out there… The mysterious Danny neighbor. Still unaccounted for, but they had his full name, and confirmation that he was *not* in Vegas. Or at least not checked in under his name at any hotel in the city.

And they still had that anonymous tip from California. Those New Bedford detectives would hopefully share some useful tidbits with Chainey.

CHAPTER SIXTY-THREE

Monday, July 2nd, 2018

FATHER COFFEDY PACED the sacristy as he continued rehearsing the words of his upcoming sermon.

He knew the crowd wasn't going to be large—today was a weekday after all—but that didn't mean his most fervent parishioners didn't deserve an inspiring message from him.

In a world where fake news, violence, and crime seemed to matter more than caring about each other, he owed it to those who came to pray with him. He took solace in the fact that the kindness of their communal words and prayers could make a difference.

He'd been told his well-chosen turns of phrases could help some see hope through dark times. His faith—and the faith of his parishioners—could positively affect the world, of that, he had no doubt. When even Father Matthews had been erroneously arrested for the murder of a young woman in the community, there was no clearer sign that the world was in clear need of help. Of *His* help, through the comforting words of his well-rehearsed sermon.

Confident his message would come out right, he moved toward his recently dry-cleaned alb hanging on the hook in front of him. He spotted the tag still stapled to the hem and pulled it off before slipping the garment over his head.

Uncertain whether his stole had also been to the dry-cleaner, he proceeded to inspect it, not wanting to look unprofessional with something as trivial as a tag sticking to his precious vestment. But what he found surprised him.

He looked around the sacristy as his mind wondered about what the item was, but also what it did.

Feeling as though it could be important, he headed down the hall to the admin office, which was empty at this time of day. But fumbling around through the items that covered the desk, he found what he was looking for: one of the detectives' business card.

He called her number from the desk phone. It rang once, twice, three times.

"Detective Murphy," she said.

"Detective, this is Father Coffedy, from St. Alban's."

"What can I do for you, Father?"

"Well, this may be nothing, but…"

"Go ahead."

"While donning my stole this morning, I noticed something unusual."

"I'm sorry. Your what?"

"My stole." A long pause followed making Father Coffedy shake his head at the lack of education in the world these days. Shouldn't detectives be more knowledgeable than that? Then again, she hadn't struck him to be much of a Christian when they'd met.

"You do know what that is, don't you?" he said in a tone he hoped was understanding but he'd heard it for what it had been: a little condescending.

She cleared her throat on the other end of the line before speaking. "Can't say that I'm familiar with the term. Is that what you call your robe?"

"No. My *robe* is called an *alb*. The *stole* is the colorful piece of fabric I wear over my alb, around my neck."

"Ah! Thanks for clarifying those terms for me."

"I noticed a little something stuck to my stole."

"Could you please describe it for me?"

"It's small and hard. Not even half an inch square. It's flat and dark gray—"

"Do you still have it?"

"Yes, I'm holding it in my hand right now."

"Thanks so much you for reporting this. Are you at St. Alban's?"

"Yes, I'm getting ready for mass."

"I'm coming to you. I need to pick it up right away."

CHAPTER SIXTY-FOUR

HE BOUGHT a copy of the Boston Globe: a souvenir for his collection. He'd heard parishioners mention something about the mayor, once again, holding a press conference. Not having a television or computer at home limited his options, but the written word was always better anyways. He'd be able to add clippings to his collection. His work was beginning to be acknowledged. All of Boston and Massachusetts would soon know of his good deeds.

But once he began reading his coverage, sitting at his kitchen table, he nearly lost it.

"'A mad killer is targeting innocent women.' What's wrong with them? Don't they *get* it? I *helped* those whores. If only their souls could sing from Heaven and tell the world they've been freed."

He tossed the paper aside, fury making his breathing ragged, then walked over to his altar and knelt down. Closing his eyes, he forced himself to calm down. He began to pray to the All Mighty, for he needed reassurance. He needed His wisdom.

"Dear Lord, give me the strength to continue the holy mission you've assigned to me. Grant me the determination and clarity of mind to choose the right people to save. Bless me with Your wisdom, Your knowledge, and Your guidance, for I am but a servant to You. Thank You, my Lord. Amen."

With his right hand, he crossed himself then got up again,

returning to the kitchen and fetching the scattered pages of the newspaper that littered the floor.

"She doesn't get it, but I'll teach her. I'll show her my process."

The detective had left her card at St. Alban's church. He could easily call her to explain it all, but what fun would there be in that? Plus it would put an end to his role as a savior of lost souls.

No, he had a much better idea.

Not only would he make her understand, he'd prove it to her.

After rummaging through a drawer to find his scissors, he cut away the picture of Detective Murphy and pinned it on his board, next to the photo of his sister, the article about Lori's Death, and that of Jessica's. The detective's face was half hidden behind her raised hands, but a house number was clearly visible in the background. He memorized it. Google could probably tell him where she lived.

Grabbing a handful of vials filled with his cleansing solution, a pair of disposable gloves, and a disposable surgeon's cap, he tossed the items in his pants pocket and headed to church. He had some research to do to find the detective. But he was confident his Lord's guidance would continue to bless him.

He would teach the detective a lesson she wouldn't live to forget.

CHAPTER SIXTY-FIVE

"SO WE KNOW how the killer has been acquiring his information," Kate said, tossing the evidence bag that contained the small bug onto Fuller's desk. "We thought only priests or close friends would have it, but now this little piece of plastic has just widened our suspect pool. Again. Anyone could have walked up to Father Coffedy and stuck this onto him. No fancy pick-pocketing skills required. I've attended mass. Even I could have stuck this little guy onto him. Not sure who would know where to buy such things, though. Even less so how to operate it and monitor the conversations."

"Fuck, guys!" said Fuller. "That's not the sort of news I want to hear. We need leads, suspects… Hell, we need to arrest the right killer already. What's the distance on this?" He raised his chin toward the device sitting on his desk.

"I showed it to an expert," Kate said. "Pretty good range as long as there's no steel or concrete in the way. Anywhere within the church would be fine."

"So any parishioner sitting on a bench, with earbuds could have been listening in?"

"Yep," Rosebud said. "Other people would have assumed they were listening to music. None the wiser."

Fuller slammed his hands on his desk and got up. "That's *not* what I want to hear from you guys!"

Kate took a step back but kept her shoulders straight. "We're following everything we've got, sir."

Fuller cracked his neck, then opened his left desk drawer to pull out an orange pill container. He tossed a couple of white tablets into his hand, then brought them to his mouth, not bothering to wash them down with any liquid. Then he dropped his entire weight back onto his chair. "What else have you got?"

Kate swallowed before speaking, knowing her words weren't going to please him more. "We're tracking down a tipster from out-of-state."

"Where?"

"California, according to the phone number."

"That ain't next door. What useful titbit could he have possibly provided?"

"*She* gave us a strangely precise detail about another case, so we're looking into it, but it's outside of our jurisdiction. New Bedford. Chainey's on it."

"What else?"

"Wang's still trying to track down Amanda's neighbor and get the sketch artist to draw the man he saw at her apartment."

"Good. I really like the sound of that one. What else?"

Kate looked at Rosebud who raised his shoulders.

"That's about it."

Fuller framed his head with his forefingers. "So did we cut off all possible leaks? Are we certain the confessions are no longer being eavesdropped on?"

"I spoke with the other two fathers and requested they check their vestments for bugs, I showed it to them."

"Did they have anything on theirs?"

"No. But their clothes had just come back from the dry-cleaners."

"That's convenient. Any chance they could all use the same dry-cleaner? Or any chance the dry cleaner for the one priest had something to do with it?"

Rosebud chimed in after shrugging and frowning. "Worth a shot. Maybe one of the employees could be involved. I'll look into that."

"Possible," Kate said. "Anyways, I told the priests to keep an eye on their clothes and contact us the minute they spot anything."

"Confessionals?" Fuller asked.

"I had them all inspected weeks ago," Kate said. "We can do it again, though."

"Do it!" barked Fuller. "And fucking find that killer before he hits again."

CHAPTER SIXTY-SIX

CHAINEY SAT on the edge of one of the tables, a thick manila file in his hands and a stoic expression on his face.

"What you got?" Kate asked before turning to see Rosebud stuffing his face with yet another chocolate muffin. "Seriously? Again?"

But Chainey began speaking, so she returned her attention to him.

"I got a copy of their case file. Well, the important bits."

"And?" Rosebud asked in between bites.

"There were quite a few young men suspected at one point or another, but all of them were crossed off the list. They still don't have a single good lead."

"Anyone connected to our current cases?"

"No. Well, Father *Miller* led the funeral service, but that's not relevant. At least I don't think so."

"And how can you say that for certain?" Kate asked, slightly annoyed that her gut had been wrong. She could have sworn something fishy was going on with their local churches. Well, something fishy that didn't involve molestation. *Those* beans had long been spilled and exposed.

"Miller's obviously not twenty-six years old. More like seventy-six or eighty-six. Plus, I checked, and he had an alibi for the day Thompson died. He was hospitalized. Confirmed with the hospital records. The man had a minor heart attack.

He left the hospital after Thompson died. He just did the service."

"Can we not catch a break?" Kate asked before exhaling loudly.

"There is one thing I found out."

"Please let it be good. Fuller's going to crucify me if we don't bring him something. Anything—"

"Crucify you?" Rosebud interjected between mouthfuls. "I think this case has been messing with your brain."

"Well, it's been weeks. Three lives have been lost, and we still have nothing to show. Not a fucking lead worth anything."

"Hold on, Murphy. We may have one. Guess what Thompson did for a living?"

"No time for games, Chainey."

"Home-school teacher."

"And?" Kate's desire to grab Chainey by the collar and give him a little shake was growing by the second. *Doesn't he get the urgency of the situation?*

"Care to venture a guess as to who he taught?" Chainey asked.

Kate could feel her face get hotter as she did her best to hold back her boiling anger. "Shit or get off the pot, Chainey!"

"Indulge me. For just one little guess." Chainey flashed his pearly whites at her and waggled his bushy eyebrows, forcing a faint smile to grow on Kate's lips, even though she fought it with all of her might.

She had to relax.

Getting upset at her colleague wasn't going to help her solve the case any faster. Plus, she was seriously exhausted. They were most probably feeling the same way.

Kate shook her head, giving up on getting Chainey to get serious. "Father Matthews?"

"You really have something against that guy, don't you?" Rosebud said as he crumpled his brown paper bag and tossed it toward the garbage can, missing his target by a solid foot.

"Who then?" Kate asked, choosing to silence the one-liner she wanted to throw at Rosebud and his serious lack of athletic skills. How had he gotten through police academy? Or did all of his health and fitness evaporate after he became a detective?

"Two young twins named Anderson and Penelope Carson."

Kate's head turned back toward Chainey. "Anderson as in Candidate Anderson?"

"The one and only."

Kate couldn't have gotten up faster if a firecracker had been lit under her ass. *Was this it?* "Did Anderson have an alibi on the day of Thompson's death?"

"Yep. Officially, he was never a suspect. No motive they could think of. He hadn't been in contact with his teacher for several years. He was questioned by the detectives and answered that"—he flipped open the file to pull from it—"he'd left home, gotten himself an apartment, and then entered seminary after their home-schooling ended. That was the last time he'd seen Mr. Thompson."

"Did they even ask him where he was the day Thompson was killed?"

"They did. They confirmed it, too. He was here in Boston, helping out with mass. Some other priest confirmed it. And no, it wasn't Father Matthews. It's not a conspiracy."

Kate sat on the edge of the table, making it lift from the other side. "Fuck!" Kate brought her palm to her forehead, pushing it up toward her hairline as though the mere motion could bring forth a stroke of genius. But nothing.

"What was the cause of death? Strangulation?" Kate asked.

"Nope. Died of a heart attack caused by some sort of poison." Chainey pulled out a photo of an old, bald man with a belly rounder than the Pillsbury Doughboy. He was curled up on the floor, laying in a pile of his own vomit.

"Do you have the toxicology report?" Kate asked, finally hopeful that something useful could come out of this.

Chainey nodded and flipped through pages in his file. "Here it is."

"Great! Let's redo our toxicology requests for all victims and include this specific blend of chemicals. With any luck, this will match our current cases, and we'll finally have results."

"That's still going to take several days. At least," Rosebud said.

"Don't I fucking know it. But what else can we do?" Kate looked at Rosebud and Chainey, both looked as exhausted as she was herself. "Did they determine how the poison was ingested?"

"They found a bottle of Californian red wine that tested positive for the same chemicals found in his body."

"Wine… That could be how our killer has been drugging our victims as well," Kate had begun pacing the floor without realizing it.

"Were there prints on Thompson's bottle?"

"Just his."

Kate continued walking the floor, her head focusing on the industrial carpet as she thought aloud. "He could have roofied their drinks, they passed out, he dragged them to their bedrooms…"

"But who's *he*? Have we eliminated women for certain now?" Chainey asked.

"Fuck if I know who our killer is," she said. "I used to think it was Matthews. But now it looks like Anderson Carson. But then again, we've got nothing on him right now. Nothing but a weak link—"

"But he's also twenty-six years old," Chainey interjected.

"Hate to break it to you," Rosebud told Chainey, "but the fact that his age matches an anonymous tip from California and that he was home-schooled by a guy who got murdered isn't enough for a warrant. You'd have to be running a lucky streak to get a judge to approve one on so little. Especially when he has an alibi for Thompson's murder and for some of the latest ones. Plus his arm's in a cast, making lifting and carrying a person upstairs nearly impossible—"

"Then again, we can't assume the killer acted alone or that the victim hadn't walked herself to her final location," Kate said. "Plus there's the bug… Anderson had easy access—"

"You said it yourself when we spoke to Fuller. Anyone could have placed it on Coffedy's robe—"

"It's a robe, right? Coffedy lectured me when I called it that!"

"What did he call it?"

"An alb or something—"

"Guys! Enough!" Chainey said, putting an abrupt end to their tangent.

"Anyways," Kate said, grateful that Chainey had stopped her. She was in no mental state to hold a straight-up conversation. "We don't have enough right now. But let's keep digging. I'll look into Anderson. Rosebud, you look into his sister. Maybe she's involved, somehow. Chainey, did the New Bedford detectives mention her?"

He shrugged. "Nope, but I didn't ask either. There might be something in this file here."

"Okay, fill me in on what else you learned about Thompson. One of the details has to mean something. We just have to find it."

CHAPTER SIXTY-SEVEN

DIGGING into Mr. Thompson's and Candidate Anderson's past turned into a task much more difficult and intriguing than Kate had anticipated. Together with Chainey, she'd found the candidate's driver's license, insurance papers for a blue Honda Civic, and a birth certificate, which led them to the discovery of the twin sister's birth *and death* certificates.

"There goes the theory she could have been involved," Kate said as the document appeared on the screen, proving that she was already dead well before Thompson got killed, let alone the current murders.

Just over a year ago, Kate realized.

If only she could find something. Anything of substance that could connect it all. At least enough to convince a judge to issue a search warrant so they could find out more.

A few phone calls and emails later, Kate started reading newly acquired legal documents pertaining to both Anderson and his sister, Penelope. The siblings had been emancipated at the age of sixteen. That little tidbit, as uncommon as it was in Massachusetts, led her down the rabbit hole she was now in. The kids had to have had really strong reasons to have been granted such a request.

So, there she was, following the parents' trails. She'd phoned in a request to get travel information from Customs. See if she could find out where they were now. Their latest departure date from the US had been over three years ago.

Best information pointed to them having entered Peru at that time.

Customs had no other information for her.

So she got on Google next, hopeful that some information about the parents and their current location could be found somewhere. She'd discovered a religious sect she'd never heard of: Explorers of Christ. According to their websites, their goal was to bring the Christian faith to isolated communities throughout the world. Photos of both the mother and father were displayed on the website, as though revered as semi-gods themselves. The spacing between the mother's eyes and her dimples made it obvious she was related to Anderson. The twin daughter had inherited the mother's blonde hair.

Their hyped-up bios listed them as having fought malaria, yellow fever, and other disabling diseases before successfully converting isolated villages that most would have called "savages" back in the explorers' days. A map showed little dots of settlements they'd converted all over Asia and Central and South America. Hovering over the colored circles provided Kate with additional information such as dialect spoken, number of people in the community, and date visited.

It was obvious spreading the Lord's word had been much more of a priority than raising their own children.

Mr. Thompson, the school teacher, had held that responsibility. But he was dead. The sister, too, was dead and the parents were God knows where trying to push their faith down the throats of people who didn't want that done to them. *But that's neither here nor there.*

It left Kate very little to go on. Why would Anderson kill his school teacher? What possible motive could he have had? That teacher was probably the closest thing to a parental figure he and his sister had had.

Unless Mr. Thompson had become too involved with the education of the children…

As suspicions of pedophilia crossed her mind, Kate realized she could have just stumbled into enough of a motive. But that thought was pulled out of thin air.

She had to find a way to prove whether or not it could have been the case.

Following Thompson's trail left her empty-handed. No

siblings, no parents, no children. The man had been an island, or so it seemed.

She didn't have much to go on, save for one tiny detail. The Andersons had owned one home until 2009, the year when the children received their emancipation.

Chances were that the address of that home would have been the address where the children lived and where Thompson had educated them.

"Look at what I found," Rosebud said, handing Kate a photocopy of a small clip from a newspaper as she was getting up from her desk.

A portrait of a blonde woman with a braid hanging over her shoulder appeared above a brief paragraph:

"Penelope died on June 1st, 2017. No funeral or service will be held but donations can be sent to the AFSP."

"What's AFSP?" Kate asked.

"American Foundation for Suicide Prevention. Isn't that the shortest obituary you've ever seen?"

Kate shrugged. "Can't say that I read them very often."

"Well, I do, and this one was written like someone was making a mockery of it."

"Or maybe they were embarrassed by the fact that she had committed suicide. Maybe she disfigured herself. Maybe they didn't want anyone to see her. Maybe they were ashamed of her suicide."

"But why pay for an obituary if they're ashamed? As far as I know, there's no legal obligation to do so in Massachusetts."

"Why don't you look into her death a bit more? See if anything suspicious comes up. Perhaps it wasn't a suicide. Maybe it was a murder after all. I'll head out to scope the neighborhood where they grew up. See if I can find people who knew the teacher way back when. Maybe they'll remember something about what happened in that home nine years ago. If I learn that some dodgy stuff was happening, that could point us to Anderson's motive. Then we'd need to figure out how he poisoned the man remotely." Kate shook her head. "I know it's a stretch."

"We've got nothing else. I'll keep digging into her past and man the phones. With a bit of luck, and a toxicology match…"

Kate walked out, letting Rosebud's words dangle in the air and inflate her hopes. They desperately needed a bit of luck.

CHAPTER SIXTY-EIGHT

THE THIRD DOOR on which Kate knocked proved the lucky one. After identifying herself and learning that the bearded man with the John Deere cap and cigarette dangling from his lips had lived at his current address since he was born, she couldn't help but get excited.

"This is probably going to sound strange, but do you recall two kids living next door to you, being homeschooled by a Mr. Thompson?"

"Heck yeah! Strange little thing they had going there, if you ask me."

"Mind if I come in and ask a few questions?"

The man shrugged as ashes dropped from his cigarette. "Sure. Don't got nothing better to do. TV's broken." He moved aside and let Kate in.

The older house reeked of tobacco and stale beer. Kate sent a quick text message to Rosebud to update him on her whereabouts and followed the man into his kitchen. A half-eaten pizza lay atop the table, house flies now having a go at it, which didn't seem to bother the man as he put his cigarette down into the ashtray and grabbed a slice.

"Have some, if you want," the man said, his mouth full.

"No thanks." She pulled her notepad out and clicked open her pen. "So you were living here back in 2009, right?"

"Yes, ma'am. Got this place from my parents when they died. I've been living here a long time. All my life."

"So, you said strange things were going on next door back then. Can you tell me a little more?"

"Heck, let me show you." He got up and grabbed what was left of his cigarette. Kate followed him to the back of his house where he used both hands to slide open a patio door. Its mechanism was in obvious need of lubrication—or perhaps replacement—Kate noted as she stepped over the crooked threshold groove to join the man outside.

"See that fence there?" he asked before inhaling from his cigarette.

"Yeah?"

"I had that put up because of the shit I saw."

"What kind of *shit*?"

"Well, it ain't my place to say… Especially since what happened to that poor girl."

"What happened to her?" Kate asked.

"You don't know? I don't mean no disrespect. But aren't you supposed to *detect* a little better than that? Are you really with the *poh-lice*?" he asked, stressing his last word.

Kate showed him her badge once more. "I know what happened to her. I'd just like to hear what you have to say about it."

"Oh. I get it." He inhaled the last of his cigarette then flicked the butt out on his yellowed grass. "She died, so I don't want to soil her reputation or nothing."

"Do you know how she died?"

"Heard she did herself in." The man's brows got crooked, then something sad—or perhaps disturbing—passed through his eyes. "Poor girl."

"Did you witness anything in that backyard that could have led her to that? Anything… inappropriate, let's say?"

"Inappropriate would be the bare minimum."

"Go on. Tell me what you saw."

"Well, that little Penelope sure grew up fast. I still remember her in her braids, wearing those pink dresses and playing with her dolls outside. She changed around the same time she forced everyone else to call her something different. I forget now. Silly nickname."

"Do you remember her brother?"

"Yeah. He was quiet. Most of the time he sat alone,

reading. The Bible of all things! But made sense with those missionaries for parents."

"Did you ever meet them?"

"A few times. Decades ago."

"What kind of people are they?"

"Mostly kept to themselves. Until she got pregnant out of nowhere. I remember how freaked out the mother had been. Not sure if the rumors I heard were true."

"What rumors?"

"Poor Mrs. Anderson was raped. Mr. Anderson wasn't the daddy of those twins."

"Really?" Kate made a note to double-check the birth records.

"Sure added with the way she treated those babies when they came out. I've seen loving mothers in my days. She was nothing like one. Then, all of sudden, this home-teacher gets here, and the missionaries leave. Never to return."

"Other than Mr. Thompson, did the children have any other adult supervision?"

"No, that man lived there alone with them after the parents left."

"So, what was the inappropriate behavior that made you want to build a fence?"

"First, it was just him drinking. Can't blame the man. He never had any adult friends coming over. I invited him over for beers once or twice, but he never accepted. But one nightly glass on the back deck soon turned to a whole bottle. But I'm not one to judge. Well, not on that."

"What did he do that had you judging him?"

"The really weird stuff began when li'l Penelope hit puberty. Or maybe shortly after. Come to think of it, maybe that's when the old teacher picked up on his drinking."

Kate's gut churned now, not just of hunger, but from the feeling that her pedophilia theory was dead on.

"Did he touch her?" Kate asked, bluntly.

The man's eyebrows went up and he scratched his beard. "Afraid t'was the other way around. If you know what I mean…"

"He abused the boy?"

"Heck no!" The man had lifted his hands as though he was

blocking himself from an impending attack. "I mean the poor teacher had his hands full with her."

Kate nearly dropped her pen. "What?"

"At first, I's about to call that number for reporting crimes against children, you know? Trying to get him away from them kids, but as I's scrolling through the phone book, I overheard sweet Penelope talk to the teacher. She was the one coming onto him. Hard. I mean, she was saying some real nasty shit. Lines taken straight from them *pornos* would be my guess. I can't imagine where else she would have heard those things. She was so sweet. Then suddenly…" He shook his head.

"How old was she?"

"I don't know. I wanna say her personality changed around the age of fifteen?"

"What kind of stuff would you see?"

"I stopped coming out here 'cause of that weird shit that was going on. Heck, that girl even came knocking on my door a few times, wearing almost nothing. Her tits looked like those of a grown woman. Barely contained in her tops." His hands made it clear the girl had been well endowed. "Never wore no bra either. Her skirts barely covered her ass."

"What did you do?"

"Fucking slammed the door on her is what I done. I ain't the type who touches a child! Told her to smarten up. Get her act together."

"Did she?"

"I don't know. She got quiet for a while. I saw her brother get on her case, too. That helped, I think. Lots of fighting between the two. Then I started seeing another boy come over. Closer to her own age, at least. But from the moans and screams that came from their house late at night, it was obvious the two were … quite close."

"When Mr. Thompson died, did the police interview you?"

"That old teacher died? When?"

"About nine months ago."

"Nope. I had no idea. But what do you mean if the police interviewed me? He didn't die of natural causes? Heart attack or something?"

"No." Kate left it at that, not wanting to mess up the other investigation. "Why would you think that?"

"Well, he was quite fat. And drank a fair bit. Those fancy cheese plates and meat platters he always brought out to snack on in the evenings."

"Do you think the teacher could have stolen money from the parents?"

"Don't think so. Spoke to him once or twice. Said the parents were wiring him money. A fair amount of money it sounded. Enough to cover those expensive snacks. And it's not like he was heading into town to party. He was with those kids all the time."

"When did you last see him?"

"Last time was the day the kids' emancipation got approved. He packed up and left right there and then. *Sayonara, señor*. Looked more than happy to leave, if you ask me."

Kate watched the pride in the man's eyes and decided not to correct his mix of Japanese with Spanish. "So that was about nine years ago," Kate said. "What happened to the kids after that day?"

"They went their separate ways. The boy wanted to become a priest, I think. They got their own apartments. She was as smart as fuck. Heck, both of them were smart. Real smart. Don't know if that smartness had come in through their genes or if that teacher was a hell of a good one, but those kids were sure smarter than they looked. I still remember the chemistry experiments they did in their backyards. They'd taken that volcano project to a whole new level. Destroyed half of their lawn that one summer. Then they focused on other things, I guess. The girl managed to make a shit load of money on the stock market during her last year here. That's how they managed to hire a lawyer to emancipate. Never saw either of them after that. Well, 'cept for her obituary. Shame they didn't hold a service. I'd have gone and paid my respects. Li'l Penelope was one sweet girl… until she hit puberty. May God help her troubled soul find peace."

~

IN THE PRIVACY of her car, Kate rang Rosebud but got his voicemail. "Rosebud, I'm heading back into town. I think we've got enough for a search warrant now. I think Anderson could have killed the teacher. His sister died, then Mr. Thompson was poisoned to death. Both kids were super smart, I just found out. He learned chemistry as a kid. Maybe enough to make poison, don't know. He could have held a grudge against the teacher. I think he could have blamed him for his sister's debauchery that led her to suicide." Her phone beeped but she ignored it just so she could finish her message to Rosebud. "Please get started on the paperwork for the warrant. I'm heading back now. Call me if you need more details."

The second she hung up, just as she started her engine, her phone rang.

"Murphy. Wang tracked Big Danny," Rosebud said. "The sketch artist worked remotely. I'm staring at Candidate Anderson."

"Fuck! We got him! I just left you a message. Get the paperwork going for the warrant, fill Fuller in, and arrange for a SWAT team. I'll be there as soon as I can."

For the first time in weeks, Kate smiled as an invigorating rush of adrenaline boomed through her body. Each heartbeat echoing in her head like a crowd cheering "Gotcha. Gotcha. Gotcha."

CHAPTER SIXTY-NINE

NO MATTER how many searches he ran in the church's database, he didn't find Kate Murphy. But Facebook proved a lot more useful. He found out who her partner was—out of marriage, unsurprisingly—then recognized that man for having seen him at one of the fundraisers a few weeks earlier. And his name linked him to his mother, an avid and devoted church member he quite liked.

Mrs. O'Brien was a good person. Well, he'd thought so until now.

As he added up the little details he'd overheard through his recordings of her confessions and mixed those with the facts he'd since uncovered, Marjorie O'Brien no longer seem like such a good Catholic.

She permitted two unmarried people to live in sin under her roof. To be fair, she had tried to get them to tie the knot—he remembered getting her a pamphlet for the church's premarital course—but she'd obviously failed. He knew better than to presume the two were saving themselves. He didn't know much about her son, Luke, except for what he'd overheard from her. But he recalled his cold behavior that day at the fundraiser. His name also didn't appear in their database, meaning that he hadn't signed the petition. He didn't care about his own community. His own neighborhood. His own brotherhood of man.

He remembered Marjorie mentioning that her son's

girlfriend had been previously married—to a horrible man she'd added, as though that was reason enough for her to get a divorce. Another sin to add to the long list they'd accumulated collectively as a "family" under one roof.

But even with technology and science on his side, he wasn't omniscient like Him. No doubt Detective Murphy had other sins to her name. And it was quite common for police officers to die at their own hands in their later years. As much as he despised her right now—for not understanding that he was his Lord's servant and not a feeble murderer as the press had erroneously labeled him—he could be the bigger man.

He could save her now before she'd eventually commit the ultimate sin on her own.

Like his sister had done. Like many police officers ended up doing.

He shook his head in an effort to ignore his deceased sister, but as though she was screaming his name out of purgatory, he could no longer ignore her cries. As scared and helpless as she sounded, her fate was no longer in his hands.

But he could help them. That family of sinners he could save.

As the bigger man that he was, he would show them the light. He'd bless them and let them see Heaven for themselves. They'd get their place by His side, as His children, freed of their sins.

The old printer spat out Mrs. O'Brien's address, as entered in the church's database. The house number matched the one he'd seen in the newspaper. The location was so convenient, too. A clear sign from God.

He checked that he still had his vials in his pocket, then he slipped a handful of rosaries into his cast. He headed to the donation bin next. Fumbling through the discarded clothes, he realized that three outfits weren't going to fit around his cast this time. One nightgown was easily concealed under the wrap that held his cast in place against his chest. But three outfits? And what would he use to cover the man's body?

He decided to skip the outfits this time. The Lord would understand. The ceremonious garb had been more for his earthly rituals than Him, he realized.

Just as he was about to leave, he thought about the man

once more. And the fact that he had three people to deal with. He'd never done a group cleansing before. Even with God on his side, he wouldn't magically grow more limbs to handle three sinners at once.

He headed to the church's maintenance closet to see if the janitor kept anything in there that could be useful. Perhaps some sort of rope.

But when he opened the door, he immediately spotted something much, much better: duct tape.

CHAPTER SEVENTY

"CAN'T BELIEVE this killer lives just a few blocks away from me!" Murphy said as she exited the car with both the arrest and search warrants in hand.

Rosebud glanced at the building where the suspect resided—a three-story structure made out of wood that hadn't received the care, paint, or attention it needed. The faded apartment doors were exposed to the elements behind the not-so-straight guardrails that ran the entire length of each floor.

Affordable rentals. Well, as affordable as Boston made them.

"Never know your neighbors, do you?" Rosebud said. "Hey, by the way, you still haven't invited me over for a drink."

"Not the time or place, Rosebud," Murphy said, looking toward a blue Honda parked across the street. "That's his car, right?"

"Yep. Probably home then. But wait, no. The man's got a broken arm. But it doesn't mean anything, unless it's a stick shift."

"We never followed up on his broken arm. He was probably faking it. Stupid of us."

"I saw his X-rays."

"On his phone. Could have been someone else's. Doesn't count. Anyways, we'll find out soon enough," Murphy said as she followed the SWAT team to the suspect's home.

Rosebud watched some of the men getting dispatched

around the back to cover all emergency exits. Even though detectives weren't allowed in until after SWAT cleared the place, the rush of excitement still flowed through his veins. Murphy had insisted on being near the building instead of waiting down the block as they normally did.

As Rosebud passed by the crime lab specialists and photographer who had also been dispatched, he spoke to them. "We'll call you in the instant SWAT clears the place."

Heads bobbed, so he ambled toward the building as he silently voiced a quick prayer for his colleagues, a habit he'd begun long ago and couldn't quit, afraid the one time he didn't do it would mark an unlucky day. Possibly someone's last. It dawned on him that maybe he was more superstitious than religious. But a prayer had never hurt anyone.

He had joined Murphy on the main floor by the time the SWAT leader pounded three loud bangs on the suspect's door two floors above them. "Boston Police! Open up!"

A loud crash echoed above and Rosebud knew the leader had forced the door open.

A few minutes later, when the all clear was given and SWAT officers started walking down the stairs, Rosebud sighed. While the thrill of potentially being the one to find and arrest the suspect was at times exhilarating, Rosebud preferred walking into a home without worrying about getting shot. Not that this particular suspect was likely to own a gun. They'd checked his file, and he hadn't used guns in his crimes. His modus operandi was more peaceful, albeit just as deadly.

The thought still made his skin crawl. How could a man of God behave in such way? What could have gone horribly wrong to twist his thoughts in such perverted ways? But his excursion down the rabbit hole of questions came to an end as the stream of SWAT officers ended and Murphy headed up. He followed.

Rosebud could hear his heartbeat in his head and feel his lungs still recovering from climbing the stairs as he watched Murphy go past the officer manning the door and enter Anderson's apartment.

Looking over the guardrail, Rosebud waved to the crime scene techs down below. They acknowledged his signal, so he ambled inside, taking in the somber home. The kitchen walls were bare, save for a cheap clock that ticked the passing seconds as though they were a punishment. Several nails stuck out from the patched-up paint—possibly from the previous tenants—and a sole crucifix hung from one of them.

The kitchen counter was a different story though. It overflowed with stuff, but not the cereal boxes, spaghetti container, or tea boxes he would have expected. No. Several unidentified bags of powders and tiny pebbles. It wasn't meth-lab quantity or paraphernalia but could easily explain the unknown drug in the vics' systems.

And there was that box of disposable gloves and another with surgeon's caps. Those explained the lack of DNA or fingerprints.

"We'll have to bag all of those and get the lab to identify the concoction he made," Murphy said, turning to look at Rosebud. "SWAT said we'll love the bedroom. I'll just have a quick peek in the bathroom. Why don't you get started in the bedroom?"

The door on the right was clearly the bathroom. A one-bedroom apartment was like hitting the jackpot when it came to easy evidence gathering.

He headed toward the left door from which shone a reddish glow but stopped in his tracks when he saw the origin of the flickering lights.

CHAPTER SEVENTY-ONE

"MOM, you won't believe what I just did," Luke said on the phone as he walked out of the store.

"I don't know, Son. Tell me?"

"I have to keep it a surprise for now, but you're going to be very proud of me."

"Did you get a promotion?"

"No, much, much better than that. Although I wouldn't turn down a raise, considering how much I just spent."

"Did you get a new car?"

"No, and no more guesses! You'll find out in due course, but I just wanted to call and thank you for pushing me in the right direction."

"Luke O'Brien, you can't just tease your poor old mom like that."

"Sorry, but I promise it's for a good cause."

"Okay then. I made something special for dinner tonight. I think you'll like it."

"What is it?" Luke asked.

"My turn to keep secrets from you." The doorbell echoed on her end. "Someone's at the door, but I haven't made it in well over a decade. Give me a second."

Luke waited, listening to the faint noise of the front lock opening, half-dreading that reporters had once again reappeared. They hadn't been by in a few days. Then he overheard his mother and her guest. "Candidate Anderson! What a surprise!"

Suddenly his mom's voice got louder, "See you soon, Luke. Gotta go."

"Bye, Mom," Luke said.

He checked the time on his watch and decided he had time to check in with Kate. He wouldn't spoil his big surprise on the phone, but he couldn't wait for her to come home tonight.

CHAPTER SEVENTY-TWO

HE CLIMBED the front steps of the brick building and rang the doorbell, waiting quietly in front of the brightly colored door. Birds chirped around him. The sun shone brightly. A mother strolled down the sidewalk, pushing a stroller.

Luck is on my side today, he thought, careful to keep his roll of duct tape behind his back.

"Candidate Anderson! What a surprise!" Mrs. O'Brien said, making him turn back to face the door.

"Hello, Mrs. O'Brien. How are you?"

She held a phone in her hand. "See you soon, Luke. Gotta go," she said into the receiver before hanging up. "To what do I owe the pleasure?"

"You didn't have to cut your call short on my behalf—"

"No, no. It was just my son. What can I do for you?"

He smiled at her, his most genuine facade. "I was just following up on the petition you signed a few weeks ago. Mind if I come in?"

She cleared the doorway, and, with a swing of her hand, let him into her home. "Please do. I'll make us coffee."

"Sounds great." He watched her close and lock the door.

"Do you mind taking off your shoes, please?" she asked with a large smile before continuing her way into another part of her home.

Her request took him a bit by surprise, but he needed to keep her happy for a few more minutes, so he obeyed. He took off his shoes, nearly exposing his tape and spilling the items he held in his cast in the process. He couldn't wait to take his prop off and get on with his program.

But everything was good. It had been so easy to be invited into her home. Now he wondered how easily she'd recognize her own sins and the sins of those she kept under her roof.

"What a delightful aroma," he said.

"That reminds me. I need to take my bird out of the oven, so it doesn't dry out!"

CHAPTER SEVENTY-THREE

WITH HIS GLOVED HAND, Rosebud flicked the light switch, but nothing happened.

"It doesn't work," a straggling member of SWAT said. "Weird fucking shit, though. Have fun!"

He walked out, leaving Rosebud alone in the room for now. In the semi-darkness, he could make out a single bed—neatly made—pushed against the wall. The standard-size room seemed immense without proper furniture. He pulled his flashlight out and turned it on, scanning the room. There wasn't even a window in here. *Isn't that against code?*

He confirmed it was just the bed, nothing underneath it. Nothing on the wall except one image of the Virgin Mary taped above the head of the bed. Well, nothing else except the large, homemade shrine that had surprised him a minute earlier.

Expecting it to hold the sick obsession of the person they were here to arrest, Rosebud approached the altar. He'd seen a few of those over the years. Enough to know that some folks were messed up. Really messed up.

On top of a small table that would normally be used in a living room as a side table, a handful of tall votive candles had been lit, the red holders coloring their light, their wax altering the scent of the room. Resting against the base of the votive and leaning against the wall was a cheap corkboard decorated with a sick man's obsession: photos, one lock of blonde hair tied with a tiny ribbon, dried flowers, newspaper clippings.

A prime fire hazard and a priceless piece of evidence.

Rosebud shone his light onto the top item on the left: a picture of two blond kids, beaming. The glare of the photo made him believe it had been printed on real photo paper.

A tiny lock of hair tied with a pink ribbon had been taped to the corner of it. The next photo his beam illuminated could have been pulled from a case file. But it wasn't one he was familiar with. A young woman in her twenties lay on her bed, one hand clutching the crucifix hanging from her neck, the other arm held an orange pill container. Her hair was tied in a braid, its tip resting over her shoulder.

Rosebud yelled out. "Murphy! Get your ass in here. Now!"

CHAPTER SEVENTY-FOUR

KATE LEFT the bathroom and ran into the bedroom after hearing Rosebud call out to her.

"What's going on? Why didn't you turn on the lights?"

"Don't work. Have a look," he said, shining his flashlight on a photo of a man with two teenagers. The boy was most likely Anderson. The hairline, the nose, the lips, the dimples in his cheeks. Sure, he was more than a decade younger on that photo, but it was him. No doubt about it. The chubby grown man's eyes had been crossed off with large Xs drawn in permanent marker.

"That has to be the sister, Penelope, and Mr. Thompson," Kate said. "Scorfosi! Come in here ASAP," she said.

He appeared next to her with his camera. "Take photos of this right now. I need to look at the back of those, but I want to keep a record of the board as we found it."

Kate and Rosebud both shone their lights as the man recorded the evidence.

"Talk about nailing *without a reasonable doubt*! Who is the woman?" Kate asked.

"All yours," the photographer said.

With her gloved hand, Kate unpinned the unknown photo and flipped it. On the back, an inscription read *Pixie, June 1, 2017*. "What the fuck?"

She flipped the next photo, the one with the man with his

eyes crossed off. The back showed *Mr. Thompson, Anderson, and Pixie, Dec 2005.*

"Pixie must be Penelope, his twin sister," Kate said.

"Never heard that nickname before, but it adds up. Did he kill her?" Rosebud asked, his eyes glued on a hand-written letter that had been pinned underneath the photo.

Kate stayed quiet, still absorbing the new information.

"This letter must have accompanied the photo," Rosebud said. "It's from someone named John. 'I know your sister's suicide must be difficult to accept for you. So I included a photo of how I found her—'"

"Who does that?" Kate asked.

"I don't know. Let's see what the letter says. 'But it's wrapped in a blank sheet, so you don't have to look at it if you don't want to. As per her wishes, her body will be cremated, and no ceremony will be held. I've attempted to contact your parents, but I've yet to succeed. Last I heard, they were in the middle of a jungle somewhere. With the passing of your sister, this is where our paths diverge. Boston has become too difficult for me to live in, so I'm leaving. I don't know where I'll go but I'm cutting ties with you forever. Consider this my goodbye letter. I hope you find it in your heart to understand my need to escape from everyone that reminds me of her. I loved your sister too much. Getting over her death will be incredibly difficult.'"

"And?" Kate asked.

Rosebud shrugged. "That's it. That's all it says."

"This doesn't make sense," Kate said. "Who does that? No decent human being would take a photo of someone they love right after finding them dead. They'd call for an ambulance, they'd call the police. They wouldn't take a photo—"

"Hold on. Do you remember when we were talking with Father Coffedy, and he said something about Candidate Anderson taking a year off for something personal? The death of his sister adds up, right? If I were in his shoes, losing my only sibling could mess me up a tad. Enough to want to put my seminary studies on hold."

"So, receiving that photo, learning of his sister's suicide, made him flip a switch in his mind? He kind of went crazy?"

"Don't know about *going* crazy. The childhood neighbor

did say he was always a bit odd. Perhaps he couldn't hold it in anymore after that."

"But why did the boyfriend send the photo to her brother?" Suddenly, without thinking, Kate's gloved hand reached for her partner's forearm. "Rosebud, I get it!"

He turned to face her, then looked down at his arm. She peeled her fingers off of it. "It's not 'Trixie' I heard on that anonymous call. It was 'Pixie!' The sister's not dead! This was all staged." She waved the photo as though it was a poor man's fan. "The boyfriend took that photo and mailed it off to her brother so they could get rid of his judgmental crap. Fucker! But now we've got all the evidence and motive we need to lock him up for life. Lori, Jessica, Mariana, and that teacher. That's four murders to his name. I need to call Fuller and get an update on whether he's been found anywhere. Maybe Chainey or Wang found and arrested him at one of the churches."

Kate pulled her phone out of her pocket and noticed a missed call and a voicemail. She ignored it for now. They could wait. She had to wrap this case up. They were so close to their finish line.

While Kate waited for Fuller to pick up, Rosebud moved his attention to the newspaper clippings. He moved closer, as though trying to read the caption below the newspaper photo. "Shit! Murphy, you're not going to like this."

"What?"

"He's gotten personal." He handed her the clipping. The caption read, *Detective Kate Murphy is leading up the serial killer case*, and Murphy's name had been underlined.

Kate's chest tightened, her heartbeat increased. Ever since she joined the force, she'd become aware of the risks associated with the job. But this here was different. It had gotten personal indeed. While she was fairly confident in her ability to defend herself, she wasn't sure if she'd just endangered those she loved. Would Luke be in danger? Or Mrs. O'Brien?

Fuller finally picked up, just as she realized something bad could be happening to either of them right now.

"Better have some good news for me, Murphy."

"Rosebud will call you right back."

Hanging up on her boss like that wasn't the smartest move,

but Kate didn't care. Her boyfriend's and his mother's lives could be on the line. Rosebud nodded and took out his phone while she reached for her radio to request that squads immediately head to her house. But no matter how many times she pressed the button and turned it off and then on, her radio wasn't coming back to life. She'd checked it earlier. Technical failure at the worst of times.

"We're heading to my place," Kate ordered. "Explain it to Fuller as I drive. Fuck, I need to call them."

She dialed Luke's number and waited but the rings went unanswered. Five. Six. Seven. "Fuck!" She ended the call then tapped her screen to listen to Luke's voicemail. It came in nearly thirty minutes ago.

"Hi, Katie. Hope you're making progress with the case. Just calling to say I love you. Oh, and heads-up. I just called Mom and that wannabe priest guy just showed up unannounced. Knowing my mom, she'll likely invite him to stay for dinner. Better get ready for some serious pre-meal blessing. Love you!"

"Fuck!" Kate yelled once more, this time anger making her want to toss her phone away, but she resisted the urge. "He's at my place!"

"Who?" Rosebud asked, moving his phone away from his mouth for a second.

"Anderson is at my place right now. Let's go!"

Rosebud nodded.

As horrible scenarios flooded Kate's mind, she heard bits and pieces of what Rosebud was relaying to Fuller. "He's got an altar with pics of the victims. And Murphy. All signs point to her being his next target. We're heading there. Yep. We're just minutes away."

Kate turned to Rosebud, who lagged behind her on the stairs. "Radio in for a couple of squads, but no lights, no sirens. We don't want to alert the killer."

She overheard him relay her request, then she dashed toward her car. She had to get there in time. She just had to.

"Rosebud! Hurry the fuck up!" she yelled as she opened the driver's door. She started the engine, watching her chubby partner do his best to reach the car. "Finally!" she said as he sat down.

Kate hit the gas before he even had time to close the door. "Keep redialing Luke's number and put it on speakerphone," she ordered, tossing her phone at him.

As she sped her way past the few intersections that separated her from Luke's home, the cabin of the car made her feel claustrophobic. With each unanswered ring that echoed out of her device, the air became more and more infused with her biggest fear.

"Hang up," she said.

Was she too late already?

CHAPTER SEVENTY-FIVE

"MOM, I'M HOME!" Luke closed the front door. Something smelled good, as usual. Onion with a hint of garlic, poultry, gravy… *Turkey?*

He took off his shoes, noting the extra pair. The priesthood candidate was still here. Good thing he had warned Kate. She was so going to dislike dinner tonight if he stuck around.

Oh shit. Turkey. I wonder if she will be okay with it now… Considering…

But at least it would be tasty, that he was sure of.

He and Kate could always eat out if turkey was a no-go. He'd deal with the wrath of his mom later. Nah. She'd understand.

Luke walked into the living room and spotted his mom lying on the couch, seemingly sleeping. "Mom?" With a few long strides, he crossed the room and knelt next to her, shaking her shoulder. Something was off.

Why would she nap with company over? Her body was warm. Bringing his index and middle finger to her neck, he felt for a pulse. It was present but weak.

Where was that priest dude? Had he gone out for help?

Luke knew he had to call an ambulance. Digging into his pant pocket, he retrieved his phone and dialed 9-1, but the device started ringing before he could press the last 1.

Caller ID read *Kate*.

He was about to swipe and answer when something smashed against the back of his head.

Darkness enveloped him as the ringtone faded away.

CHAPTER SEVENTY-SIX

ROSEBUD AND KATE arrived at the scene at the same time as a patrol car parked a few houses down. Kate exited the vehicle and darted to meet the two officers that had just gotten out of theirs. Digging into her jacket's inner pocket, she pulled out the sketch that Rosebud had shared with her.

"That's our suspect." She pointed to her house. "That's my home. My boyfriend and his mom are possibly inside with him. I'm going in the front, as though I was just coming home. Rosebud"—she turned to see him arrive, out of breath—"there's an entrance around the back. I'll disarm the alarm on the backdoor. Depending on where he is, I may not be able to unlock the backdoor without him seeing me, but there's a spare key hidden in the bucket that holds the clothespins." She turned to the patrol officers. "You'll follow me through the front door. I don't expect him to be armed. He uses an unknown drug or poison on his victims. If there's an antidote, he's the only one who knows, so do *not* kill him. Getting him to talk may be the only way to save the other people in the house."

The other people. The ones I care most about in the whole world.

"And let's stay silent to keep the element of surprise," Kate added.

Inhaling deeply, Kate motioned for Rosebud to head around the back of the house, and she climbed up the front stairs, the two officers in tow, her heart threatening to burst in her chest. She couldn't lose them. Not Luke or his mom. No. She simply couldn't let that happen.

She unlocked the front door, drew her weapon, and stepped into the home, doing her best to push aside the dread. Something really nice reached her nostrils. Mrs. O'Brien had once again cooked them a feast. Here was hoping everyone would live to enjoy it. She had to act swiftly.

The clutter of shoes at her feet included an unknown pair. Black. Men's shoes that weren't Luke's. The killer was still here. All Kate could do was hope he hadn't taken action yet. And keep her shoes on, ready to outrun the guy or kick him where it hurt.

"Luke? Mrs. O'Brien?" she called out, pretending to act normally, but she didn't lock the door. She motioned for the officers to head upstairs.

Beeps echoed in the entrance hall as she turned off the alarm they kept activated on the backdoor.

Nobody had replied to her greeting. While expected, it didn't make the dread any easier to take. How bad was it? The killer couldn't have already…

She didn't dare finish her thought.

The officers upstairs had two bedrooms and two bathrooms to clear so Kate left the entrance hall and entered the living room, checking everything around her.

Nobody was here.

She continued advancing through the room, checking Luke's office door as she passed it. It had been left open.

Clear.

That left the kitchen and the downstairs' half bath. She could continue moving across the room and reach the kitchen that way, or she could backtrack to the entrance, go down the hall, check the half-bath and then enter the kitchen from the back, next to the backdoor entrance. There was no way for her to unlock that backdoor without being seen by the killer if he was in the kitchen.

She still didn't know if the killer acted alone. Rosebud would eventually find his way in, even though the key was hard to find among the clothespins. Plus the other officers would join her downstairs if they hadn't found him or an unknown accomplice upstairs. They would check that half-bath.

So, with a deep inhalation, she stepped forward and turned to face the opening to their kitchen and dining room.

But as she peeked into the kitchen, her fears became real.

Mrs. O'Brien and Luke had both been tied to kitchen chairs, their limp bodies held up with duct tape. On the table in front of them rested a turkey, a carving knife next to it.

Luke's head was tilted backward, and so was his mom's. Kate had to blink for a second as flashes from her parents' kitchen came back. Between blinks, she saw blood on the walls. The turkey. The knife. The duct tape. Everything reminded her of that fateful day. The multiple knife wounds her parents had suffered in their sudden demise. Twenty-three years suddenly disappeared, merging with her present.

But she blinked her hallucinations away as her heart boomed in her chest. Her current reality didn't show any evidence of blood. At least not yet.

Between Luke and Mrs. O'Brien stood Anderson, a wide grin on his face.

"And our third sinner finally joins us," he said.

Both of his arms were extended in a way that reminded Kate of the preaching position. Elbows lowered but hands up and facing away from his body. The troublesome part was what he held in each of his hands.

Two vials—their lids gone—hovered threateningly just above Luke and Mrs. O'Brien's gaping mouths.

"Put those vials away," Kate said, her gun aimed at him.

"I won't."

Kate's instincts and training told her to end the threat, to shoot for the center of the target, but she refrained from firing. While she wasn't worried about her marksmanship, she didn't want to risk having those vials spill their contents into her loved ones' mouths as Anderson fell to the ground. Not knowing what he had in those vials changed everything. Would an ambulance get here in time? Would the doctors even know how to counteract whatever the vials contained?

"What did you do to them?" she asked, doing her best to notice any movement with Luke's and Mrs. O'Brien's chests.

"Gun down, then we'll talk."

Kate didn't obey; she changed topics instead. "So, no broken arm?"

He squinted and frowned. "I broke it years ago. I kept the cast as a souvenir. Came in handy these past few weeks."

Her weapon still aimed squarely at him, Kate glanced at the table once more. Beside the damn turkey lay the pieces of his discarded cast. Each half showed a straight edge, where a saw had been used to cut the cast, then two smaller latches had been added. A tiny part of her admired his ingenuity. With the brace holding the cast in place over his shoulder, none of that had been visible. The X-rays he'd so proudly shown to Rosebud had probably been old ones, of which he'd taken new photos, so they'd appear in his recent timeline.

"Gun down, Detective," he repeated.

Kate knew she wasn't in any imminent physical danger herself, but she feared for what he'd already given Luke and Mrs. O'Brien. She needed to learn more about the drug or poison he used.

"Not until you prove to me that they are both still alive."

"They're alive. Not for long, but for now." An evil smile grew on his lips.

"What did you do to them?"

"I gave her some of my cleansing medicine. He came in a little too soon, so I had to hit him on the head."

Although Kate couldn't be sure, she figured he'd brought three vials, one for each of them. "Why are you doing this?"

"In general or this here?" he asked.

Anderson was testing her patience. Her finger feeling the trigger, she hoped he'd move his vials just a bit so she could shoot him.

"Here," Kate said. "Lori. Jessica. Mariana. All of it!"

"This, here, is for you. You are misrepresenting my work. You need to learn my real purpose. To understand it. If you won't lower your gun, then please join me for a toast."

The arrogance in the man's voice made his distorted sense of grandeur palpable.

She had to get Anderson to move those vials. She couldn't believe he was still holding them. His elbows being bent probably made it a less strenuous a posture to maintain than if his arms had been held out straight.

"But why Lori? Why Jessica? Mariana?"

"All sinners. I know firsthand what happens when

corruption and sin enter a person's soul. It's a slippery slope that ends nowhere but Hell."

"Was it why you also targeted Amanda? What was her sin?"

He flinched at the mention of her name.

"What had she done that was so bad?"

He shook his head and something unsettling and deeply unnerving shone in his eyes. "I am simply a servant of the Lord saving fragile souls before it's too late. They start off with the sin of the flesh, then drugs and alcohol, then…"

"Then suicide? Like Penelope?"

One of his eyebrows rose. "What? How do you know about her?"

"That's my job. You think your sister, Penelope, or Pixie, is rotting in Hell?"

His voice descended nearly an octave as rage flashed in his eyes. "She is, unfortunately. That is what happens when people commit suicide. I'm her twin. I know. I can feel the flicker of the burning flames against my skin when I think of her. I've seen where her despair took her, and I want to save other souls before they reach that point."

"Because suicide is bad, and the worst possible thing anyone could ever do?"

"Yes!"

"Worse than murder?"

His crazed eyes looked up. "The Lord has been speaking to me." His hands—and the dangerous vials he'd been holding—reached toward the ceiling, so Kate took her opportunity.

She fired a single shot. His body fell backward and the vials he'd been holding crashed onto the tiled floor.

Kate walked toward the man, still aiming her gun at him. His face contorted as his hands reached toward his shoulder. Blood seeped from the wound she'd inflicted, rapidly staining the area around his left collarbone.

Rosebud and the other two officers joined her in the kitchen and she heard other people rushing into her home, shouting their BPD identity as they stormed in.

Kate met Anderson's eyes and shook her head at the deranged man lying at her feet. "The Lord—"

"Don't you dare speak his name in vain," he said, his voice tainted with agony. "You ingraaaate!"

One of the patrol officers got to the floor and began attending to Anderson's wounds now that he was no longer a threat to others.

Radios crackled around her as Rosebud reported the situation to Fuller who had nearly arrived at the scene. The other officer radioed for medical assistance.

Kate turned her attention to Luke and his mom. Kate checked Luke's pulse first, then his head. A bump was already growing. He could have a concussion.

She checked Mrs. O'Brien next. Her pulse was weak, but present.

She allowed relief to wash over her. They'd soon be in good hands. The threat to her family was gone. She looked at Anderson again as the officer continued applying pressure to the wound to stop the bleeding.

"Just so you know, your sister isn't rotting in Hell," Kate told Anderson. "She's in California. Maybe those L.A. sun rays hitting her skin are the flickering flames you've been feeling."

"No!" he winced. "Impossible. The photo—"

"Enough of this. Anderson Carson," Kate announced with a booming voice, "you're under arrest for the murders of Eliah Thompson, Lori Davis, Jessica Stephenson, Mariana Gomez Alvarez, and attempted murders of Amanda McCutcheon, Luke O'Brien, and Mrs.—" Kate corrected herself upon hearing her words aloud, "and Marjorie O'Brien."

Anderson hissed at her, and Kate turned away from him to stare at her loved ones once more. Mrs. O'Brien wore a peaceful expression, oddly enough. Kate crossed her fingers, hoping that the drug would soon wear off and leave Luke and her without any repercussion—or recollection of what had happened.

CHAPTER SEVENTY-SEVEN

Monday, July 16th, 2018

A COUPLE of days in the hospital had been enough to grant both Luke and his mother a clean bill of health. While Kate was drowning in paperwork, Luke had suggested getting out of her way. Plus, he really wanted nothing to do with the press who'd been following them around nonstop the instant they'd left the hospital.

A last-minute getaway took care of the newspaper reporters and allowed Kate to wrap up her work without distraction. How she loved a man that got her like that, a man who not only loved her but also understood that her job was simply part of her. In her mind, there was no calling in sick when real lives were on the line.

Her job made her feel alive more than anything in the world. She was making a difference. A tiny one, sure, but a difference nonetheless. The case had yet to go through the courts, but the district attorney was confident in the evidence the detectives had collected. Anderson was recovering from his wound and would live to face justice for his acts. She was happy about that.

And she was ecstatic about the press no longer having an interest in her.

Other than a few chauffeurs holding names on placards, the airport was mostly families and friends waiting for their loved ones. A young blonde positioned herself just in front of Kate with a large gift-wrapped box in her hands. No doubt a gift for whomever she was picking up at the airport. As Kate reveled in the satisfaction of knowing that Candidate Anderson wouldn't be targeting women such as that girl any longer, she allowed herself to feel the buzzing energy of the crowd around her, letting it energize her. Normally, her training left her tense and prepared for the worst in crowds. Anywhere. That just came with the job. But right now, surrounded with the excited gossip of strangers chitchatting, making nervous conversation while waiting for their loved ones to appear, she decided to pretend the world was safe, for just a few minutes.

And how dearly did she want to see her loved ones right now.

It had been ten days already since they'd left to go on an all-inclusive holiday to the Riviera Maya.

Her phone rang, bringing her back to the present. The number indicated it was out-of-state. *California.*

"Detective Murphy," she answered.

"Detective, I'm Officer Juarez from the L.A. police. We found Penelope Carson. Goes under the name of Pixie Browne now. I just wanted to let you know. Tracked down the phone she used to make the call. It was a diner. The waitress identified her once we showed her a photo."

"Are you going to charge her with fraud?" Kate asked, knowing fair well that she had staged her own death but that in itself wasn't a crime. The steps she'd taken next, to restart her life, had been.

"They falsified documents, so we'll have to."

"Who's *they*?"

"She and her boyfriend. They schemed together and fled from Massachusetts together, leaving all of their friends and relatives behind. I guess they really wanted out. It's a hell of a lot of work to fake your own death."

"Having met her brother, I could understand why. But please be lenient with the prosecution. She was crucial in solving a major case here."

"Will do."

"Great work, and thanks for taking the time to call and keep me posted."

Kate hung up, smiling as she watched a stream of suntanned passenger come out of the automated doors.

When she saw the man she loved wheeling two suitcases behind him, smiling at his mother who was digging something out from her purse, Kate's chest filled with warmth, as though the sun had just risen and now shone its happy rays on her, pushing away the worries of the world.

They were back. She had her team—her de facto family—by her side again.

Luke looked up, perhaps feeling Kate's intense stare. He beamed. Tiny wrinkles adorned the corners of his eyes behind his glasses. He sped up his pace as he approached her. Letting go of the bag handles, he wrapped his arms around Kate and breathed in her scent.

"How I've missed you, Katie," he whispered. "Next time, you're coming with me. Just you and me. A real vacation under the sun." He pulled away just enough to kiss her. Their lips merged into a passionate kiss that transcended words. Kate felt whole again in Luko's arms.

"What about me? Don't I get my welcome-back hug?" Mrs. O'Brien asked.

CHAPTER SEVENTY-EIGHT

Tuesday, July 17th, 2018

LUKE AWOKE, fearing for his life, darting up to a sitting position in bed.

"You okay, babe?" Kate mumbled next to him.

"Yeah. Go back to sleep."

The tables had turned. Since the day he'd got the big bump on his head—although he didn't recall much of it—he'd started having nightmares. At first, he kept reliving the discovery of his mom, passed out on the couch. But lately, his mom's role had somehow been recast, through whatever subconscious trick his mind liked to play. The same scenario unfolded in his head, but Kate was the one on the couch, passed out.

Or perhaps dead.

He always woke up before he could check her pulse.

If the past few weeks had taught him anything, it was that life was too short. Too short for playing around. Too short for not daring to go for what he wanted. Too short for not doing his best at being truly happy.

"Kate? Are you awake?"

She mumbled, then opened her eyes and rubbed her face. "What's wrong?"

"Just nightmares."

She rubbed her arm against his back. "You know that hypnotherapist?"

"Yeah…"

"I think it helped. I don't have as many nightmares these days. Maybe it can help you, too."

"Maybe. But there's something else that can help. And a lot more."

Her eyelids kept drooping, sleep trying to take over once more. But he needed her to stay awake and have this conversation now.

Luke pulled the cord on his nightstand lamp.

"Whoa! What's that for? What did I ever do to you?" she asked.

He turned to look at her. She was blinking, her elbow raised, her hand up to block some of the light.

But he knew—well, he hoped—she'd soon forgive him for his impulsivity and rude awakening. Opening the drawer of his nightstand, he retrieved the tiny box he'd purchased two weeks ago. He did his best to hide it in his large hand.

He hopped over her, placing his knees on the outside of her stretched out legs before pecking a kiss on her lips. He leaned back and grinned at her.

"What's going on?" Kate asked. Confusion spread over her face as her eyes went from the alarm clock to Luke's expression.

"Kate, you are a hell of an amazing woman. I can't believe how lucky I am to be part of your life. I don't know how I'd live without you. You left my life once when we were teenagers, and I'm still amazed that our paths somehow crossed again. I love you so much. Much more than you'll ever know."

Kate brought a hand over her heart, her face twisting into that weird sad-happy expression he knew too well. "I love you too, Luko—"

"Wait, there's more."

Luke's heart bounced in his chest, its beat increasing by the second. He brought forward the closed fist that held the precious box worth five months of his wages, and flipped it open. "Kate Murphy…" His glance left the ring to meet her wide-open green eyes. Sleep had fully dissipated now. Her mouth was agape.

Luke hoped her surprised look was a good indication. "Will you make me the happiest man on earth and marry me?"

She inhaled a ragged breath then wrapped her arms around him.

"Hell, yes!"

CHAPTER SEVENTY-NINE

WHILE LUKE POURED a hefty serving of wine in everyone's glasses, Mrs. O'Brien placed the meatloaf on the table then sat down and grabbed Kate's hand—presumably to get ready with the pre-meal prayer—but Kate was taken aback when Mrs. O'Brien lifted her hand close to her face.

"It's truly a gorgeous ring. I can't believe my Luke is going to make an honest woman out of you, finally!"

"Mom! Quit it with your outdated expressions. People don't have to get married to be honest or respectable these days!"

"Say whatever you want. I'm excited! You two committing to tying the knot is the best gift I could have ever asked for."

"Better than accompanying you to those fundraisers?"

"Much, much better."

"Should have done it sooner, then," he said.

"Luke!"

"You know I'm just kidding, Mom."

"Enough of this. Let's bless this meal," Mrs. O'Brien began but Kate's phone rang in the distance.

"I'm sorry, Mrs. O'Brien." Kate got up and left the table.

"Kate!"

"I'm sorry, *Marjorie*." Kate stepped out of the room and overheard Luke as she dug into her purse.

"Let it go, Mom. Those mealtime calls come with the job. You won't change her."

Kate smiled. She appreciated having a partner—a fiancé—as supportive as Luke, but her grin disappeared when she recognized the area code.

"Hello?"

"Detective Murphy, it's Sheriff Ramsay. I won't take much of your time, but we've identified the man from the letters."

His unexpected words made her blood flow faster through her veins. Her breathing sped up. "And?"

"The DNA from the glue matched a man in one of our databases, but we haven't been able to locate him. As far as the records are concerned, he seems to have disappeared off the grid. No one has seen or heard from him in decades."

"Oh." Kate felt her shoulders slump, along with her hopes.

"But there's also no obituary to be found."

"What are you saying?" Kate asked.

"You gave us a new lead. It's no longer a cold case, but we don't know if we'll ever find out anything about this man. Congratulations on that serial killer, by the way."

"Thanks. What's the man's name, if I may?"

"Ethan Thibodeau."

"Thanks, Sheriff. I really appreciate you taking the time to call and let me know," Kate said before hanging up.

She stared mindlessly at her phone while letting the new-found knowledge sink in. A name. She now had a name. That was something, right? Worth all the sleepless nights and worries?

Debatable. But a name was progress. And progress was always good. The sheriff and his team would eventually find him. Or she could work on it in her spare time…

"Are you joining us now?" Luke called out.

"Yes, I'm coming." She put her phone away then returned to the kitchen, her eyes spotting the dent in the wall where her bullet had stopped its trajectory. The subtle mark had become her daily reminder to spend time with those she loved.

She took her seat and grabbed the hands of Luke and his mom. Her family.

"Please, let me?" Kate asked as Mrs. O'Brien was about to speak.

A line split her brows as she looked at her son, then she turned to face Kate and shrugged. "If you wish."

"Thank you for allowing me to share my life with Luke and Marjorie." Mrs. O'Brien squeezed Kate's hand at the mention of her first name. "Thank you for keeping them safe on that terrible day. Thank you to all my colleagues who helped us catch him in time—"

"Katie," Mrs. O'Brien muttered. "You're supposed to bless the food—"

Mrs. O'Brien yelped in pain.

Kate looked at Luke. "You kicked your mom?"

"Go on," Luke said, his eyes wide, his face stern even though he was turning crimson.

"Thank you to … Marjorie for preparing a delicious meal for us. She always cooks with love and I'm very grateful to have her in my life. I'm very grateful to have Luke be so patient and understanding with me. I love you," she said, squeezing his hand. "Thank you to all those farmers who grew the ingredients we needed. Thank you for everything you do to feed us. May this delicious meal and the conversations we'll share replenish us, both body and mind. Thank you, Universe."

"Amen."

TO BE CONTINUED...

...in more police procedural mysteries/thrillers featuring Kate Murphy as she pursues her detective career in Boston and continues to make progress with her family's case.

In the mean time, if you haven't read the prequels, here's more information about them:

The Last Hope (Prequel novel)

Officer Kate Murphy's uncle is like a father to her. When he's arrested for murder, she's his only hope.

After a few off-the-record conversations with Luke, an awkwardly attractive forensic technician, Kate knows something doesn't add up. And when a host of politicians and homeless people begin to die all over the Northeast, Kate suspects they're somehow connected to her uncle's case.

To prove the innocence of the man who took her in after her parents were murdered, Kate must make an incredible leap of faith. But she's not prepared for the stunning discovery that calls everything into question.

The Last Hope is a gripping techno-thriller with some sci-fi elements and a dash of romance. If you like mind-bending whodunits, sizzling sex scenes, and tenacious heroines, then you'll love this thrilling yet unconventional police procedural.

Buy your copy today!

https://books2read.com/km2

~

The Last Lies (Prequel novella that precedes The Last Hope)

A woman in a man's world.
An enemy she never saw coming.

Police officer Kate Murphy thought she'd left her tumultuous past behind when she married Matt, but nothing could be further from the truth.

As problems and **deceptions pile up** both at home and at work, a disturbingly high number of **animal deaths begin to spread** in and around Boston. Kate will have to **unravel a web of lies** and connect the dots to solve the case and regain control over her life.

If you like dramatic police procedurals with characters who grow and become stronger as the story progresses, then you'll love this fast-paced yet emotional mystery.

Buy your copy today.
https://books2read.com/km1

~

If you'd like to read more stories from C.C. Jameson, please post a review where you bought this book. The more reviews, the faster C.C. can quit the dreaded day job and write more stories for you to read and enjoy.

Thank you for taking the time to read and review this book.

Join C.C.'s reader group to receive regular updates: http://ccjameson.com

THANK YOU

I would like to thank my family and friends for believing in me. In particular, I'd like to thank my parents who let me stay at their cottage so I could work on this book in a peaceful setting. I'd like to thank Sébastien and Patrick, who helped me navigate through police procedural problems as well as Claire and Rachael, my editor and proofreader, for making this story reach its full potential.

And thanks to all my readers, especially those who leave a review. **You are the best!**

AUTHOR'S NOTES

DEAR READER,

I hope you enjoyed ***The Last Amen***. In an effort to create a story that would be fast-paced, entertaining, and emotionally satisfying, I took artistic liberties with some of the police procedures involved in the story you just read.

Since I keep learning more and more about what real cops and detectives do, it wouldn't surprise me if the next book in the ***Kate Murphy Mystery*** series gets a bit closer to real life.

If you want to learn more about me, get regular updates about my life as a wanderlust, self-employed nomad, please join my reader group. You'll also be notified when my next book is ready so you can purchase it at its discounted launch price.

You can join my reader group by subscribing to my mailing list here: http://ccjameson.com/join-my-reader-group-the-last-amen/

(It's free, and you can unsubscribe anytime.)

Keep it real,
Be true to yourself,

C.C. Jameson
March 6, 2019
http://ccjameson.com

ABOUT THE AUTHOR

C.C. Jameson is an ex-military officer now wanderlust-driven author. Other than politically unstable countries, those with visa restrictions, or where only the wealthy can live, no place is out of bounds for the single, adventurous author.

At the time of publication, C.C. lived somewhere along the coast of Mexico, where blue skies meet turquoise waters, and cold beers and lime margaritas reign as the best thirst quenchers.

C.C. loves spending time alone in nature and writing at home. Hobbies include listening to live music, learning new languages, reading tons of books, and making up stories for readers to enjoy.

The name C.C. Jameson was born out of two authors' imaginations while chatting at a bar somewhere in Florida. Drinking was involved, of course, because it's one of C.C.'s favorite activities and a *must* for the introverted author while in social situations. As for the C.C. part, it corresponds to the author's real first initial, but doubled because it sounded better. Plus, that's how many people refer to *Canadian Club*.

So, C.C. Jameson is not just an anonymous author's pen name, it's a drinking name, too.

Learn more at http://ccjameson.com.

facebook.com/ccjamesonauthor

twitter.com/ccjamesonauthor

amazon.com/author/ccjameson

goodreads.com/CCJameson

bookbub.com/authors/c-c-jameson

BOOK CLUB

SUGGESTED DISCUSSION TOPICS

If you choose to read this book as part of your book club, the following questions could help trigger some interesting discussions.

The themes and topics hinted at in this book are broad and may offend some readers. The views expressed by the characters in this book do not necessarily represent the author's views on such topics.

The Seal of Confession

The information heard by clergy members during confessions cannot be shared with the police. That's a fact.

Do you believe exceptions should be made? For example, if someone confesses to having committed a serious crime and the police fear other crimes are planned, do you think laws should be created to force various religious leaders to disclose those confessions in order to save other lives?

Do you foresee a future where certain/all religious rights might be taken away due to public safety reasons?

If you were the member of clergy who heard the confession and knew the person expected to kill/hurt/endanger more people but your religious vows prevented you from revealing this information for fear of being excommunicated. What would you do?

Defining Sins

What is a *sin*?

Where do you draw the line?

What is acceptable behavior?

Suicide

The topic is often taboo, and possibly for good reasons. We don't know if the person sitting next to us was affected by it. Did their spouse/child/friend commit suicide?

Being the person to discover a loved one's dead body most definitely qualifies as a traumatizing experience, so perhaps some people avoid talking about it so those unfortunate people won't have to relive their trauma every time the topic comes up.

How do you feel about suicide?

Is it an acceptable way to end one's life? And if so, under what circumstances?

When a person no longer takes any pleasure in living (and has been feeling that way for years), should he or she have the right to put an end to it? Should a person remain alive just to please others?

If you were to place all sins on a scale, where would suicide rank?

Suicide prevention hotline:

https://suicidepreventionlifeline.org/

Helping Your Community

In the book, the priests decided to raise funds to help the poor. What programs are available within your community to help those in need?

Do you volunteer?

We only have limited time and a limited budget. How do you determine if a cause is worth supporting with your time and/or money?

Discuss ways you can help improve your community.

Made in the USA
Middletown, DE
15 November 2019